Around the World in 80 Days

AROUND THE WORLD IN 80 DAYS

Jules Verne

Translated by Jacqueline and Robert Baldick

First published in this translation
by J. M. Dent & Sons in 1968
This illustrated edition first published in Armada in 1989
This edition published in 1993
by Diamond Books
77-85 Fulham Palace Road,
Hammersmith, London W6 8JB

Printed and bound in Great Britain by BPCC Hazells Ltd.

Contents

CHAPTER ONE

*In which Phileas Fogg and Passepartout mutually accept
each other, one as master, the other as servant*

In 1872 No 7 Savile Row, Burlington Gardens – the house
in which Sheridan died in 1816 – was occupied by Phileas
Fogg Esq. He belonged to the Reform Club of London,
and although he seemed to take care never to do anything
which might attract attention, he was one of its strangest
and most conspicuous members.

Thus one of England's greatest orators had been followed by this Phileas Fogg, an enigmatic personage about
whom nothing was known except that he was a man of
honour and one of the finest gentlemen in English high
society.

It was said that he bore a certain resemblance to Byron –
in his looks, for his feet were irreproachable – but he was
a Byron with a moustache and side-whiskers, an impassive
Byron who could have lived a thousand years without
growing old.

Undoubtedly an Englishman, Phileas Fogg might not
have been a Londoner. He had never been seen at the
Stock Exchange, nor at the Bank, nor in any of the offices
in the City. No ship owned by Phileas Fogg had ever
entered the London docks. The gentleman was not on any
board of directors. His name never echoed round the
Temple, or Lincoln's Inn, or Gray's Inn. He never pleaded
in the Court of Chancery, the Court of Queen's Bench, the
Court of Exchequer or an Ecclesiastical Court. He was
neither manufacturer nor trader, neither merchant nor
gentleman farmer. He belonged neither to the Royal
Society of Great Britain, nor the London Society, nor the

Workmen's Society, nor the Russell Society, nor the Western Literary Society, nor the Law Society, nor that Society of United Arts and Sciences which enjoys the patronage of Her Gracious Majesty. In short, he belonged to none of the countless associations which pullulate in the English capital, from the Harmonica Society to the Entomological Society, founded with the principal aim of destroying harmful insects.

Phileas Fogg was a member of the Reform Club, and that was all.

If anyone should wonder how such a mysterious gentleman could have been admitted to that honourable association, the answer is that he had been recommended by Messrs Baring Brothers, with whom he had open credit. He enjoyed a certain standing due to the fact that his cheques were regularly cashed on sight from a current account which was invariably in credit.

Was this Phileas Fogg a rich man? Undoubtedly. But not even the best informed could say how he had made his fortune, and Mr Fogg was the last person one could ask. In any case he was no spendthrift, but nor was he a miser, for whenever some noble, useful or worthy cause was in need of funds, he would furnish the necessary money quietly and even anonymously.

In short, nobody could be less communicative than this gentleman. He spoke as seldom as possible, and seemed all the more mysterious for his silence. Admittedly his life was open to the light of day, but his habits followed such a rigid pattern that a dissatisfied imagination sought for something behind them.

Had he travelled? That seemed very likely, for nobody knew the map of the world better than himself. No place was so out of the way that he did not appear to have special knowledge of it. Sometimes, in a few brief, clear words, he corrected the countless conjectures going round the Club concerning travellers who had gone astray or disappeared; he furnished the most likely explanations, and his words were so often justified by events that he might have been gifted with second sight. He was a man who must have travelled everywhere – in thought if not in fact.

What was quite certain was that Phileas Fogg had not left London for many a long year. Those who had the honour of knowing him rather better than the rest maintained that nobody could claim ever to have seen him anywhere but on the direct route he took every day from his home to his Club. His only pastimes were reading the papers and playing whist. At that silent game, so appropriate to his nature, he often won, but his winnings never went into his purse, and formed a large part of his contributions to charity. Besides, it should be added that Mr Fogg obviously played for the sake of playing, and not to win. For him the game was a combat, a struggle against difficulty, but a struggle that suited his character, in that it involved no movements, no effort, no fatigue.

So far as was known, Phileas Fogg had neither wife nor children – which may be the case with the best of men – but nor – which is more unusual – was he believed to have any relatives or friends. Phileas Fogg lived alone in his house in Savile Row, which nobody ever entered. Nothing was known about his domestic life. A single servant attended to all his needs. Lunching and dining at the Club at fixed times, always in the same room and at the same table, he never invited any of his fellow members to join him, and never entertained any guests. He went home only to go to bed on the stroke of midnight, and never made use of the comfortable accommodation which the Reform Club places at the disposal of its members. Out of every twenty-four hours, he spent ten at home, either asleep or making his toilet. If he took a walk, it was invariably to pace with a regular step around the mosaic floor of the entrance hall, or around the circular gallery beneath the dome with its blue glass windows and supported by twenty Ionic columns in red porphyry. When he lunched or dined, his table was supplied from the succulent stocks of the Club's kitchens, larder, pantry, fish tanks and dairy. It was the Club's servants, solemn personages dressed in tailcoats and wearing soft-soled shoes, who served him his meals in dishes of special porcelain and on Saxony table linen of the finest quality. It was the Club's unique crystal decanters which contained his sherry, his port, or his claret spiced with maidenhair syrup and cinnamon. Finally it was the Club's ice – ice brought at great expense from the lakes of America – which kept his beverages suitably cool.

If to live in this style is to be eccentric, it must be admitted that there is something to be said for eccentricity!

Without being sumptuous, the house in Savile Row was extremely comfortable. On account of its occupant's unchanging habits, there was little enough for the only servant to do, but Phileas Fogg expected him to be absolutely punctual and regular. That very day, 2nd October, he had dismissed James Foster, who had committed the offence of bringing him shaving water at eighty-four degrees Fahrenheit instead of eighty-six and he was now waiting for his successor, who was supposed to call between eleven and half past.

Squarely seated in his armchair, his feet together like those of a soldier on parade, his hands resting on his knees, his body erect and his head high, Phileas Fogg was watching the progress of the hands of his clock – a complicated timepiece which recorded not only the hours, the minutes and the seconds, but also the day, the date and the year. On the stroke of half past eleven, in accordance with his daily habit, Mr Fogg would leave the house and go to the Reform Club.

At that moment there was a knock at the door of the little room in which Phileas Fogg was sitting.

James Foster, the servant whom he had just dismissed, appeared on the threshold.

"The new servant," he said.

A young man of about thirty came in and bowed.

"You are French and your name is John?" Phileas Fogg asked him.

"Jean, if Monsieur does not mind," answered the new-comer, "Jean Passepartout, a nickname which has stuck to me because of my natural aptitude for getting out of scrapes. I think I may claim to be an honest fellow, Monsieur, but to be quite frank, I've had several occupations. I've been an itinerant singer, a circus rider, a trapeze artist like Léotard and a tightrope walker like Blondin. Then, to make my talents more useful, I became a teacher of gymnastics. Finally, I was a sergeant fireman in Paris, where I was concerned in some quite remarkable fires. But it's five years now since I left France. I wanted to have some experience of domestic life, so I became a valet in England. Well, finding myself out of work and hearing that Monsieur Phileas Fogg was the most punctilious and the most sedentary gentleman in the United Kingdom, I have come to you, Monsieur, in the hope of leading a quiet life in this house and forgetting the very name of Passepartout . . ."

"I have no objection to the name of Passepartout," the gentleman replied. "You have been personally recommended to me, and I have had good reports of you. You know my terms?"

"Yes, Monsieur."

"Good. What time is it?"

"Eleven twenty-two," replied Passepartout, after taking a huge silver watch out of the depths of his pocket.

"Your watch is slow," said Mr Fogg.

"Begging Monsieur's pardon, that is impossible."

"Your watch is four minutes slow. Never mind. It is enough to take note of the error. So from this moment, eleven twenty-six in the morning of this Wednesday, the second of October, 1872, you are in my service."

Having said this, Phileas Fogg stood up, picked up his hat in his left hand, placed it on his head like an automaton, and went out without another word.

Passepartout heard the street door shut once: that was his new master going out. Then he heard it shut again: that was his predecessor, James Foster, going out in his turn.

Passepartout was alone in the house in Savile Row.

CHAPTER TWO

In which Passepartout is convinced that he has at last found his ideal

"Upon my word," Passepartout said to himself, feeling slightly taken aback. "I've seen people in Madame Tussaud's who have just as much life in them as my new master!"

During the few moments he had just spent with Phileas Fogg, Passepartout had made a swift but careful study of his future employer. He was a man who seemed about forty, with a fine tall figure, none the worse for a slight paunch, fair hair and side-whiskers, an unlined forehead with no wrinkles at the temples, a somewhat pale complexion and excellent teeth. He appeared to posses in the highest degree what physiognomists call "repose in action", a quality common to all those who get things done without any ostentation. Calm and phlegmatic, with a clear steady gaze, he was the perfect example of those self-possessed Englishmen so often to be found in the United Kingdom, and whose slightly academic posture has been so perfectly rendered by Angelica Kaufmann in her paintings. Seen in his various activities, this gentleman gave the impression of a well-balanced and accurately regulated being, as perfect as a chronometer by Leroy or Earnshaw. This was because Phileas Fogg was indeed exactitude personified, as could be clearly seen from his hands and feet, for with man as with the animals, the very limbs are expressive of the passions.

Phileas Fogg was one of those people who are mathematically precise, never in a hurry and always ready, as sparing of their steps as of all their movements. He never took a stride too many, always going by the shortest route. He never wasted a glance on the ceiling. He never allowed himself a superfluous gesture, and had never been seen moved or disturbed. He was the least hurried person in the world, but he always reached his destination in time. It is easy to understand why he lived alone and so to speak outside society: he knew that in life one must make allowances for friction, and as friction imposes delay he avoided all social contact.

As for Jean, nicknamed Passepartout, he was a true Parisian of Paris. During the five years he had spent in England and been a valet in London, he had sought in vain for a master to whom he could become attached.

Passepartout was not one of those steely-eyed, hard-faced valets depicted by Molière or Lesage, forever shrugging their shoulders and turning up their noses. No, Passepartout was a good fellow with a likeable face, and somewhat full lips, always ready for food or kisses, a gentle, helpful young man with the sort of round head one likes to see on a friend's shoulders. He had blue eyes, a ruddy complexion, and a face full enough to allow him to see his own cheekbones. With his broad chest, his sturdy figure and his strong muscles, he had a Herculean strength which the athletic activities practised in his youth had developed to an admirable degree. His brown hair was rather unruly; if the sculptors of antiquity had known eighteen different ways of arranging Minerva's hair, Passepartout knew only one of dealing with his: three strokes of the comb and that was that.

The most elementary prudence forbids one to say whether this fellow's expansive character would harmonize with that of Phileas Fogg. Would Passepartout be the basically methodical servant his master required? Only time would tell. After spending his youth, as we have seen, in a somewhat wayward fashion, he longed to settle down, and as he had heard people praise the methodical nature and proverbial coldness of the English gentleman, he had come to seek his fortune in England. So far, however, fate had served him ill. Nowhere had he found a place where he could take root. He had served a dozen masters, but each had been whimsical, eccentric, mad about women or mad about travel — two passions which no longer suited Passepartout. His last employer, young Lord Longsferry, MP, after spending his nights in the Haymarket Oyster Rooms, had been brought home all too often on policemen's shoulders; and when Passepartout, who above all else wanted to be able to respect his master, had ventured a few respectful comments, these had been badly received and he had given notice. In the meantime he had heard that Phileas Fogg, Esq, was looking for a servant, and he made enquiries about this gentleman. A personage whose life was so regular, who never stayed out at night, who never travelled, who never went away, even for a day, could not help but appeal to him. He had therefore offered his services and been engaged.

Half past eleven having struck, Passepartout found himself alone in the house in Savile Row, and promptly began to inspect it from cellar to attic. This clean, neat, austere, puritanical house, well organized for domestic service, pleased him greatly. It was like a beautiful snail's shell, but a shell lighted and warmed by gas. Passepartout had no difficulty in finding the room assigned to him on the second floor, and it suited him perfectly. Electric bells and speaking tubes kept him in touch with the rooms on the first floor and the *entresol*, and on the mantelpiece there was an electric clock synchronized with the clock in Phileas Fogg's bedroom, so that both timepieces recorded the same second at the same moment.

"This is just what I wanted!" Passepartout said to himself.

In his room he also found a notice fixed above the clock. This was a list of his daily duties. From eight in the morning, the regulation hour at which Phileas Fogg arose, to half past eleven, the hour at which he left home to go and lunch at the Reform Club, it gave every detail of his servant's duties: Tea and toast at 8.23, shaving water at 9.37, dressing his master's hair at 9.40, and so on. Then from half past eleven in the morning until midnight – the hour at which the methodical gentleman went to bed – everything was set down, provided for, regulated. Passepartout took pleasure in studying this programme and committing its various details to memory.

As for his master's wardrobe, that was excellently devised and marvellously complete. Every pair of trousers, every jacket and waistcoat, bore a number which was repeated in a register of entries and withdrawals, showing the date on which, according to the season of the year, each garment was to be worn. The shoes were similarly tabulated and recorded.

In short, this house in Savile Row, which must have been a temple of disorder when it had been occupied by the illustrious but dissipated Sheridan, was comfortably furnished in a style which denoted a comfortable income. There was no library and there were no books, for these would have been useless to Mr Fogg, since he had at his disposal the Reform Club's two libraries, one devoted to literature and the other to politics and law. In the bedroom

17

there was a medium-sized safe which was proof against fire and theft alike. There were no weapons anywhere in the house, no instruments of war or hunting. Everything in the place denoted the most peaceful habits.

After a detailed examination of the house, Passepartout rubbed his hands, beamed all over his face, and said joyfully:

"This suits me down to the ground! This is just what I wanted! We'll get on famously, Mr Fogg and me! He's a methodical stay-at-home, a real machine! Well, I shan't be sorry to serve a machine!"

CHAPTER THREE

In which Phileas Fogg joins in a conversation which may cost him dear

Phileas Fogg had left his house in Savile Row at half past eleven. After putting his right foot before his left foot five hundred and seventy-five times and his left foot before his right foot five hundred and seventy-six times, he arrived at the Reform Club, an enormous edifice built in Pall Mall at a cost of not less than a hundred thousand pounds.

He promply made his way to the dining room, whose nine windows opened on to a beautiful garden with trees already gilded by the autumn, and sat down at his usual table, which was laid for lunch. This meal consisted of an *hors-d'oeuvre*, poached fish with Reading sauce of the first quality, underdone roast beef flavoured with mushroom ketchup, a rhubarb and gooseberry tart and a piece of Cheshire cheese, the whole washed down with a few cups of an excellent tea especially blended for the Reform Club's kitchen.

At twelve forty-seven he got up and made for the morning room, a sumptuous apartment adorned with richly framed paintings. There a servant handed him an uncut copy of *The Times*, which he unfolded with a sureness of touch which showed considerable familiarity with that delicate operation. The reading of this paper took Phileas Fogg until three forty-five, and the reading of the *Standard*, which followed it, until dinner. This meal was taken in the same conditions as lunch, with the addition of Royal British sauce.

At twenty to six Phileas Fogg reappeared in the morning room and became engrossed in the *Morning Chronicle*. Half an hour later various members of the Reform Club came in and went over to the fireplace, where a coal fire was burning. They were Phileas Fogg's usual partners, fanatical whist players like himself: the engineer Andrew Stuart, the bankers John Sullivan and Samuel Fallentin, the brewer Thomas Flanagan, and Walter Ralph, one of the directors of the Bank of England – all rich men who were highly respected, even in a club which counts among its members the leaders of industry and finance.

"Tell us, Ralph," said Thomas Flanagan, "what news is there of that robbery?"

"Well," replied Andrew Stuart, "the bank can say goodbye to its money."

"On the contrary," said Walter Ralph, "I hope that we'll be able to lay our hands on the robber. Some highly skilled police inspectors have been sent to all the principal ports in America and Europe, and that fellow will be hard put to it to give them the slip."

"So they've got a description of the robber, have they?" asked Andrew Stuart.

"To begin with, he isn't a robber," Walter Ralph replied gravely.

"What! He isn't a robber, a fellow who makes off with fifty-five thousand pounds in banknotes?"

"No," answered Ralph.

"You mean he's a manufacturer?" said John Sullivan.

"The *Morning Chronicle* assures us that he's a gentleman."

The person who provided this information was none other than Phileas Fogg, whose head emerged from the flood of paper surrounding him as he exchanged greetings with his fellow members.

The incident in question, which all the newspapers in the United Kingdom were eagerly discussing, had taken place three days before, on 29th September. A wad of banknotes to the value of fifty-five thousand pounds had been taken from the chief cashier's table at the Bank of England.

To anyone who expressed surprise that such a theft could have been committed so easily, Walter Ralph merely replied that at the time the cashier had been busy recording a deposit of three shillings and sixpence, and that nobody could be expected to keep his eye on everything.

However, it should be pointed out in explanation that that admirable establishment the Bank of England appears to be extremely concerned about the dignity of the public. It has no guards, no commissionaires, no grills! Gold, silver and banknotes are left lying about, at the mercy, as it were, of the first comer, for it would not do to cast suspicion on the honesty of any passer-by. One of the most observant students of English behaviour actually tells how one day, when he happened to be in one of the rooms at the Bank, he was impelled by curiosity to make a closer examination of a gold ingot weighing seven or eight pounds, which was lying on the cashier's table. He picked it up, examined it, and passed it to his neighbour, who passed it on to someone else, so that the ingot was passed from hand to hand all the way down a dark corridor. It was only half an hour later that it returned to its place, and during that time the cashier had not so much as raised his head.

But on 29th September things had not happened in quite the same way. The wad of banknotes did not return, and when the splendid clock above the drawing office struck five and the offices were closed, the Bank of England had no option but to enter fifty-five thousand pounds into the profit and loss account.

Once the theft had been duly established, some of the finest detectives in the country were sent to all the principal ports – Liverpool, Glasgow, Le Havre, Suez, Brindisi, New York and so on – and were promised a reward of two thousand pounds in the event of success, plus five per cent of whatever sum was recovered. Pending the result of the inquiry which had immediately been opened, these inspectors were instructed to scrutinize all the travellers who arrived or departed.

These precautions were necessary because, according to the *Morning Chronicle*, there was reason to believe that the thief did not belong to any organized gang of criminals. On that 29th September, a well-dressed gentleman, with good manners and a distinguished appearance, had been observed walking up and down the withdrawals room in which the theft had occurred. Inquiries had made it possible to draw up an exact description of this gentleman, and this was promptly sent to every detective in the United Kingdom and on the Continent. A few good souls – of whom Walter Ralph was one – accordingly felt they had grounds for hoping that the thief would not escape.

As might be expected, this crime was the principal topic of conversation in London and indeed throughout England, and there were fierce arguments as to the likelihood of the Metropolitan Police being successful. It will therefore not surprise the reader to find the members of

. . . this crime was the principal topic of conversation throughout England . . .

the Reform Club talking about the same question, especially as their number included one of the Bank's directors.

The worthy Walter Ralph refused to admit any doubt as to the success of the investigation, thinking that the reward offered was bound to stimulate the zeal and intelligence of the police. But his fellow member Andrew Stuart was far from sharing this confidence, and the argument therefore continued after they had taken their places round the card table, Stuart opposite Flanagan and Fallentin, opposite Phileas Fogg. While they were playing, nobody spoke, but between rubbers the interrupted conversation was resumed more vehemently than before.

"I maintain," said Andrew Stuart, "that the chances are in the thief's favour, for he must be a very clever fellow."

"Nonsense!" retorted Ralph. "There isn't a single country in the world where he can take refuge."

"Really?"

"Where do you think he could go, then?"

"I haven't the faintest idea," replied Andrew Stuart, "but after all, the world is a big place."

"It used to be," said Phileas Fogg in an undertone. "Will you cut, sir?" he added, passing the cards to Thomas Flanagan.

During the rubber the discussion was suspended, but Andrew Stuart soon revived it, saying:

"What do you mean by saying it used to be? Has the world shrunk by any chance?"

"Of course it has," replied Walter Ralph. "I agree with Mr Fogg. The world has grown smaller, since you can go round it ten times faster now than you could a hundred years ago. And in the case we are discussing, that will enable inquiries to be carried out much more quickly."

"And the thief to get away much more easily!"

"Your turn to play, Mr Stuart," said Phileas Fogg.

But the incredulous Stuart remained unconvinced, and when the rubber was over he went on:

"I must say, Mr Ralph, that you have found an amusing way of proving that the world has shrunk! So because you can now travel round it in three months . . .'

"In no more than eighty days," said Phileas Fogg.

"That's correct, gentlemen," added John Sullivan. "In eighty days, now that the section of the Great Indian Peninsular Railway between Rothal and Allahabad has been opened. This is how the *Morning Chronicle* works out the journey:

From London to Suez via Mont Cenis and Brindisi, by rail and steamer	7 days
From Suez to Bombay, by steamer	13 days
From Bombay to Calcutta, by rail	3 days
From Calcutta to Hong Kong, by steamer	13 days
From Hong Kong to Yokohama, by steamer	6 days
From Yokohama to San Francisco, by steamer	22 days
From San Francisco to New York, by rail	7 days
From New York to London, by steamer and rail	9 days
TOTAL	80 days

"Yes, eighty days!" exclaimed Andrew Stuart, inadvertently trumping his partner's ace. "But that doesn't allow for bad weather, head winds, shipwrecks, derailments and so on."

"Allowing for everything," replied Phileas Fogg, as he went on playing, for this time the discussion was showing no respect for the game.

"Even if the Hindus or the Indians rip up the rails?" cried Stuart. "Even if they stop the trains, loot the luggage vans and scalp the passengers?"

"Allowing for everything," repeated Phileas Fogg. And putting down his cards, he added: "Two winning trumps."

Andrew Stuart, whose turn it was to deal, picked up the cards and said:

"In theory you are right, Mr Fogg, but in practice . . ."

"In practice too, Mr Stuart."

"I'd like to see you do it."

"That depends only on yourself. Let's go off together."

"Heaven forbid!" exclaimed Stuart. "But I'm willing to bet four thousand pounds that a journey like that, made under those conditions, is impossible."

"On the contrary, it's perfectly possible," replied Mr Fogg.

"Well then, prove it!"

"Travel round the world in eighty days?"

"Yes."

"All right."

"When?"

"Straight away."

"This is ridiculous!" cried Andrew Stuart, who was beginning to be annoyed at his partner's insistence. "Look, let's get on with our game."

"Then you must start again," said Phileas Fogg, "because that was a misdeal."

Andrew Stuart gathered up the cards feverishly, then suddenly put them down on the table.

"Very well, Mr Fogg, I agree," he said. "Yes, I'll bet four thousand pounds . . ."

"Steady on, my dear Stuart," said Fallentin. "You can't be serious."

"When I say I'll bet," replied Andrew Stuart, "I'm always serious."

"Very well," said Mr Fogg. Then, turning to his fellow members, he went on:

"I have twenty thousand pounds deposited at Baring's. I'm willing to risk them . . ."

"Twenty thousand pounds?" exclaimed John Sullivan. "Twenty thousand pounds which any unforeseen delay could make you lose!"

"The unforeseen does not exist," was all that Phileas Fogg replied.

"But, Mr Fogg, this period of eighty days is calculated as an absolute minimum."

"Properly employed, a minimum is quite enough."

"But if you are to avoid exceeding it, you'll have to leap with mathematical precision from trains on to steamers, and from steamers on to trains!"

"I shall leap with mathematical precision."

"You must be joking!"

"The unforseen does not exist," was all that Phileas Fogg replied

"A good Englishman never jokes about something as serious as a bet," replied Phileas Fogg. "I will bet twenty thousand pounds against anyone who wishes to take up the wager that I will travel round the world in not more than eighty days, in other words nineteen hundred and twenty hours or one hundred and fifteen thousand two hundred minutes. Will you accept the bet?"

"We accept," replied Messrs Stuart, Fallentin, Sullivan, Flanagan and Ralph, after a brief confabulation.

"Very well," said Mr Fogg. "The Dover train leaves at eight forty-five. I shall take it."

"This very evening?" asked Stuart.

"This very evening," replied Phileas Fogg. "So," he added, consulting a pocket calendar, "as today is Wednesday, the second of October, I must be back in London, in this very room in the Reform Club, on Saturday, the 21st December, at eight forty-five in the evening. Failing which, the twenty thousand pounds standing to my credit with Baring Brothers will belong to you, gentlemen, *de facto* and *de jure*. Here is my cheque for that sum."

A record of the bet was drawn up and signed immediately by the six participants. Phileas Fogg had lost nothing of his composure. He had certainly not made his bet for the sake of winning, and he had staked only twenty thousand pounds – half his fortune – because he foresaw that he might have to spend the other half in order to bring this difficult, not to say impossible, project to a successful conclusion. As for his adversaries, they seemed somewhat upset, not because of the amount involved, but because they felt certain scruples about accepting a bet in such conditions.

The clock struck seven, and the others suggested stopping the game so that Mr Fogg could get ready for his journey.

"I'm always ready!" replied that phlegmatic gentleman. And as he dealt the cards, he said:

"Diamonds are trumps. Your turn to lead, Mr Stuart."

CHAPTER FOUR

In which Phileas Fogg astonishes his servant Passepartout

At seven twenty-five Phileas Fogg, having won twenty guineas at whist, took leave of his fellow members and walked out of the Reform Club. At seven fifty he opened the door of his house and walked in.

Passepartout, who had studied his programme conscientiously, was somewhat surprised to see Mr Fogg guilty of the inexactitude of appearing at this unexpected hour. According to the notice his master was not due to return until the stroke of midnight.

Phileas Fogg went straight up to his bedroom and then called out:

"Passepartout."

Passepartout made no reply. That summons could not be meant for him. It was not the right time.

"Passepartout," Mr Fogg repeated, without raising his voice.

Passepartout appeared.

"That's the second time I called you," said Mr Fogg.

"But it isn't midnight," replied Passepartout, taking out his watch.

"I know," said Phileas Fogg, "and I am not blaming you. In ten minutes we leave for Dover and Calais."

A sort of grimace appeared on the Frenchman's round face. He told himself he could not have heard aright.

"Monsieur is going on a journey?" he asked.

"Yes," replied Phileas Fogg. "We are going round the world."

Passepartout, his eyes wide open, his eyebrows and eyelids raised to their full extent, his arms hanging loosely, his body drooping, showed all the signs of astonishment carried to the point of stupefaction.

"Round the world?" he murmured.

"In eighty days," said Mr Fogg. "So we haven't a moment to lose."

"But what about the trunks?" said Passepartout, unconsciously wagging his head from side to side.

"No trunks. Just a travelling bag. Inside, two woollen shirts and three pairs of stockings. The same for you. We shall buy what we need on the way. Take my macintosh and my travelling rug downstairs. Make sure you have some stout shoes. Though we shall be doing little or no walking. Off you go."

Passepartout would have liked to reply, but he could not. He left Mr Fogg's room and went up to his own. There he slumped on to a chair, and using a colloquial expression from his own country, said to himself:

"Well I'll be blowed! And I came here looking for a quiet life!"

Working mechanically, he made his preparations for the journey. Round the world in eighty days! Was he dealing with a madman? No . . . Perhaps it was a joke? They were going to Dover, well and good. To Calais, all right. After all, that shouldn't annoy a fellow who hadn't trodden the soil of his native country for five years. Perhaps they would even go to Paris, and really he would be quite glad to see that great capital again. But surely a gentleman who counted every pace he took would stop there. Yes, no doubt, but the fact remained that he was going away, this gentleman who had so far been such a stay-at-home!

By eight o'clock Passepartout had packed the modest travelling bag which contained his wardrobe and that of his master. Then, still sorely troubled in mind, he left his room, carefully shut the door and joined Mr Fogg.

Mr Fogg was ready. Under his arm he had *Bradshaw's Continental Railway, Steam Transit and General Guide*, which was to provide him with all the information he needed for his journey. He took the travelling bag out of Passepartout's hands, opened it, and slipped into it a thick wad of those splendid banknotes which are accepted all over the world.

"You haven't forgotten anything?" he asked.

"Nothing, Monsieur."

"My macintosh and my travelling rug?"

"Here they are."

"Good. Take this bag."

Mr Fogg handed the bag to Passepartout.

"And take good care of it," he added. "There's twenty thousand pounds inside."

The bag nearly slipped out of Passepartout's hands, as if the twenty thousand pounds were in gold and weighed a ton.

Master and servant then went downstairs and the street door was double-locked behind them.

A line of cabs stood at the end of Savile Row. Phileas

Fogg and his valet got into one of them, which set off swiftly for Charing Cross Station, one of the terminals of the South-Eastern Railway.

At twenty past eight the cab stopped at the station entrance. Passepartout jumped out. His master followed him and paid the driver. At that moment a poor beggar woman, holding a child by the hand, standing barefoot in the mud, and wearing a tattered shawl over her rags and a dilapidated hat from which hung a pitiful feather, came up to Mr Fogg and asked him for alms.

Mr Fogg took out of his pocket the twenty guineas he had just won at the whist table, and gave them to her.

"Here, my good woman," he said, "I am glad I met you."

Then he walked on.

Passepartout felt his eyes growing moist. His master had gone up in his affection.

Followed by his servant Mr Fogg went straight into the entrance hall of the station where he told Passepartout to buy two first class tickets for Paris. Then, looking round, he saw his five fellow members of the Reform Club.

"Gentlemen," he said, "I am leaving, and when I get back the various visas entered into a passport I am taking with me for that purpose will enable you to verify my itinerary."

"Oh, Mr Fogg," Walter Ralph protested politely, "there's no need for that. We shall rely on your honour as a gentleman."

"It's better this way," said Mr Fogg.

"You haven't forgotten when you are due back?" asked Andrew Stuart.

"In eighty days," replied Mr Fogg. "On Saturday the 21st of December 1872, at eight forty-five in the evening. *Au revoir*, gentlemen."

At eight forty Phileas Fogg and his servant took their

seats in the same compartment. At eight forty-five a whistle sounded and the train started moving.

It was a dark night and the fine drizzle was falling. Phileas Fogg, sitting in his corner, remained silent. Passepartout, still dazed and bewildered, was unconsciously hugging the travelling bag containing the banknotes.

But before the train had reached Sydenham he let out a positive cry of despair.

"What's the matter?" asked Mr Fogg.

"It's that ... in my hurry ... my anxiety ... I forgot ...'

"What?"

"To turn out the gas lamp in my bedroom!"

"Well, young man," Mr Fogg replied coldly, "it is burning at your expense!"

CHAPTER FIVE

In which a new share is quoted on the London Exchange

When he left London Phileas Fogg probably had little idea what a stir his departure would cause. News of the bet spread first of all through the Reform Club and produced a positive sensation among the members of that honourable body. Then, from the Club, that sensation was passed on to the papers by way of the reporters, and from the papers to the London public and that of the entire United Kingdom.

This "journey round the world business" was discussed, argued about, and analysed with as much heat and passion as if it were another *Alabama* affair. Some sided with Phileas Fogg, while the rest – and they soon formed a considerable majority – came out against him. Travelling round the world, otherwise than in theory and on paper, in this minimum of time, and with the means of transport available, was not only impossible, it was utter folly.

The Times, the *Standard*, the *Evening Star*, the *Morning Chronicle*, and a score of other leading papers declared themselves against Mr Fogg. Only the *Daily Telegraph* gave him a certain measure of support. Phileas Fogg was generally dismissed as a maniac and a lunatic and his fellow members of the Reform Club were criticized for having accepted this bet, which could only have been made by a man whose mental faculties were deteriorating.

Impassioned but logical articles were published on the question. The interest which the English take in everything connected with geography is well known, so that there was not a single reader, to whatever class he belonged, who did not devour the columns devoted to Phileas Fogg's enterprise.

To begin with, a few bold spirits – mostly women – were on his side, especially when the *Illustrated London News* published a portrait of him, taken from the photograph deposited in the archives of the Reform Club. A few men, too, ventured to say: "Why not, after all? We've seen stranger things than that!" These were chiefly readers of the *Daily Telegraph*. But soon it became obvious that that paper itself was beginning to weaken.

On 7th October a long article appeared in the Report of the Royal Geographical Society. It examined the question from every point of view and clearly demonstrated the utter folly of the enterprise. According to this article, everything was against the traveller, both man-made obstacles and natural obstacles. To succeed in this venture required a miraculous concordance between times of departure and times of arrival, a concordance which did not and could not exist. In Europe, where the distances involved were relatively small, one could at a pinch rely on trains arriving on time; but when they took three days to cross India and seven to cross the United States, how could anyone base all his hopes of success on their punctuality? Mechanical failures, derailments, hold-ups, bad weather and snowdrifts – wasn't everything against Phileas Fogg? When he was at sea, wouldn't he find himself, during the winter, at the mercy of wind and fog? It was not so unusual, after all, for the fastest ocean liners to suffer delays of two or three days. And it would need only one delay for the chain of communications to be irreparably broken. If Phileas Fogg were to miss a steamer, even if it were by only a few hours, he could have to wait for the next, and this in itself would compromise his journey irrevocably.

This article caused a great stir. Nearly all the papers reprinted it and odds on Phileas Fogg fell steeply.

During the first few days after his departure, considerable sums of money had been wagered on his chances of success. England is of course famous for her gamesters, creatures more intelligent and refined than ordinary gamblers, and betting is second nature to the English. Accordingly, not only did the members of the Reform Club lay heavy bets for or against Phileas Fogg, but the general public joined in the game. Phileas Fogg's name was entered into a sort of studbook as though he were a racehorse. He was also converted into stock, which was quoted on the Stock Exchange. "Phileas Foggs" were asked for and offered at par or at a premium, and tremendous business was done in them. But five days after his departure, when the article in the Report of the Royal Geographical Society appeared, offers of shares started pouring in. Phileas Foggs declined. They were offered in bundles, first of five, then of ten, and soon buyers would only take them in twenties, fifties or hundreds!

Only one supporter remained faithful to him. This was the old paralytic Lord Albemarle. Tied to his armchair, the old peer would have given his whole fortune to go round the world, even if the journey had taken ten years, and he wagered five thousand pounds in Phileas Fogg's favour. And when the futility as well as the folly of the enterprise was pointed out to him, he simply replied: "If the thing can be done, it's right and proper that the first to do it should be an Englishman!"

That was the position, then, with Phileas Fogg's supporters becoming fewer and fewer. Everybody, not unreasonably, seemed to be siding against him; the odds against him had risen to one hundred and fifty to two hundred. Then, seven days after his departure, a completely unexpected incident occurred which reduced the odds in his favour to nil.

That day, in fact, at nine o'clock in the evening, the Commissioner of the Metropolitan Police received a telegram which read:

Suez to London
Rowan, Commissioner of Police, Scotland Yard.
Am shadowing bank robber Phileas Fogg. Send warrant for arrest immediately Bombay.

Inspector Fix.

The effect of this telegram was immediate. The respectable gentleman disappeared to give place to the bank robber. His photograph, deposited at the Reform Club with those of all his fellow members, was carefully examined. It corresponded, feature by feature, with the description of the bank robber which the police investigation had produced. People recalled the mysterious circumstances of Phileas Fogg's life, his isolation and his sudden departure, and it seemed obvious that this individual, on the pretext of a journey round the world for a senseless wager, had

34

no other aim than to throw the English police off the scent.

CHAPTER SIX

In which Inspector Fix shows signs of understandable impatience

These were the circumstances in which the telegram about Phileas Fogg had been despatched.

On Wednesday, 9th October, the steamer *Mongolia* of the P & O Line, a screw-propelled steel ship with a spar deck, of two thousand eight hundred tons with engines of five hundred horsepower, was expected at Suez at eleven in the morning. The *Mongolia* travelled regularly between Brindisi and Bombay, by way of the Suez Canal. She was one of the Company's fastest ships, and she had always beaten the regulation speeds, namely ten knots between Brindisi and Suez and nine and a half knots between Suez and Bombay.

Waiting for the arrival of the *Mongolia*, two men were

walking up and down the quay in the midst of the crowd of natives and foreigners who throng that town, once an insignificant village, but now assured of a splendid future by Monsieur de Lesseps' great work.

One of these two men was the British Consul at Suez, who – in spite of the pessimistic forecasts of the British Government and the sinister prophecies of the engineer Stephenson – saw English ships passing through the Canal every day, and thus shortening by half the old route from England to India round the Cape of Good Hope.

The other was a thin little man with a rather intelligent face and a nervous habit of knitting his brows with remarkable frequency. Through his long lashes there shone a pair of bright eyes whose brilliance he could extinguish at will. At the moment he was showing certain signs of impatience, pacing up and down and quite unable to keep still. This man was called Fix, and was one of those English detectives who had been sent to all the important ports after the robbery at the Bank of England. He had been instructed to scrutinize all the travellers who passed through Suez and to shadow anyone who looked suspicious, pending the arrival of a warrant for his arrest.

Two days earlier, Fix had received from the Commissioner of the Metropolitan Police the description of the presumed bank robber, namely the distinguished, well-dressed gentleman who had been observed in the Bank.

The detective, naturally tempted by the large reward offered for the man's arrest, was therefore awaiting the arrival of the *Mongolia* with understandable impatience.

"And you say, sir," he asked for the tenth time, "that the ship can't be long now?"

"No, Mr Fix," replied the Consul. "She was sighted yesterday off Port Said, and the hundred miles along the canal are nothing for such a fast ship. As I've already told you, the *Mongolia* has always won the bonus of twenty-five pounds which the Government grants every time a ship gains twenty-four hours on the official times."

"This steamer comes straight from Brindisi?" asked Fix.

"Yes, from Brindisi, where she picked up the mail for India. She left there on Saturday at five in the afternoon. So be patient, she can't be long now. But I really don't know how, from the description you've been given, you'll be able to recognize your man, if in fact he is on the *Mongolia*."

"Oh, you sense those people more than you recognize them," replied Fix. "You have to have a special instinct, a sixth sense supplemented by sight, smell and hearing. I've arrested more than one of those gentlemen in my time, and provided my bank robber is on board, I can guarantee that he won't slip through my fingers."

"I hope he won't, Mr Fix, for it was a serious robbery."

"A magnificent robbery," the inspector answered enthusiastically. "Fifty-five thousand pounds! We don't often have a windfall like that! Our robbers are setting their sights very low nowadays, and the Jack Sheppard breed is dying out. They get themselves hung nowadays for a few shillings."

"Mr Fix," said the Consul, "I like the way you talk and I wish you every success; but as I've said before, I fear that in the present circumstances you'll find it very difficult. You must be aware that according to the description you've been given, that robber of yours looks exactly like an honest man."

"Sir," the inspector replied dogmatically, "the great robbers always look like honest men. So that people who look like scoundrels have only one course to follow, and that's to remain honest, otherways they'd be arrested straight away. Honest faces are the very ones you've got to look at carefully. It's a difficult job, I admit, and it's not a trade any more but an art."

It can be seen that the aforementioned Fix was not entirely free of vanity.

Meanwhile the activity on the quay had been gradually growing. Sailors of various nationalities, merchants, ship-brokers, stevedores and fellahs were crowding on to it; the steamer's arrival was obviously not far off.

The weather was quite fine but the east wind had chilled the air. A few minarets stood out above the town in the pale sunshine. Towards the south a jetty nearly two miles long stretched like an arm across the Suez roadstead. On the surface of the Red Sea several fishing boats and coasting vessels were tossing about, a few of them with something of the elegant structure of the galleys of old.

As he moved among the crowd, Fix, out of professional habit, kept scanning the faces of the passers-by.

"Is that steamer never coming?" he exclaimed as he heard the port clock strike half past ten.

"She can't be far away," replied the Consul.

"How long will she stay in Suez?" asked Fix.

"Four hours. Just long enough to take on coal. From Suez to Aden, at the far end of the Red Sea, is just over thirteen hundred miles, and she must have plenty of fuel."

"And from Aden she goes straight to Bombay?" asked Fix.

"Yes, without putting in anywhere."

"Well," Fix went on, "if the robber has come this way on this ship he must be planning to land at Suez, so as to reach one of the Dutch or French colonies in Asia by some other route. He must know that he wouldn't be safe in India, because that's British territory."

"Unless he's a very clever man," replied the Consul. "As you know, an English criminal is always better hidden in London than he would be abroad."

After making this remark, which gave the detective considerable food for thought, the Consul went back to his office a little way off. The inspector remained alone, a prey to nervous impatience, and with the strange presentiment that his robber was none the less on the *Mongolia*. And indeed, if the scoundrel had left England with the idea of travelling to the New World, the route through India, not so closely watched or so easy to watch as that across the Atlantic, was sure to have obtained his preference.

Fix was not left to his thoughts for long before some shrill blasts of a whistle announced the steamer's arrival. The whole horde of stevedores and fellahs rushed towards the quay in tumult which seemed to bode no good for the limbs and clothing of the passengers. At the same time a dozen or so boats pushed off from the shore and went to meet the *Mongolia*.

Soon the hull of the *Mongolia* came into sight between the banks of the canal, and as eleven o'clock was striking she entered the roadstead, with a loud noise of letting off steam.

There were a good many passengers on board. Some of them stayed on deck gazing at the picturesque panorama of the town; but most of them came ashore in the boats which had come alongside the *Mongolia*.

Fix carefully scrutinized everyone who set foot on shore.

Just then one of the passengers came up to him, after vigorously pushing away the fellahs who were plying him with offers of help, and asked Fix very politely if he could tell him where to find the British Consulate. At the same time he produced a passport which he apparently wished to have stamped with a British visa.

Fix instinctively took the passport and glanced rapidly through the description it contained.

He gave an involuntary start, and the sheet of paper trembled in his hand. The description given in the passport was identical with the one he had received from the Commissioner of the Metropolitan Police.

"This passport isn't yours, is it?" he asked the passenger.

"No," the other replied. "It's my master's."

"And where is your master?"

"He has remained on board."

"But," the inspector went on, "he will have to go to the Consulate in person to establish his identity."

"What, is that necessary?"

"Absolutely essential."

"And where are the Consul's offices?"

"There, at the corner of the square," replied the inspector, pointing to a house two hundred yards away.

"Then I'll go and fetch my master, though he won't be at all pleased at having to come ashore."

With these words the passenger bowed to Fix and went back on board the steamer.

CHAPTER SEVEN

Which once again shows the futility of passports for police purposes

The inspector hurried down the quay to the Consulate, where at his urgent request, he was immediately admitted to the Consul's presence.

"Sir," he said, without any preamble, "I have strong reasons for believing that our man is a passenger on board the *Mongolia*."

And Fix reported the conversation he had had with the servant about the passport.

"Well, Mr Fix," replied the Consul, "I would quite like to see that scoundrel's face, but I rather doubt whether he'll come to my office if he's what you think he is. A thief doesn't like leaving traces of his journey behind him, and besides that, passports are no longer compulsory."

"Sir," replied the inspector, "if he's as clever as I think he is, he'll come here all right."

"To have his passport visa'd?"

"Yes. Passports are no use except to annoy honest people and assist the escape of scoundrels. I can assure you that this passport will be in order, but I very much hope you won't visa it . . ."

"And why not?" retorted the Consul. "If the passport is in order, I have no right to refuse my visa."

"Still, sir, I have to keep this man here until I get a warrant for his arrest from London."

"Ah, that's your business, Mr Fix," said the Consul. "But I cannot . . ."

The Consul did not finish his sentence, for at that moment there was a knock at the door, and the office boy showed in two strangers, one of whom was none other than the servant who had spoken to the inspector on the quay.

His companion was in fact his master, who produced his passport and laconically asked the Consul to be good enough to visa it.

The Consul took the passport and read it carefully, while from a corner of the room Fix studied the stranger, or rather devoured him with his eyes.

"You are Mr Phileas Fogg?" asked the Consul, when he had finished reading the passport.

"Yes, sir," replied the gentleman.

"And this man is your servant?"

"Yes. A Frenchman called Passepartout."

"You have come from London?"

"Yes."

"And where are you going?"

"To Bombay."

41

"Very well, sir. You know that a visa is a useless formality and that we no longer insist on seeing passports?"

"I know that, sir," replied Phileas Fogg, "but I want to be able to prove by your visa that I have been through Suez."

"All right, sir."

And after signing and dating the passport, the Consul stamped it with his seal. Mr Fogg paid the appropriate fee, bowed stiffly and went out, followed by his servant.

"Well?" asked the inspector.

"Well," replied the Consul, "he looked perfectly honest."

"Maybe," said Fix, "but that isn't the point. Don't you think, sir, that phlegmatic gentleman resembles in every particular the robber whose description I've been given?"

"I agree, but as you know, all descriptions . . ."

"I'm going to make sure," said Fix. "That servant strikes me as being less inscrutable than his master. What's more, he's a Frenchman, and they can't help talking. I'll see you later, sir."

With these words, the inspector went out to look for Passepartout.

Meanwhile, Mr Fogg, after leaving the Consulate, had gone back to the quay. There he gave some orders to his servant, took a boat back to the *Mongolia*, and went down to his cabin. Then he took out his notebook, which contained the following record:

Left London, Wednesday 2 October, 8.45 p.m.
Arrived Paris, Thursday 3 October, 7.20 a.m.
Left Paris, Thursday, 8.40 a.m.
Arrived Turin by way of Mont Cenis, Friday 4 October, 6.35 a.m.
Left Turin, Friday, 7.20 a.m.
Arrived Brindisi, Saturday 5 October, 4 p.m.

Sailed on the *Mongolia*, Saturday 5 p.m.
Arrived Suez, Wednesday 9 October, 11 a.m.
Total of hours spent: 158½, or 6½days.

Mr Fogg wrote down these dates on an itinerary divided into columns, showing, from 2nd October to 21st December, the month, the day of the month, and the day of the week of his scheduled and actual arrival at each of his principal ports of call – Paris, Brindisi, Suez, Bombay, Calcutta, Singapore, Hong Kong, Yokohama, San Francisco, New York, Liverpool and London – enabling him to calculate how much time he had gained or lost at every stage of his journey.

This methodical itinerary thus constituted a complete record, so that Mr Fogg always knew whether he was ahead of his schedule or lagging behind. On this Wednesday, 9th October, he therefore noted down his arrival at Suez, which, since it was in accordance with the scheduled time, represented neither gain nor loss.

Then he had lunch served in his cabin. As for seeing the town, the idea never occurred to him, for he was the sort of Englishman who, on his travels, gets his servant to do his sightseeing for him.

CHAPTER EIGHT

In which Passepartout talks rather more freely, perhaps,
than is wise

Fix soon caught up with Passepartout, who was strolling along the quay and looking about him, for he at least did not feel under any obligation not to see anything.

"Well, my friend," Fix said, accosting him, "have you had your passport visa'd?"

"Oh, so it's you, Monsieur," replied the Frenchman. "Yes, thank you, everything's in order."

"And you're having a look round?"

"Yes, but we are going so fast that I feel as if I were travelling in a dream. So this is Suez, is it?"

"Yes."

"In Egypt?"

"Yes, in Egypt."

"And in Africa?"

"In Africa."

"In Africa!" repeated Passepartout. "I can't believe it. Just think, Monsieur, I thought we were going no farther than Paris, but all I saw of that splendid capital was from twenty past seven to twenty to nine in the morning, between the Gare du Nord and the Gare de Lyon, through the windows of a cab and in driving rain! It was such a shame! I'd have loved to see Père Lachaise and the Champs Elysées circus!"

"Then you're in a hurry, are you?" asked the inspector.

"I'm not, but my master is. That reminds me, I must buy some socks and shirts. We left London without any trunks, and nothing but a travelling bag."

"I'll take you to a bazaar where you'll find everything you want."

"Monsieur," said Passepartout, "this is really very kind of you."

They set off together, with Passepartout still talking.

"Whatever happens," he said, "I must make sure I don't miss the boat."

"You've got plenty of time," replied Fix. "It's only twelve o'clock.'

Passepartout took out his big watch.

"Twelve o'clock?" he said. "Get along with you! It's eight minutes to ten."

*Passepartout took out his big watch . . . "Get along with you!
It's eight minutes to ten"*

45

"Your watch is slow," replied Fix.

"My watch? A family heirloom, which has come down to me from my great-grandfather? Why, it doesn't vary by as much as five minutes a year. It's a real chronometer!"

"I see what the trouble is!" said Fix. "You are still keeping London time, which is two hours behind Suez time. You must be careful to set your watch by the midday hour of each country."

"Me? Mess about with my watch?" exclaimed Passepartout. "Never!"

"Well then, it won't agree with the sun."

"So much the worse for the sun, Monsieur! It's the sun that will be wrong!"

And with a proud gesture the good fellow put his watch back in his pocket.

A few moments later Fix asked him:

"So you left London in a hurry?"

"I should say we did! Last Wednesday Mr Fogg came home from his club at eight in the evening – which is quite unusual for him – and three-quarters of an hour later we were off."

"But where is your master going?"

"Straight ahead! He's going round the world!"

"Round the world?" exclaimed Fix.

"Yes, in eighty days! It's a bet, he says, but between you and me I don't believe a word of it. That would be ridiculous. There must be some other reason."

"So he's a bit of an eccentric, this Mr Fogg of yours?"

"It looks like it."

"And he must be a rich man?"

"Obviously, and he's brought a nice little nest egg with him, in brand new banknotes. He isn't stingy with his money on the way, either. Why, he has promised the *Mongolia*'s chief engineer a splendid bonus if we get to Bombay well ahead of time."

"You have known your master for a long time, I suppose?"

"Me?' replied Passepartout. "No, I only entered his service on the day we set off."

It is easy to imagine what effect these replies were bound to produce on the inspector's mind, which was already overexcited.

This hasty departure from London shortly after the robbery, this large sum of money which Fogg had brought with him, this anxiety to reach some distant country as quickly as possible, this pretext of an eccentric wager – all this inevitably confirmed Fix in his theory. He went on encouraging the Frenchman to talk and soon discovered that the young man knew nothing about his master, that the latter lived a solitary life in London, that he was reputed to be rich although nobody knew where his wealth came from, that he was an inscrutable individual and so on. At the same time Fix acquired the conviction that Phileas Fogg did not intend landing at Suez, and that he really was going on to Bombay.

"Is it a long way to Bombay?" asked Passepartout.

"Quite a long way," answered the inspector. "It will take you another ten days by sea."

"And you can tell me where Bombay is?"

"In India."

"In Asia?"

"Of course."

"Blast! You see, there's something worrying me, and that's my lamp."

"What lamp?"

"My gas lamp. I forgot to turn it off and it's burning at my expense. I've worked it out that it's costing me two shillings every twenty-four hours, which is exactly sixpence more than I earn. So you can see that if the journey goes on much longer . . ."

It may be doubted whether Fix understood this business

of the gas, because he had stopped listening: he was making up his mind. He and the Frenchman had reached the bazaar, where he left his companion to do his shopping, telling him to be sure not to miss the boat. He then hurried back to the Consulate.

Now that he was sure of his facts, Fix had recovered all his composure.

"Sir," he said to the Consul, "there's no doubt about it. I've got my man. He's passing himself off as an eccentric who's trying to travel round the world in eighty days."

"Then he's a clever fellow," replied the Consul. "He's counting on getting back to London, after putting the police forces of both continents off his scent."

"We'll see about that," said Fix.

"But you're sure you're not making a mistake?" the Consul asked again.

"No, I'm not making a mistake."

"Then why was this robber so anxious to get a visa to prove that he had been through Suez?"

"I've no idea, sir," replied the inspector. "But listen to this."

And in a few words he reported the salient points of his conversation with Fogg's servant.

"Appearances are certainly all against this man," said the Consul. "What do you propose to do?"

"Send a telegram to London asking for a warrant for his arrest to be sent to me at once in Bombay. Then I'll take a berth on the *Mongolia*, shadow my robber to India, and there, on British soil, I'll accost him politely with my warrant in one hand and the other on his shoulder."

Having coldly stated his intentions, the inspector took leave of the Consul and went to the telegraph office, where he sent the Commissioner of the Metropolitan Police the telegram with which the reader is already acquainted.

A quarter of a hour later Fix went on board the *Mongolia*, with just a bag in his hand, but well provided with money, and before long the ship was speeding under full steam over the waters of the Red Sea.

CHAPTER NINE

In which the Red Sea and the Indian Ocean favour Phileas Fogg's designs

The distance between Suez and Aden is exactly 1,310 miles, and the Company's schedules allow their steamers 138 hours to cover it. The *Mongolia*, which was under full steam, was making such good progress that she was sure to arrive ahead of her scheduled time.

Most of the passengers who had come on board at Brindisi were bound for India. Some were going to Bombay and the others to Calcutta, but the latter were going by way of Bombay, for now that a railway ran right across the Indian peninsula, it was no longer necessary to sail round past Ceylon.

These passengers on the *Mongolia* included members of the Indian Civil Service and Army officers of all ranks. Some of the latter belonged to the regular Indian Army, while the rest were in command of the native Sepoy troops. They were all well paid, even though the British Government had now taken over the rights and obligations of the East India Company: second lieutenants received £280 a year, brigadiers £2,400 and generals £4,000. The pay of Civil Servants was even higher: the most junior members of the Indian Civil Service were paid £480 a year, magistrates £2,400, judges £10,000, governors £12,000 and the Governor General over £24,000.

Apart from these public servants there were a number

of young men possessed of ample funds, on their way to found businesses in distant parts. All these people lived well on board the *Mongolia*. The Purser, the Company's trusted servant and the Captain's equal at sea, did things in style. At breakfast, at lunch at two o'clock, at dinner at half past five and at supper at eight, the tables sagged under the dishes of fresh meat and other food from the steamer's stores. The ladies – there were a few on board – changed their dresses twice a day, and there was music, and even dancing, whenever the sea allowed it.

But the Red Sea, like all long narrow gulfs, is extremely capricious and often very rough. When the wind blew from the Asian or the African coast, the *Mongolia*, like a long spindle with a screw, was caught on the beam, and rolled terribly. Then the ladies vanished, the pianos fell silent, and songs and dances ceased at the same moment, Yet in spite of squall and swell, the steamer, impelled by her powerful engines, forged steadily ahead towards the straits of Bab-el-Mandeb.

Meanwhile, what was Phileas Fogg doing? It might be thought that, uneasy and anxious, he was worrying about changes in the wind which might impede the ship's progress, about the tumultuous swell which might damage the engines, and indeed about all the possible accidents which might compel the *Mongolia* to put into some port and thus compromise the success of his journey.

He was doing nothing of the sort, or at least, if he thought of these possibilities, he showed no sign of it. He was still the impassive gentleman, the imperturbable member of the Reform Club to whom no incident or accident could come as a surprise. He seemed to be no more affected than the ship's chronometers, and he was rarely seen on deck. He appeared to have little desire to observe that Red Sea, so rich in memories, which had witnessed the first notable happenings in the history of mankind. He did not try to identify the curious towns scattered along its shores, their picturesque outlines sometimes standing out on the horizon. He did not even give a thought to the perils of that Gulf of Arabia of which the ancient historians, Strabo, Arrian, Arthemidorus and Edrisi, always spoke with horror, and upon which the navigators of old never ventured without first consecrating their voyage by means of propitiatory sacrifices.

Then what was this strange fellow doing, imprisoned on board the *Mongolia*? First, since neither pitching nor rolling could ever upset such a wonderfully organized machine, he ate four hearty meals a day. Then he played whist, for he had found some partners as enthusiastic as himself: a tax collector on his way to take up his post at Goa, a clergyman, the Reverend Decimus Smith, who was returning to Bombay and a brigadier general of the British Army, who was rejoining his brigade at Benares. These three passengers were just as devoted to whist as Mr Fogg, and they played together for hours on end, no less silently than himself.

As for Passepartout, seasickness had no power over him. He had a cabin forward and, like his master, took his meals conscientiously. It must be said that this journey, under these conditions, no longer caused him the slightest displeasure. He was completely reconciled to it. He was well-fed, he had comfortable quarters, and he was seeing the world. Besides, he kept telling himself that all this nonsense would come to an end in Bombay.

The day after they left Suez, 10th October, he was not at all displeased to meet on deck the obliging person whom he had asked for information when he had gone ashore in Egypt.

"If I'm not mistaken," he said, greeting him with his most amiable smile, "you are the gentleman who so kindly acted as my guide at Suez?"

"Why yes," replied the detective. "I remember you. You are the servant of that eccentric Englishman . . ."

"That's right, Monsieur . . .?"

"Fix."

"Monsieur Fix," replied Passepartout. "I am delighted to find you on board. But where are you going?"

"Why, to Bombay, like you."

"That's splendid! Have you ever made this trip before?"

"Several times," replied Fix. "I'm one of the Company's agents."

"So you know India well?"

"Quite well," answered Fix, who did not want to commit himself.

"And is it a curious sort of place?"

"Very curious. Mosques, minarets, temples, fakirs, pagodas, tigers, snakes, dancing girls! But you'll have time to see the country, I hope?"

"I hope so too, Monsieur Fix. After all, it's out of the question for a sane man to spend his life jumping from a steamer on to a train and from a train on to a steamer, on the pretext of going round the world in eighty days! No, all these antics will come to an end in Bombay, you can be sure of that."

"And is Mr Fogg keeping well?" asked Fix in a casual tone of voice.

"Very well indeed, Monsieur Fix. So am I, for that matter. I'm eating like an ogre who's been on a fast. It's the sea air."

"But I never see your master on deck."

"Never. He isn't interested in the view."

"You know, Mr Passepartout, this alleged journey round the world in eighty days might well be a cover for some secret mission . . . a diplomatic mission perhaps."

"I wouldn't know about that, Monsieur Fix, and to tell the truth, I wouldn't give half-a-crown to find out."

After this meeting Passepartout and Fix often chatted together, for the inspector was anxious to get into the confidence of Mr Fogg's servant. This, he thought, might prove useful in the future, so he often treated him to a few glasses of whisky or pale ale in the *Mongolia*'s bar. The good fellow accepted these drinks quite naturally and even returned the compliment, so as not to be behindhand, for he considered Fix to be a very good sort.

Meanwhile the steamer was making rapid progress. On the 13th they sighted Mocha, with a few green palm trees standing out above its girdle of ruined walls. Farther off, in the mountains, there stretched vast fields of coffee bushes. The sight of this famous town delighted Passepartout, and he even thought that with its circular walls and dismantled fort standing out like a handle, it looked like a huge coffee cup.

During the following night the *Mongolia* passed through the straits of Bab-el-Mandeb, whose Arabic name means the Gate of Tears, and the next day, the 14th, she put in at Steamer Point, northwest of the Aden roadstead, to take on a fresh supply of coal.

This fuelling of steamers at such distances from the centres of production was a very serious business. For the P & O Company alone it meant an expense of eight hundred thousand pounds a year, for coal dumps had to be established in several ports, and in those distant regions coal came to four pounds a ton. The *Mongolia* had another 1,650 miles to cover before reaching Bombay, and she had to remain for four hours at Steamer Point to fill her bunkers.

But this delay could not have the slightest effect on Phileas Fogg's programme, for he had allowed for it. Besides, instead of reaching Aden only on the morning of 15th October, the *Mongolia* had arrived in the evening of the 14th, which represented a gain of fifteen hours.

Mr Fogg and his servant went ashore, as the former wanted to have his passport visa'd. Fix followed him without being noticed. Once the formality of the visa had been completed, Phileas Fogg went back on board to continue his interrupted game of whist.

As for Passepartout, he strolled about, as was his custom, among the Somalis, Banyans, Parsees, Jews, Arabs and Europeans who made up Aden's population of twenty-five thousand inhabitants.

He admired the fortifications which made this town the Gibraltar of the Indian Ocean, and some magnificent cisterns on which the English engineers were still working, two thousand years after the engineers employed by King Solomon.

"Very curious, very curious," he said to himself as he went back on board. "I can see that it isn't a bad idea to travel, if you want to see something new."

At six in the evening the *Mongolia* was churning up the waters of the Aden roadstead with the blades of her screw, and before long she was speeding across the Indian Ocean. She had 168 hours in which to cover the distance between Aden and Bombay, and the sea proved favourable to her. A steady wind blew from the northwest, and her sails were brought into service to supplement the screw. With greater power, the ship rolled much less. The ladies came up on deck wearing new dresses, and the singing and dancing started up again.

The voyage thus turned out very agreeably, and Passepartout was delighted with the pleasant companion chance had put in his way in the person of Fix.

On Sunday, 20th October, about midday, the Indian coast was sighted, and two hours later the pilot came on board. On the horizon a line of hills stood out against the sky, providing a fitting background to the sea, and soon the rows of palm trees which covered the city of Bombay became clearly visible. The steamer entered the roadstead formed by the offshore islands of Salsette, Colaba, Elephanta and Butcher, and at half past four she came alongside the quays of Bombay.

At that moment Phileas Fogg was coming to the end of the thirty-third rubber of the day, and he and his partner, by means of a bold move, took all thirteen tricks and finished off this splendid voyage with a magnificent slam.

The *Mongolia* was not due in Bombay until 22nd October, and now she had arrived on the 20th. This represented a gain of two days since Phileas Fogg's departure from London, and he methodically noted this down in his itinerary, in the gains column.

CHAPTER TEN

In which Passepartout get off lightly with the loss of his shoes

Everyone knows that India, that great reversed triangle with its base in the north and its apex in the south, covers an area of 1,400,000 square miles, over which a huge population is unevenly distributed. The British Government at that time wielded effective power over part of this vast country, with a governor general in Calcutta, governors in Madras, Bombay and Bengal, and a lieutenant governor at Agra.

But British India, properly so called, covered an area of only 700,000 square miles, with a population of between a hundred and a hundred and ten million. In other words there was still a large part of the country over which the Queen's Government had no authority. Indeed, in the dominions of certain ferocious and greatly feared rajahs in the interior, Hindu independence was still absolute.

From 1756, when the first English settlement was founded on the site now occupied by the city of Madras, until the year when the great mutiny of the Sepoys broke out, the famous East India Company was all-powerful. It gradually annexed various provinces obtained from the rajahs in return for annuities, of which little or nothing was ever paid, and it appointed its own governor general and all its civil or military employees. But now the East India Company had ceased to exist, and the British possessions in India were under the direct authority of the Crown.

Thus the general appearance, the way of life and the ethnographical divisions of the peninsula were changing every day. Formerly people travelled about India by all the ancient means of locomotion: on foot, on horseback, in carts, wheelbarrows and palanquins, on men's backs, in coaches and so on. But now fast steamers plied on the Indus and the Ganges; and a railway right across the peninsula, joined by branch lines along its entire length, brought Bombay within three days' journey of Calcutta.

This railway did not cross India in a straight line. The distance between Bombay and Calcutta, as the crow flies, is not more than one thousand to eleven hundred miles, and trains travelling at only average speed would not take three days to cover it; but this distance was increased by at least a third by the detour the railway made to Allahabad in the north.

This, very roughly, is the route taken by the Great Indian Peninsular Railway. Leaving the island of Bombay, it went through Salsette, joined the continent opposite Tannah, crossed the chain of the Western Ghauts, ran northeast as far as Burhanpur, struck across the semi-independent territory of Bundelkhand, went north to Allahabad, turned east to meet the Ganges at Benares, turned away slightly and, going southeast again at Burdwan and the French town of Chandernagore, reached its terminus at Calcutta.

It was half past four in the afternoon that the passengers

56

on the *Mongolia* landed in Bombay, and the train for Calcutta was due to leave on the stroke of eight. Accordingly Mr Fogg took leave of his whist partners, went ashore, sent his servant to do some shopping, giving him strict instructions to be at the station before eight, and, with that regular step of his which marked the seconds like the pendulum of an astronomical clock, set off for the passport office.

As for the wonders of Bombay – the town hall, the splendid library, the forts and docks, the cotton market, the bazaars, the mosques and synagogues, the Armenian churches and the magnificent pagoda on Malabar Hill, with its two polygonal towers – he never thought of seeing any of them. He likewise ignored the masterpieces of Elephanta, the mysterious hypogea hidden away to the southeast of the harbour, and those admirable remains of Buddhist architecture, the Kanheria Grottoes on Salsette Island.

No, Phileas Fogg saw nothing whatever. After leaving the passport office, he went quietly to the station, where he ordered dinner. Among other dishes, the head waiter thought fit to recommend a stew made from "native rabbit" which he praised highly.

Phileas Fogg ordered some of this stew and tasted it conscientiously; but in spite of the highly spiced sauce served with it, he found it detestable.

He rang for the head waiter.

"Sir," he said, looking him in the eye, "is this really rabbit?"

"Yes, milord," the rascal replied brazenly, "jungle rabbit."

"And you are sure this rabbit didn't mew when it was killed?"

"Mew, milord? A rabbit mew? I swear to you . . ."

"Sir," said Mr Fogg coldly, "do not swear, and

"And you are sure this rabbit didn't mew when it was killed?"

remember this: there was a time in India when cats were regarded as sacred animals. That was a good time."

"For cats, milord?"

"And possibly for travellers too!"

With these words Mr Fogg quietly went on with his dinner.

Shortly after Mr Fogg had come ashore, Mr Fix had likewise left the *Mongolia* and hurried to the headquarters of the Bombay police.

He established his identity as a detective, and explained the mission which had been entrusted to him and his situation with regard to the presumed robber. Had they received a warrant of arrest from London? They had received nothing. And indeed, the warrant which had been sent off after Fogg's departure could not possibly have arrived yet.

Fix was extremely put out. He tried to persuade the Chief of the Bombay Police to give him a warrant for

Fogg's arrest. The Chief of Police refused. This was a matter for the Metropolitan authorities, and they alone were legally empowered to issue a warrant. This strict regard for principle and rigorous observance of the law are in perfect accord with English tradition, which allows no arbitrary action where individual freedom is concerned.

Fix did not press the matter, realizing that he would have to resign himself to waiting for the warrant. But he resolved not to let the inscrutable scoundrel out of his sight while he was in Bombay. Like Passepartout he had no doubt that Phileas Fogg would stay there for a while, and this would give the warrant time to arrive.

However, after receiving his master's latest instructions on leaving the *Mongolia*, Passepartout had realized that what had happened at Suez and Paris would also occur in Bombay: that their journey would not end there, but would go on at least as far as Calcutta, and perhaps even further. And he began to wonder whether this wager of Mr Fogg's might not be perfectly serious after all, and whether he who longed for a quiet life might not be forced by fate to go round the world in eighty days.

Meanwhile, after buying some shirts and socks, he was strolling about the streets of Bombay, which were crowded with the common people. In the midst of Europeans of all nationalities, there were Persians with pointed bonnets, Bunhyas with round turbans, Sindes with square caps, Armenians in long robes and Parsees in black mitres. It happened to be a festival of these Parsees or Ghebers, direct descendants of the followers of Zoroaster who are the most industrious, most highly civilized, most intelligent and most austere of the Hindus, and who at that time included the richest native merchants of Bombay. That day they were celebrating a sort of religious carnival, with processions and entertainments at which dancing girls, dressed in pink gauze decorated with gold and silver, danced, gracefully but with perfect modesty, to the sound of viols and the beating of tambourines.

That Passepartout watched these curious ceremonies with eyes and ears wide open to see and hear, and that his expression and attitude were those of the greenest booby imaginable, goes without saying.

Unfortunately for himself and for his master, the success of whose journey he risked compromising, his curiosity took him to unseemly lengths. For after seeing something of that Parsee carnival, Passepartout was on his way to the station when, passing in front of the magnificant pagoda on Malabar Hill, he had the unhappy idea of looking inside.

There were two things he did not know: first of all that there are certain Hindu pagodas which Christians are strictly forbidden to enter, and secondly that the faithful themselves may not enter without first leaving their shoes outside. It should be added in this connection that the British Government, as a matter of policy, respected and enforced respect for the native religion down to its most trivial details, punishing very severely anyone who offended against the practices of that religion.

Passepartout went into the Malabar Hill pagoda like any tourist, without meaning any harm, and was admiring the dazzling Brahmin ornamentation, when he was suddenly knocked down on the sacred flagstones. Three priests, their eyes blazing with anger, flung themselves upon him, tore off his shoes and socks, and started raining blows upon him, at the same time uttering wild cries.

Strong and agile as he was, the Frenchman sprang to his feet. With a punch and a kick he knocked down two of his adversaries, whose long robes hampered their movements, then rushing out of the pagoda as fast as his legs could carry him, he soon left behind the third Hindu, who had dashed after him, stirring up the mob as he went.

At five to eight, only a few minutes before the train was

due to leave, Passepartout arrived at the station, hatless, barefoot, and without the parcel containing his purchases, which he had lost in the scuffle.

Fix was there on the platform. Having followed Mr Fogg to the station, he had realized that the scoundrel was going to leave Bombay, and promptly made up his mind to follow him to Calcutta, and even farther if necessary. Passepartout did not see Fix, who was standing in the shadows, but Fix overheard the brief account of his adventures which Passepartout gave his master.

"I trust that this will not happen again," was all that Phileas Fogg said in reply, as he took his seat in one of the carriages.

The poor fellow, barefoot and dejected, followed his master without saying a word.

Fix was about to enter another carriage when an idea suddenly struck him and made him change his mind.

"No, I'll stay here," he said to himself. "An offence committed on Indian soil . . . I've got my man."

At that moment the engine gave a loud whistle and the train disappeared into the darkness.

CHAPTER ELEVEN

In which Phileas Fogg buys a mount at a fabulous price

The train had left Bombay punctually. There were a fair number of passengers, including a few officers, some Indian Civil Servants and some opium and indigo traders whose business required their presence in the eastern part of the peninsula.

Passepartout was travelling in the same compartment as

The train entered the extensive mountain chain of the Western Ghauts

his master, and there was a third passenger in the opposite corner. This was Sir Francis Cromarty, one of Mr Fogg's partners during the passage from Suez to Bombay, who was now going to join his troops garrisoned near Benares.

A tall, fair-haired man of about fifty, Sir Francis Cromarty had greatly distinguished himself in the last Sepoy revolt. He could almost have been described as a native of India, for he had lived there since early youth, and had only rarely returned to his homeland. He was a man of learning, and would gladly have furnished information about the customs, history and organization of India if Phileas Fogg had been the sort of man to ask for it. But that gentleman asked for nothing. He was not travelling: he was describing a circumference. He was a solid body following an orbit round the terrestrial globe in accordance with the laws of mechanics. Just then he was calculating once again the hours he had spent since leaving London, and he would have rubbed his hands if it had been in his nature to make a useless gesture.

Sir Francis Cromarty had not failed to notice the eccentricity of his travelling companion, although he had only been able to study him while playing whist and between rubbers. He had therefore been led to wonder whether a human heart could really beat beneath that cold exterior, and whether Phileas Fogg possessed a soul alive to the beauties of nature and to moral aspirations. He rather doubted it. Of all the strange human beings the brigadier had ever met, not one could be compared to this product of the exact sciences.

Phileas Fogg had not concealed his plan to travel round the world from Sir Francis Cromarty, nor the conditions in which the journey was being made. The brigadier saw the wager only as an eccentric caprice, serving no useful purpose and therefore lacking that *transire benefaciendo* which should guide any reasonable man. If the odd fellow continued in this way, he would obviously go through life without doing anything for himself or for anybody else.

An hour after leaving Bombay, the train had crossed Salsette Island, passing over the viaducts, and was speeding across the continent. At Callyan it left on the right the branch line which goes through Kandallah and Poona towards southeast India, and came to Pauwell. There it entered the extensive mountain chain of the Western Ghauts, whose base is of trap and basalt, and whose highest peaks are thickly wooded.

From time to time Sir Francis Cromarty and Phileas Fogg exchanged a few words, and at one point the brigadier, reviving a conversation which kept flagging, said:

"A few years ago, Mr Fogg, you would have suffered a delay here which would probably have upset your time-table."

"Why, Sir Francis?"

"Because the railway stopped at the foot of these mountains, which had to be crossed in palanquins or on ponies to Kandallah on the other side."

"That delay would not have upset my programme in the slightest," replied Mr Fogg. "I have provided for the possibility of certain obstacles."

"All the same, Mr Fogg," the brigadier continued, "you risked having some trouble on your hands with this fellow's adventure."

Passepartout, his feet wrapped in his travelling rug, was fast asleep and had no idea that they were talking about him.

"The British Government is extremely strict about that sort of offence, and rightly so," Sir Francis went on. "It insists above all on respect for the religious customs of the Hindus, and if your servant had been caught . . ."

"Well, Sir Francis," replied Mr Fogg, "if he had been caught he would have been convicted, he would have served his sentence, and then he would have gone quietly back to Europe. I fail to see how that matter could have delayed his master."

Here the conversation lapsed once more.

During the night the train crossed the Ghauts and passed through Nassik. The next day, 21st October, found it speeding across the relatively flat countryside of the Khandeish. The land was well cultivated and dotted with villages, above which the minarets of the pagodas stood out like the church steeples in European villages. This fertile region was irrigated by a great many small streams, most of them direct or indirect tributaries of the Godavari.

Waking up, Passepartout looked out of the window, scarcely able to believe that he was crossing the land of the Hindus, in a train of the Great Peninsular Railway. The idea seemed incredible, yet nothing could be more real! The engine, controlled by the hand of an English driver and stoked with English coal, was puffing out its smoke over plantations of cotton, coffee, nutmeg, clove and pepper. Its steam wound in spirals round clumps of palm trees, between which he could glimpse picturesque bungalows, a few abandoned monasteries known as *viharis* and wonderful temples enriched by the inexhaustible ornamentation of Indian architecture. Then came vast expanses of land stretching as far as the eye could see, jungles in which there was no lack of snakes and tigers, terrified by the whistling of the engine, and finally forests cleft by the railway line and still frequented by elephants, which gazed pensively at the train with its dishevelled plume of smoke.

During the morning the travellers crossed the sinister region beyond Malligam which was so often stained with blood by the sectaries of the goddess Kali. Not far away rose Ellora with its splendid pagodas, and famous Aurungabad, the ferocious Aurungzeb's capital, now merely the chief town of one of the provinces detached from the Nizam's kingdom. It was over this area that Feringhea, chief of the Thugs and king of the Stranglers, used to hold sway. These murderers, joined together in an elusive association, strangled victims of all ages in honour of the goddess of Death, without shedding a drop of blood, and there was a time when it was impossible to turn up the earth anywhere here without finding a corpse. The British Government had undoubtedly succeeded in effecting a notable reduction in the number of these murders, but the terrifying association was still in existence and still at work.

At half past twelve the train stopped at Burhanpur, where for an exorbitant price Passepartout was able to buy a pair of Indian slippers decorated with false pearls, which he put on with unconcealed vanity.

The travellers ate a hasty lunch and then set off again for Assurghur, passing briefly along the banks of the

Tapty, a little river which flows into the Gulf of Cambray, near Surat.

This is a suitable point at which to reveal the thoughts then occupying Passepartout's mind. Until his arrival in Bombay he had believed, not without reason, that things would go no further. But now that they were travelling at full speed across India, his outlook changed completely. He recovered his old spirit, with all the wild fancies of his youth. Now he took the master's plans seriously: he believed in the reality of the wager, and hence in this journey round the world and this time limit which had not to be exceeded. Indeed, he was already worrying about possible delays, and accidents which might happen on the way. He felt personally involved in this wager, and trembled at the thought that he might have compromised it by his unpardonable stupidity the previous day. Moreover, being much less phlegmatic than Mr Fogg, he was much more anxious. Over and over again he counted the days which had gone by, cursed the train whenever it stopped, and mentally criticized Mr Fogg for not having promised the engine driver a bonus. The good fellow did not know that, while this was possible on the steamer, it could not be done on a train, whose speed is governed by the time-table.

Towards evening they entered the defiles of the Sutpur Mountains, which separate the territory of Khaidish from that of Bundelkhand.

The next day, 22nd October, in reply to a question from Sir Francis Cromarty, Passepartout looked at his watch and said it was three in the morning. And indeed, as this precious watch was still set by the Greenwich meridian, which was now nearly seventy-seven degrees to the west, it was bound to be, and in fact was, four hours slow.

Sir Francis accordingly corrected the time given by Passepartout, repeating what Fix had already told him. He tried to make him understand that the watch had to be set by each new meridian, and that as he was constantly travelling eastwards, in other words towards the sun, the days were shorter by four minutes for every degree he covered. It was all in vain. Whether the stubborn fellow had understood the brigadier's explanation or not, he obstinately refused to put his watch on and insisted on keeping it at London time. This was an innocent fad, in any case, which could not harm anyone.

At eight in the morning, fifteen miles short of Rothal, the train stopped in the middle of a vast clearing, on the edges of which there stood a few bungalows and work-men's huts. The guard walked along the train shouting:

"All change!"

Phileas Fogg looked at Sir Francis Cromarty, who did not seem to know what to make of this halt in the heart of a forest of tamarinds and khajours.

Passepartout, who was equally surprised, jumped down on to the track and came back almost at once exclaiming:

"Monsieur, there's no more railway!"

"What do you mean?" asked Sir Francis.

"I mean that the train doesn't go any farther!"

The brigadier got out at once, and Phileas Fogg followed him unhurriedly. Both of them questioned the guard.

"Where are we?" asked Sir Francis.

"At the hamlet of Kholby," the guard replied.

"Do we stop here?"

"Of course. The railway isn't finished . . ."

"What! It isn't finished?'

"No. There's still about fifty miles of track to be laid from here to Allahabad, where the line starts again."

"But the papers announced the complete opening of the railway!"

"Well, the papers were wrong, sir."

"But you issue tickets from Bombay to Calcutta!" said Sir Francis, who was beginning to get angry.

"That's true," replied the guard. "But the passengers

know very well that they have to find their own means of transport from Kholby to Allahabad."

Sir Francis Cromarty was furious, and Passepartout would have liked to knock the guard down, although it was not his fault. He did not dare to look at his master.

"Sir Francis," said Mr Fogg, "if you are agreeable we will see about finding a way of getting to Allahabad."

"But Mr Fogg, isn't this delay bound to upset your plans?"

"No, Sir Francis; it was provided for."

"What! You mean to say that you knew that the line . . ."

"Not at all, but I knew that some obstacle or other would crop up sooner or later on my way. Now there is no harm done. I have two days in hand which I can sacrifice. There's a steamer which leaves Calcutta for Hong Kong at noon on the twenty-fifth. Today is only the twenty-second, and we shall get to Calcutta in time."

There was nothing to be said in reply to a statement made with such complete assurance.

It was only too true that the railway went no farther. The papers are like certain watches which have a craze for going too fast, and they had announced the completion of the railway prematurely. Most of the travellers were aware of this break in the line, and on getting out of the train they had seized upon all the vehicles of various types which the hamlet could provide – four-wheeled palki-garis, carts drawn by zebus, a sort of humpbacked oxen, carriages which looked like perambulating pagodas, palanquins, pony carts and so on. The result was that Mr Fogg and Sir Francis Cromarty, after searching the village from end to end, returned without having found anything.

"I shall walk," said Phileas Fogg.

Passepartout, rejoining his master at that moment, pulled an expressive face as he looked at his splendid but quite inadequate slippers. Fortunately he too had been making enquiries, and with some hesitation he said:

"Monsieur, I think I've found a means of transport."

"What is it?"

"An elephant! An elephant belonging to an Indian who lives a hundred yards from here."

"Let us go and see the elephant," replied Mr Fogg.

Five minutes later, Phileas Fogg, Sir Francis Cromarty and Passepartout came to a hut adjoining a paddock enclosed by a high fence. In the hut there was an Indian, and in the paddock an elephant. At their request the Indian took Mr Fogg and his two companions into the paddock.

There they found themselves in the presence of a half-tamed animal which its owner was rearing not as a beast of burden but as a beast of combat. With this aim in view, he had begun to change the animal's naturally gentle character so as to bring it gradually to that paroxysm of fury which the Hindus call *mulsh,* by feeding it for three months on sugar and butter. This treatment might seem unlikely to produce such a result, but it is nonetheless used with success by elephant trainers. Fortunately for Mr Fogg the elephant in question had only just been put on this diet, and so far *mulsh* had not developed.

Like all its fellows, Kiouni — that was the animal's name — could travel rapidly for a long time, and in the absence of any other sort of mount, Phileas Fogg decided to use it.

But elephants are expensive in India, where they are beginning to become scarce. The males, which are the only elephants suitable for circus fighting, are greatly sought after. As these animals breed rarely once they have been tamed, they can only be obtained by hunting. Consequently their owners take the greatest care of them, and when Mr Fogg asked the Indian if he was willing to let him hire his elephant, the man flatly refused.

Fogg persisted and offered the considerable sum of ten

pounds an hour for the use of the beast. This was refused. Twenty pounds? Another refusal. Forty pounds? Yet another refusal. Passepartout gave a start at every increase, but the Indian was not to be tempted.

Yet it was a handsome offer. Assuming the elephant took fifteen hours to get to Allahabad, that would be six hundred pounds it would bring its owner.

Without showing the slightest excitement, Phileas Fogg then suggested buying the animal from the Indian and made an opening offer of a thousand pounds.

The Indian, possibly scenting a splendid bargain, refused to sell.

Sir Francis Cromarty took Mr Fogg aside and urged him to think before going any farther. Phileas Fogg replied that he was not in the habit of acting without thinking, that after all it was a wager of twenty thousand pounds that was at stake, that he had to have this elephant, and that he was going to have it, even if he had to pay twenty times what it was worth.

Mr Fogg went back to the Indian, whose little eyes, shining with greed, made it clear that for him it was only a question of how much he could get. Phileas Fogg offered in succession twelve hundred pounds, then fifteen hundred, then eighteen hundred, and finally two thousand. Passepartout, normally ruddy-cheeked, was pale with emotion.

At two thousand pounds the Indian gave in.

"By my slippers," exclaimed Passepartout, "here's somebody who puts a good price on elephant meat!"

Once the transaction had been completed, all that remained was to find a guide. This proved to be a simpler matter. A young Parsee with an intelligent face offered his services, which Mr Fogg accepted, promising him a large fee which could only stimulate his intelligence.

The elephant was brought out and equipped without delay. The Parsee, who was an expert *mahout*, covered the elephant's back with a sort of saddlecloth and fixed on each of its sides a rather uncomfortable howdah. Phileas Fogg paid the Indian in banknotes taken out of the famous travelling bag, an operation which hurt Passepartout as much as if they had been extracted from his own bowels. Then Mr Fogg offered to take Sir Francis Cromarty to Allahabad, an offer which the brigadier accepted. One more traveller was not likely to tire the gigantic animal.

Some provisions were bought at Kholby, and Sir Francis Cromarty took his seat in one of the howdahs, Phileas Fogg in the other. Passepartout sat astride on the saddlecloth between his master and the brigadier, and the Parsee perched himself on the elephant's neck. At nine o'clock the animal left the hamlet and plunged straight into the dense forest of palm trees.

CHAPTER TWELVE

In which Phileas Fogg and his companions venture through the forests of India, and what ensues

In order to shorten the journey, the guide left on his right the unfinished railway line, for because of the capricious ramifications of the Vindhai Mountains this line did not follow the direct route which it was in Phileas Fogg's interest to take. The Parsee, who was familiar with the roads and paths of the region, claimed to be able to gain twenty miles by cutting across the forest, and they took his word for it.

Phileas Fogg and Sir Francis Cromarty, enclosed up to their necks in their howdahs, were badly shaken about by

71

the brisk trot of the elephant, which the *mahout* was driving hard. But they endured this discomfort with true British phlegm, talking very little and scarcely able to see each other.

As for Passepartout, perched on the animal's back and receiving the full force of every jolt, he took good care to follow his master's advice not to put his tongue between his teeth, for otherwise it would have been bitten clean off. Now flung forward on to the elephant's neck and now thrown backwards on to its rump, the good fellow kept bouncing about like a clown on a trampoline. But he laughed and joked as he was flung about, and every now and then he produced a piece of sugar from his bag which the intelligent Kiouni took with the end of his trunk, without interrupting its regular trot for a single moment.

After two hours' progress the guide stopped the elephant and gave it an hour's rest. The animal first of all quenched its thirst at a nearby pool, and then began devouring some branches and shrubs. Sir Francis Cromarty did not complain about this halt, for he was tired out, but Mr Fogg looked as fresh as if he had just got out of bed.

"He must be made of iron!" said the brigadier, looking at him admiringly.

"Of wrought iron," replied Passepartout, as he started preparing a hasty lunch.

At noon the guide gave the signal for departure. The country soon took on a very wild appearance. The dense jungle gave place to copses of tamarinds and dwarf palms, and then to vast arid plains, bristling with stunted shrubs and strewn with great boulders of syenite. The whole of this part of upper Bundelkhand, little visited by travellers, was inhabited by a fanatical people hardened to the most terrible practices of the Hindu religion. The British had been unable to establish complete control over this region, subject as it was to the influence of the rajahs, whom it would have been difficult to reach in their inaccessible fastnesses in the Vindhia Mountains. Several times they caught sight of gangs of fierce-looking Indians who made angry gestures as they saw the huge quadruped speeding by. The Parsee did his best to avoid them, for he regarded them as dangerous customers. They saw few animals in the course of that day, only a few monkeys which scampered away with countless antics and grimaces, to Passepartout's huge delight.

One thought in particular among many others was worrying the young man. What would Mr Fogg do with the elephant when he reached Allahabad? Take it with him? That was impossible. The cost of transport added to the purchase price would make the animal ruinously expensive. Would he sell it then, or set it free? The worthy animal deserved every consideration. If by some chance Mr Fogg decided to make his servant a present of it, he would not know what to do. This possibility kept tormenting him.

By eight in the evening the main range of the Vindhias had been crossed, and the travellers stopped for the night in the ruined bungalow at the foot of the northern slopes.

That day they had covered about twenty-five miles, and they had another twenty-five miles to travel before reaching Allahabad.

The night was cold, so the Parsee lit a fire of dry branches, whose heat was much appreciated. Supper consisted of the provisions bought at Kholby, and the travellers ate like the tired, exhausted men they were. The conversation, which began with a few disjointed sentences, soon ended in loud snores. The guide kept watch beside Kiouni, who went to sleep standing up, leaning against the trunk of a sturdy tree.

The night passed without incident. The silence was occasionally broken by a few roars from cheetahs and panthers, mingled with the shrill chattering of monkeys, but the carnivorous animals confined themselves to roaring and made no hostile demonstration against the inmates of the bungalow. Sir Francis Cromarty slept heavily, like a gallant soldier overcome by fatigue. Passepartout had a restless night, reliving in his dreams the jolts he had suffered the previous day. As for Mr Fogg, he slept as peacefully as if he had been in his quiet house in Savile Row.

At six in the morning they set off again, the guide hoping to reach Allahabad that very evening. Mr Fogg would thus lose only part of the forty-eight hours he had gained since the beginning of his journey.

As they descended the last slopes of the Vindhias, Kiouni resumed his swift stride. About noon the guide skirted the little town of Kallinger, on the Cani, one of the tributaries of the Ganges. He always kept clear of inhabited places, feeling safer in those deserted plains which mark the first depressions of the great river basin. Allahabad was now less than twelve miles away to the northeast. They made a halt beneath a clump of banana trees, whose fruit, as wholesome as bread, and, according to travellers, "as tasty as cream", was greatly appreciated.

At two o'clock the guide entered a dense forest through which they would have to travel for a distance of several miles. He preferred to keep under cover of the trees. So far they had had no unpleasant encounters, and it looked as if the journey would be completed without incident when the elephant, showing signs of uneasiness, stopped in its tracks.

It was then four o'clock.

"What's the matter?" asked Sir Francis Cromarty, looking out of his howdah.

"I don't know, sir," replied the Parsee, listening to a vague murmur coming through the dense foliage.

A few moments later this murmur became more distinct. It was like a concert, still far away, of human voices and brass instruments.

Passepartout was all eyes and ears. Mr Fogg waited patiently, without saying a word.

The Parsee jumped down, tied the elephant to a tree and plunged into the thickest part of the wood. He returned a few minutes later, saying:

"A procession of Brahmins is coming this way. We must keep out of sight if we can."

The guide untied the elephant and led it into a thicket, advising the travellers not to dismount. He for his part held himself in readiness to remount quickly, if flight should be necesssary. But he thought that the procession of the faithful would go by without seeing him, for he was completely hidden by the dense foliage.

The discordant noise of voices and instruments drew nearer. Monotonous chants mingled with the beating of drums and the clash of cymbals. Soon the head of the procession appeared beneath the trees, about fifty yards from the position occupied by Mr Fogg and his companions, who could easily distinguish through the branches the curious personnel of this religious ceremony.

First came some priests, wearing mitres and dressed in long embroidered robes. They were surrounded by men, women and children chanting a sort of dirge, interrupted at regular intervals by the tom-toms and cymbals. Behind them came a car with wide wheels whose spokes and felloes were shaped like interlaced serpents. It was drawn by four richly caparisoned zebus and carried a hideous statue. It had four arms, a body coloured dark red, haggard eyes, tangled hair, a protruding tongue and lips tinted with henna and betel. Round its neck was a collar of death's heads, and round its loins a belt of severed hands. It stood erect on a prostrate giant without a head.

Sir Francis Cromarty recognized the statue.

"The goddess of Kali," he murmured, "the goddess of love and death."

"Of death perhaps, but of love never!" said Passepartout. "The ugly hag!"

The Parsee motioned to him to keep quiet.

Around the statue there leaped and danced and writhed a group of old fakirs, painted with stripes of ochre and covered with cross-shaped incisions from which their blood was oozing drop by drop. These were the stupid fanatics, who, in the great Hindu ceremonies, would still throw themselves under the car of Juggernaut.

Behind them a few Brahmins, in all the splendour of their oriental robes, were dragging along a woman who was scarcely able to stand. She was a young woman, with a skin as white as that of any European. Her head, neck, shoulders, ears, arms, fingers and toes were weighed down with jewels, necklaces, bracelets, earrings and rings. A gold-spangled tunic covered with a thin muslin veil revealed the outline of her figure.

In sharp contrast to the sight presented by this young woman, some guards walked behind her, armed with naked sabres at their belts and with long damascened pistols, and carrying a corpse on a palanquin.

This was the body of an old man, dressed in the splendid garb of a rajah. As in his lifetime, he wore the turban embroidered with pearls, the robe of silk and gold thread, the belt of diamond-studded cashmere and the magnificent weapons of an Indian prince.

Some musicians and a troop of fanatics, whose shouts occasionally drowned the deafening din of the instruments, brought up the rear.

Sir Francis Cromarty observed all this pomp with a singularly sad expression, and turning to the guide he said:

"A suttee."

The Parsee nodded and put a finger to his lips. The long procession slowly wound it way beneath the trees, and soon its last ranks disappeared into the depths of the forest.

76

Little by little the singing died away. There were a few more shouts in the distance, and then at last all this uproar was followed by a profound silence.

Phileas Fogg had heard what Sir Francis had said, and as soon as the procession had disappeared he asked:

"What is a suttee?"

"A suttee, Mr Fogg," replied the brigadier, "is a human sacrifice, but it is a voluntary sacrifice. That woman you have just seen will be burnt at dawn tomorrow."

"Oh, the scoundrels!" exclaimed Passepartout, unable to repress a cry of indignation.

"And what about that corpse?" asked Mr Fogg.

"That is the body of her husband the prince," replied the guide. "He was one of the independent rajahs of Bundelkhand."

"What!" said Phileas Fogg, without any trace of emotion in his voice. "Are these barbarous customs still practised in India, and haven't the English been able to suppress them?"

"In the greater part of India," replied Sir Francis, "these sacrifices are no longer carried out, but we have no influence over these wild regions, and least of all over this territory of Bundelkhand. The entire northern slope of the Vindhias is the scene of incessant killing and looting."

"Poor woman!" murmured Passepartout. "To be burnt alive!"

"Yes, burnt alive," said the brigadier. "But if she weren't you can't imagine what a wretched state she would be reduced to by her relatives. They would shave off her hair, feed her on just a few handfuls of rice, and spurn her completely. She would be treated as an unclean creature and left to die in some corner like a mangy dog. So it's often the prospect of such an appalling existence, much more than love or religious fanaticism, which drives these unfortunate creatures to death. Sometimes, however, the sacrifice is really voluntary, and it requires the forcible intervention of the Government to prevent it. For instance, a few years ago, when I was living in Bombay, a young widow came and asked the Governor for permission to be burnt with her husband's body. As you may imagine, the Governor refused. But then the widow left the town, took refuge on the territory of an independent rajah, and there succeeded in carrying out her wishes."

While the brigadier was telling this story, the guide kept shaking his head, and when Sir Francis had finished speaking he said:

"The sacrifice due to take place at dawn tomorrow is not a voluntary one."

"How do you know?"

"It's a story that everybody in Bundelkhand knows," replied the guide.

"But the poor woman seemed to be offering no resistance," observed Sir Francis.

"That's because they had drugged her with the fumes of hemp and opium."

"But where are they taking her?"

"To the pagoda of Pilagi, two miles from here. She will spend the night there waiting for the hour of the sacrifice."

"And when will that sacrifice take place?"

"Tomorrow, at the first sign of day."

With these words the guide led the elephant out of the thicket and hoisted himself on to the animal's neck. But just as he was about to urge it forward by means of a special whistle, Mr Fogg stopped him and, speaking to Sir Francis Cromarty, said:

"What if we were to rescue that woman?"

"Rescue that woman, Mr Fogg!" cried the brigadier.

"I've still got twelve hours to spare, I can use them for that."

"Good Lord! So you have got a heart!" exclaimed Sir Francis.

"Sometimes," was all that Phileas Fogg replied. "When I have time."

CHAPTER THIRTEEN

In which Passepartout proves once again that Fortune favours the bold

The plan was a daring one, bristling with difficulties and possibly impracticable. Mr Fogg was going to risk his life, or at least his liberty, and consequently the success of his journey. But he did not hesitate. What is more, he found a determined ally in Sir Francis Cromarty.

As for Passepartout, he was ready for anything and entirely at their disposal. His master's plan excited his enthusiasm. He felt there was a heart and soul under that icy exterior. He was beginning to like Phileas Fogg.

There remained the guide. What would he decide? Wouldn't he be likely to side with the Hindus? Failing his help, they must at least make sure of his neutrality.

Sir Francis Cromarty put the question to him frankly.

"Sir," replied the guide, "I am a Parsee, and that woman is a Parsee. I am ready to do whatever you wish."

"Good," said Mr Fogg.

"All the same," the Parsee went on, "I must warn you that we are not only risking our lives if we are caught, but also horrible tortures. So consider that carefully."

"It has all been considered," replied Mr Fogg. "I suppose we must wait until nightfall before we begin the rescue?"

"I think so too," answered the guide.

The good Indian then proceeded to give them a few

particulars about the victim. She was a famous beauty of the Parsee race, the daughter of a rich Bombay merchant. She had been given an English education in that city, and from her manners and her breeding could be taken for a European. Her name was Aouda.

Left an orphan, she had been married against her will to that old rajah of Bundelkhand. Three months later she had been widowed. Knowing the fate which awaited her, she had escaped, but she had been recaptured immediately, and the rajah's family, who had an interest in her death, had condemned her to this sacrifice from which it seemed she had no escape.

This story could only confirm Mr Fogg and his companion in their generous resolve. They decided that the guide should take the elephant towards the pagoda of Pillagi and get as close to it as possible

Half an hour later they halted in a copse five hundred yards from the pagoda. They could not see the building itself, but the howls of the fanatics were clearly audible.

Methods of reaching the victim were then discussed. The guide knew this pagoda, in which he asserted the young woman was imprisoned. Could they enter it through one of the doors when the whole crowd was plunged in a drunken stupor, or would they have to make a hole in one of the walls? That could be decided only at the time and on the spot. But one thing was quite certain, and that was that the abduction would have to be carried out that very night, and not at daybreak when the victim was taken out to die. At that moment no human intervention could possibly save her.

Mr Fogg and his companions waited for the night. As soon as darkness fell, about six o'clock, they decided to carry out a reconnaissance around the pagoda. The last cries of the fakirs were then dying away. According to their custom, the Indians should have sunk into the drunken slumber produced by *bhang*, liquid opium mixed with an infusion of hemp, and it might be possible to slip between them and reach the temple.

Followed by Mr Fogg, Sir Francis Cromarty and Passepartout, the Parsee moved noiselessly forward through the forest. After crawling for ten minutes under the branches, they reached the bank of a little river, and there, by the light of resin burning at the tips of iron torches, they saw a great pile of wood. This was the funeral pyre, made of costly sandalwood and already soaked in perfumed oil. On the top lay the embalmed body of the rajah, which was to be burnt at the same time as the widow. A hundred yards from this pyre stood the pagoda, whose minarets could be seen above the treetops in the dusk.

"Come on!" whispered the guide.

And more cautiously than ever, he silently slid through the tall grass, followed by his companions.

Nothing now broke the silence save the murmur of the wind in the branches.

Soon the guide stopped at the edge of a clearing lit by a few resin torches. The ground was strewn with groups of sleeping figures overcome by drunkenness. It looked like a battlefield with dead soldiers. Men, women and children were mingled together. Here and there a few drunkards were breathing noisily.

Between the trees the temple of Pillagi loomed vaguely in the background. But to the guide's great disappointment, the rajah's guards were keeping watch at the doors by the light of smoky torches, and pacing up and down with drawn swords. It was reasonable to assume that the priests were likewise keeping watch inside.

The Parsee went no farther. Recognizing the impossibility of entering the temple by force, he led his companions back.

Phileas Fogg and Sir Francis Cromarty had likewise realized that it was futile to try anything in that direction. They stopped and consulted together in whispers.

"Let's wait," said the brigadier. "It's only eight o'clock, and these guards may fall asleep too."

"Yes, that is a possibility," replied the Parsee.

Phileas Fogg and his companions accordingly stretched out at the foot of the tree and waited.

Time seemed to drag endlessly. Now and then the guide left them to see what was happening at the edge of the wood. The rajah's guards were still keeping watch in the glow of the torches, and a vague light was filtering through the windows of the pagoda.

They waited till midnight, but there was no change in the situation. The same watch was being kept outside, and it was obvious that they could not count on the guards' falling asleep. They had probably been spared the intoxication produced by *bhang*. It was therefore necessary to adopt another course of action and to try to enter the pagoda by making a hole in the wall. It remained to be seen whether the priests were watching over their victim as carefully as the soldiers were guarding the temple door.

After a final conversation the guide said that he was ready to start. Mr Fogg, Sir Francis and Passepartout followed him, and they made a fairly long detour to get to the back of the pagoda.

At about half past twelve they reached the foot of the walls without having met anyone. No watch was being kept on this side, but then there were no doors or windows to watch.

The night was dark. The moon, then in its last quarter, had barely risen above the horizon, which was shrouded with thick clouds. The height of the trees made the darkness deeper than ever.

But it was not enough to have reached the foot of the walls: they still had to make an opening in them. For this operation Phileas Fogg and his companions had absolutely nothing but their pocket knives. Fortunately the temple walls were built of bricks and wood which could not be

82

difficult to penetrate. Once the first brick had been removed, the others would come away easily.

They set to work, making as little noise as possible. The Parsee on one side and Passepartout on the other began loosening the bricks, so as to make an opening two feet wide.

The work was progressing when a cry rang out inside the temple, and almost immediately other cries responded from outside.

Passepartout and the guide stopped at once. Had they been heard? Had the alarm been given? The most elementary prudence urged them to withdraw, which they did at the same time as Phileas Fogg and Sir Francis Cromarty. Once again they crouched down under cover of the woods, waiting for the alarm, if it had been given, to die down, and ready, in that event, to resume their work.

But then their hopes were dashed as some guards appeared at the rear of the pagoda and stationed themselves there so as to prevent anyone from approaching.

It would be difficult to describe the disappointment of the four men, thus interrupted in their work. Now that they could not reach the victim, how could they save her? Sir Francis Cromarty started biting his nails. Passepartout was beside himself, and the guide had some difficulty in calming him down. The impassive Fogg waited without showing any emotion. "Is there nothing we can do but go?" the brigadier asked in a whisper.

"Yes, there is nothing else we can do," replied the guide.

"Wait," said Fogg. "It will be soon enough if I get to Allahabad before noon tomorrow."

"But what can you hope to do?" asked Sir Francis. "In a few hours it will be daylight, and . . ."

"Perhaps the opportunity which has escaped us will occur again at the last moment."

The brigadier would have liked to be able to read Phileas Fogg's eyes. What did this cold Englishman have in mind? Did he mean to rush towards the young woman just as the sacrifice was taking place, and snatch her openly from her executioners?

That would be sheer madness and he found it hard to believe that this man was as mad as that. Nevertheless, Sir Francis Cromarty agreed to wait until the end of this terrible drama. However, the guide would not leave his companions in the place where they had taken refuge, but led them to the front of the clearing. There, sheltered by a clump of trees, they could keep an eye on the sleeping groups.

In the meantime, Passepartout, who was perched on the lowest branches of a tree, was pondering an idea which, after flashing through his mind like lightning, had finally taken root.

He had begun by telling himself that it was utter madness, but now he kept muttering: "After all, why not? It's a chance, maybe the only one, and with brutes like that . . ."

Without formulating his idea any more clearly than that, Passepartout soon started crawling with the suppleness of a snake along the lower branches of the tree, the ends of which hung down towards the ground.

The hours went by, and eventually a few lighter shades announced the approach of day, though it was still very dark.

The moment had come. A sort of resurrection took place among the slumbering crowd. The groups of people came to life. Tom-toms sounded. Chants and cries broke out anew. The hour had come when the unfortunate woman was to die.

Sure enough, the doors of the pagoda opened and brighter light escaped from the interior. In the vivid glare, Mr Fogg and Sir Francis Cromarty could see the victim being dragged outside by a couple of priests. It even seemed to them that the poor woman, shaking off her drunken stupor in obedience to a supreme instinct of self-preservation, was trying to escape from her executioners. Sir Francis Cromarty's heart gave a leap, and as he grasped Phileas Fogg's hand in a convulsive movement, he found that it was holding an open knife.

At that moment the crowd began to move. The young woman, who had fallen back into the torpor produced by the fumes of hemp, passed by among the fakirs, who were escorting her with their religious chants.

Phileas Fogg and his companions, mingling with the last ranks of the crowd, followed her.

Two minutes later they reached the river bank and stopped less than fifty yards from the funeral pyre, on which the rajah's body was lying. In the semi-darkness they saw the victim stretched out, completely inert, beside her husband's corpse.

Then a torch was applied, and the wood, soaked with oil, caught fire at once.

Sir Francis Cromarty and the guide had to hold back Phileas Fogg, who, in a moment of noble folly, was trying to dash towards the pyre . . .

But he had already thrust them aside when the scene was suddenly transformed. A cry of terror arose, and the whole crowd fell to the ground, stricken with horror.

So the old rajah was not dead, for he could be seen suddenly rising up like a ghost, picking up the young woman in his arms, and coming down from the pyre surrounded by wreaths of smoke which lent him a spectral appearance! Seized with sudden terror, fakirs, guards and priests lay there with their faces to the ground, not daring to raise their eyes and look at such a miracle.

The insensible victim was carried along in the strong arms which held her, without appearing to tire them. Mr Fogg and Sir Francis Cromarty were still on their feet, but the Parsee had bowed his head, and no doubt Passepartout was no less astounded.

Seized with terror they lay with their faces to the ground

The resuscitated rajah came forward in this way to where Mr Fogg and Sir Francis were standing, and there said curtly:

"Let's clear off!"

It was Passepartout himself who had crept towards the pyre in the midst of the thick smoke! It was Passepartout who, taking advantage of the darkness, which was still profound, had snatched the young woman from the jaws of death! It was Passepartout who, playing his part with lucky boldness, had walked right through the panic-stricken crowd!

A moment later all four had disappeared into the wood, and the elephant was carrying them off at a brisk trot. But shouts, cries, and even a bullet which made a hole in Phileas Fogg's hat, told them that their ruse had been discovered.

Sure enough, the old rajah's body was now clearly visible on the blazing pyre. The priests, recovering from their fright, had promptly rushed into the forest, followed by the guards. A volley had been fired, but the abductors

86

fled swiftly, and in a few moments they were out of reach of bullets and arrows.

CHAPTER FOURTEEN

In which Phileas Fogg travels down the whole length of the splendid valley of the Ganges without even thinking of seeing it

The bold abduction had been successful. An hour later Passepartout was still chuckling over his triumph. Sir Francis Cromarty had shaken hands with the daring fellow, and his master had said: "Well done," which in his mouth was praise indeed. To this Passepartout had replied that all the credit in this business belonged to his master. All that he had done was to have a "funny" idea, and he kept laughing at the thought that for a few moments he, Passepartout, former gymnast and one-time sergeant in the fire brigade, had been an elderly embalmed rajah and the husband of a charming widow.

As for the young woman, she had known nothing of what had happened. Wrapped in the travelling rugs, she was resting in one of the howdahs.

In the meantime the elephant, directed with considerable skill by the Parsee, was making swift progress through the forest, although it was still dark. An hour after leaving the pagoda of Pillagi, it was crossing a vast plain, and at seven o'clock the party halted. The young woman was still in a state of complete prostration. The guide made her swallow a few mouthfuls of brandy and water, but she was to remain in this drugged stupor a little longer.

Sir Francis Cromarty, who knew the effects of the

intoxication produced by inhaling the fumes of hemp, felt no anxiety on her account.

But while the brigadier had no doubts about the young woman's recovery, he felt far less confident about her future. He did not hesitate to tell Phileas Fogg that if Aouda remained in India she would inevitably fall once more into the hands of her executioners. These fanatics had connections throughout the peninsula, and in spite of the British police they would be sure to recapture their victim, whether in Madras, Bombay or Calcutta. And in support of this warning Sir Francis cited a similar incident which had recently occurred. In his opinion the young woman would not be really safe until she had left India.

Phileas Fogg replied that he would bear these remarks in mind and take the necessary steps.

About ten o'clock the guide announced that they had reached Allahabad. There the interrupted railway line began again, with trains covering the distance between Allahabad and Calcutta in less than twenty-four hours. Phileas Fogg would therefore arrive in time to take a steamer due to leave for Hong Kong at noon the following day, 25th October.

The young woman was left in a waiting room at the station, and Passepartout was sent to go and buy various articles of clothing for her – a dress, a shawl, some furs and so forth, indeed anything he could find. His master gave him unlimited credit.

Passepartout set off straight away to explore the streets of Allahabad. The "City of God" is one of the most revered places in India, as it stands at the junction of two holy rivers, the Ganges and the Jumna, whose waters attract pilgrims from all over the peninsula. It is of course common knowledge that, according to the legend of the Ramayana, the Ganges rises in heaven, from which it flows down to earth through the grace of Brahma.

While he did his shopping, Passepartout soon saw all

there was to be seen of the city, once protected by a splendid fort, which had been turned into a state prison. Formerly an industrial and trading centre, Allahabad no longer had either commerce or industry. Passepartout hunted around for a draper's shop, as if he had been in Regent Street close to Farmer and Co, but in vain. All he could find was a secondhand shop kept by an unscrupulous old Jew, from whom he bought the articles he needed, a plain dress, a voluminous cloak and a magnificent otterskin pelisse, for which he had no hesitation in paying seventy-five pounds. He then returned in triumph to the station.

Aouda was beginning to recover consciousness. The effect of the drugs to which the priests of Pillagi had subjected her was gradually wearing off, and her beautiful eyes were regaining all their Indian softness.

When the poet king, Usaf Addaul, celebrates the charms of the Queen of Ahmehnagara, he expresses himself in these terms:

"Her gleaming hair, evenly parted, frames the harmonious contours of her delicate white cheeks, radiant in their smooth freshness. Her ebony brows have the shape and power of the bow of Kama, the god of Love, and beneath her long silky lashes, in the black pupils of her great limpid eyes, swim the purest reflections of heavenly light, as in the holy lakes of Himalaya. Her small, white, even teeth shine between her smiling lips like dewdrops in the half-closed heart of a pomegranate flower. Her dainty ears with their symmetrical curves, her rosy hands, her little feet, rounded and tender as lotus buds, shine with the brilliance of the finest pearls of Ceylon, the most splendid diamonds of Golconda. Her slim, supple waist, which a single hand can encircle, sets off the elegant curve of her rounded loins and the rich beauty of her bosom, in which blossoming youth displays its most perfect treasures, and beneath the silken folds of her tunic she seems to have been modelled in pure silver by the divine hand of Vicvacarma, the immortal sculptor."

Without all this embroidery, it is sufficient to say that Aouda, the widow of the Rajah of Bundelkhand, was a charming woman in the full European sense of the word. She spoke excellent English, and the guide had not exaggerated when he asserted that this young Parsee woman had been transformed by her upbringing.

The train was now about to leave Allahabad, and the Parsee was waiting. Mr Fogg paid him his agreed wages, without a farthing extra. This rather surprised Passepartout, who knew all that his master owed to the guide's devotion. The Parsee had, in fact, willingly risked his life in the Pillagi affair, and if the Hindus ever heard of this, he would find it difficult to escape their vengeance.

There also remained the question of Kiouni. What was to be done with an elephant bought at such a price?

But Phileas Fogg had already made up his mind on this question.

"Parsee," he said to the guide, "you have given me devoted service. I have paid for your service, but not for your devotion. Would you like to have this elephant? If so, it is yours."

The guide's eyes shone.

"Your honour is giving me a fortune!" he exclaimed.

"Take it, guide," replied Mr Fogg, "and I shall still be in your debt."

"Splendid!" cried Passepartout. "Take it, friend! Kiouni is a fine, brave animal!"

And going up to the elephant, he held out a few lumps of sugar, saying:

"Here you are, Kiouni, here you are!"

The elephant gave a few grunts of satisfaction. Then, coiling its trunk round Passepartout's waist, it lifted him as high as its head. Passepartout, not in the least frightened, patted the animal, which gently replaced him on the ground, and in response to the worthy Kiouni's "trunk-shake" the good fellow gave it a hearty handshake.

A few moments later, Phileas Fogg, Sir Francis Cromarty and Passepartout, installed in a comfortable railway carriage, whose best seat was occupied by Aouda, were travelling at full speed towards Benares. The distance between this town and Allahabad is eighty miles at the most, and it was covered in two hours.

During this journey the young woman regained consciousness completely as the stupefying fumes of the *bhang* wore off.

How astonished she was to find herself in this railway carriage, dressed in European clothes, and in the company of travellers who were complete strangers to her!

To begin with, her companions lavished attention on her and revived her with a few drops of brandy; then the brigadier told her what had happened. He dwelt on the devotion shown by Phileas Fogg, who had not hesitated to risk his life to save her, and on the happy outcome of the adventure, due to Passepartout's bold imagination.

Mr Fogg let him speak without saying a single word, but Passepartout, overcome by shyness, kept saying that "it wasn't worth mentioning".

Aouda thanked her rescuers effusively, more with her tears than with her words. Her beautiful eyes interpreted her gratitude even better than her lips. Then, as her thoughts took her back to the scenes of the suttee, and her gaze fell once more upon that land of India where so many dangers still faced her, she shuddered with terror.

Phileas Fogg realized what was passing through her mind. To reassure her he offered, though very coldly, to take her to Hong Kong, where she could stay until this affair had blown over.

Aouda accepted the offer gratefully. As it happened she had a relative living at Hong Kong, a Parsee like herself, and one of the leading merchants in that city.

91

At half past twelve the train came to a halt at Benares. The Brahmin legends maintain that this city stands on the site of ancient Kasi, which was formerly suspended in space like Mahomet's tomb, between the zenith and the nadir. But in these more realistic days, Benares, which orientalists called the Athens of India, rested quite prosaically on the ground, and Passepartout caught a brief glimpse of its brick houses and wattle huts which gave it an utterly desolate appearance, without any trace of local colour.

This was where Sir Francis Cromarty had to leave them, for the troops he was rejoining were encamped a few miles to the north of the town. The brigadier accordingly bade Phileas Fogg farewell, wishing him every possible success, and expressing the hope that he might make this journey again one day in a less original, but more profitable way. Mr Fogg gave his fingers a gentle squeeze in response. Aouda's leave-taking was more affectionate. Never, she said, would she forget what she owed Sir Francis Cromarty. As for Passepartout, he was honoured with a hearty handshake and, deeply moved, asked himself where and when he might be able to be of service to the brigadier. Then they parted.

After Benares the railway followed the valley of the Ganges for a while. The weather was fairly clear, and through the windows of their carriage the travellers could see the varied landscape of Behar, the mountains covered with greenery, fields of barley, maize and wheat, streams and ponds inhabited by greenish alligators, well-kept villages and forests which were still green. A few elephants and some zebus with big humps came to bathe in the waters of the sacred river, as well as some parties of Hindus of both sexes, who in spite of the lateness of the season and the already chilly temperature piously performed their holy ablutions. These devotees, bitter enemies of Buddhism, are fervent followers of the Brahmin religion, with its divine trinity, Vishnu, the sun-god, Shiva, the divine incarnation of the natural forces, and Brahma, the supreme master of priests and lawgivers. What must Brahma, Shiva and Vishnu have thought of this anglicized India, when some steamboat went screeching by, churning up the sacred waters of the Ganges and startling the gulls skimming its surface, the turtles teeming on its banks, and the faithful stretched out along its shores!

The whole of this panorama went by like a flash, its details often hidden by a cloud of white steam. The travellers had only a brief glimpse of the fort of Chunar, twenty miles southeast of Benares, an ancient stronghold of the rajahs of Behar; of Ghaziput and its important rose-water factories; of Lord Cornwallis's tomb standing on the left bank of the Ganges; of the fortified town of Buxar; of Patna, a large industrial and commercial city and the principal centre of the opium trade in India; and of Monghyr, a more than European town, as English as Manchester or Birmingham, famous for its iron foundries and its edge tools and side arm factories, and whose tall chimneys stained Brahma's sky with black smoke – a brutal attack on the land of dreams.

Then night fell, and the train sped onwards in the midst of the roaring of tigers, the growling of bears and the howling of wolves which fled before the engine; and nothing more was seen of the wonders of Bengal – Golconda, the ruins of Gour, Murshidabad, once a metropolis, Burdwan, Hugli and Chandernagore, that French outpost on Indian territory over which Passepartout would have been proud to see his country's flag flying.

At last, at seven in the morning, they arrived in Calcutta. The steamer for Hong Kong was not due to weigh anchor before noon, so that Phileas Fogg had five hours to spare. According to his timetable, he was supposed to arrive here on 25th October, twenty-three days after leaving London, and he had arrived on the appointed day. He was therefore neither behind nor ahead of his schedule. Unfortunately, the two days he had gained between London and Bombay had been lost, as we have seen, in crossing the Indian peninsula — but we may reasonably assume that Phileas Fogg did not regret them.

CHAPTER FIFTEEN

In which the bag holding the banknotes is once again lightened by a few thousand pounds

When the train came to a stop in the station, Passepartout was the first to get out of the carriage. He was followed by Mr Fogg, who helped his young companion on to the platform. Phileas Fogg intended to go straight to the Hong Kong steamer, in order to see Aouda comfortably installed for the voyage. He did not wish to leave her as long as she was in a country so full of danger for her.

Just as Mr Fogg was about to leave the station, a policeman came up to him and said:

"Mr Phileas Fogg?"

"That is my name."

"Is this man your servant?" asked the policeman, pointing to Passepartout.

"Yes."

"Will both of you kindly come along with me."

Mr Fogg showed no sign of surprise. This policeman was a representative of the law, and the law is sacred to all Englishmen. Passepartout, like a true Frenchman, tried to argue, but the policeman tapped him with his truncheon, and Phileas Fogg motioned to him to obey.

"May this young lady come with us?" asked Mr Fogg.

"She may," replied the policeman.

He led Mr Fogg, Aouda and Passepartout to a *palkigari*, a sort of four-wheeled carriage with four seats, drawn by two horses, and it was driven off. Nobody spoke during the journey, which lasted about twenty-minutes.

The *palkigari* drew up in front of a house which looked unpretentious but which was obviously not a private residence. The policeman told his prisoners – for that is what they were – to get out, led them into a room with barred windows, and told them:

"You will appear before Judge Obadiah at half past eight." Then he went out and shut the door.

"Well, they've caught us!" exclaimed Passepartout, dropping on to a chair.

Speaking to Mr Fogg and trying in vain to conceal her emotion, Aouda said straight away:

"Sir, you must leave me! It is on my account that you are being prosecuted! It is because you rescued me!"

Phileas Fogg merely replied that this was impossible. It was inconceivable that he should be prosecuted because of that business of the suttee. How would the plaintiffs dare to come foward? There must be a mistake. Mr Fogg added that in any case he would not abandon the young woman, but would take her to Hong Kong.

"But the boat leaves at noon!" observed Passepartout.

"We shall be on board before noon," was all that the imperturbable gentleman replied.

He spoke with such assurance that Passepartout could not help saying to himself:

"Yes, of course, there's no doubt about that! We shall be on board before noon!" But he was far from reassured.

At half past eight the door opened. The policeman reappeared and ushered the prisoners into the next room. This was a courtroom in which the public benches were already occupied by a fairly large number of Europeans and natives.

Mr Fogg, Aouda and Passepartout sat down on a bench facing the seats reserved for the judge and the clerk of the court.

This magistrate, Judge Obadiah, a stout, rotund man, entered almost at once, followed by the clerk. He took down a wig hanging on a nail and briskly put it on.

"The first case!" he said.

But then, putting his hand on his head, he exclaimed: "Here! This isn't my wig!"

"No, your worship, it's mine," replied the clerk.

"My dear Mr Oysterpuff, how do you expect a judge to dispense justice properly wearing a clerk's wig!"

The wigs were duly exchanged. During these preliminaries Passepartout was fuming with impatience, for the hands of the big courtroom clock seemed to be moving round the dial terribly fast.

"The first case!" repeated Judge Obadiah.

"Phileas Fogg?" said Oysterpuff.

"Here," replied Mr Fogg.

"Passepartout?"

"Present!" replied Passepartout.

"Good!" said Judge Obadiah. "Prisoners at the bar, for two days the police have been looking for you on every train from Bombay."

"But what are we accused of?" cried Passepartout, losing patience.

"You will soon find out," replied the judge.

"Sir," said Mr Fogg at this point, "I am a British subject and I am entitled . . .'

"Have you been ill-treated in any way?" asked Judge Obadiah.

"Not in the least."

"Good! Show in the plaintiffs."

At the judge's order a door opened and three Hindu priests were shown in by an usher.

"Just as I thought!" muttered Passepartout. "Those are the scoundrels who were trying to burn our young lady!"

The priests stood in front of the judge, and the clerk of the court read out a charge of sacrilege against Phileas Fogg and his servant, who were accused of violating a place consecrated by the Brahmin religion.

"You have heard the charge?" the judge asked Phileas Fogg.

"Yes, sir," replied Mr Fogg, looking at his watch, "and I admit it."

"Ah! You admit it?"

"I admit it, and I am waiting for these three priests to admit in their turn what they were going to do at the pagoda of Pillagi."

The priests looked at each other. They seemed unable to make head or tail of what the defendant was saying.

"Why, yes!" Passepartout burst out impetuously. "At that pagoda at Pillagi, where they were going to burn their victim."

The priests showed fresh astonishment, while Judge Obadiah looked utterly astounded.

"What victim?" he asked. "Burn whom? In the heart of Bombay?"

"Bombay?" exclaimed Passepartout.

"Yes, Bombay. This has nothing to do with the pagoda of Pillagi, but the pagoda of Malabar Hill in Bombay."

"And as evidence," added the clerk, "here are the desecrator's shoes." And he placed a pair of shoes on his desk.

"My shoes!" cried Passepartout, who was so surprised that he could not keep back this involuntary exclamation.

The confusion which had taken place in the minds of master and servant may well be imagined. They had completely forgotten that incident of the Bombay pagoda, and it was that very incident which had brought them before the Calcutta magistrate.

Inspector Fix had in fact realized the advantage he could derive from that unfortunate affair. Delaying his departure for twelve hours, he had appointed himself adviser to the priests of Malabar Hill; he had promised them heavy damages, knowing very well that the British Government treated this kind of offence very severely; then he had sent them off by the next train in pursuit of the desecrators.

But because of the time spent in rescuing the young widow, Fix and the Hindus reached Calcutta before Phileas Fogg and his servant, whom the magistrates, notified by telegram, had been supposed to arrest as soon as they got off the train. It is easy to imagine Fix's disappointment when he learnt that Phileas Fogg had not yet reached the capital, for he was forced to suppose that his robber had stopped at one of the stations along the Peninsular Railway and taken refuge in the northern provinces. For twenty-four hours, a prey to mortal anxiety, Fix lay in wait for him at the station. Imagine then his joy when, that very morning, he saw him getting out of a carriage, admittedly in the company of a young woman whose presence he could not understand. He promptly pointed him out to a policeman, and that is how Mr Fogg, Passepartout and the widow of the Rajah of Budelkhand, were brought before Judge Obadiah.

If Passepartout had been less preoccupied with his case, he would have noticed the detective in a corner of the courtroom, following the proceedings with an interest easy to understand – for in Calcutta, as in Bombay and at Suez, he was still without his warrant.

In the meantime, Judge Obadiah had taken note of the confession blurted out by Passepartout, who would have given all he possessed to take back his rash words.

"The facts are admitted?" asked the judge.

"They are admitted," Mr Fogg replied coldly.

"Inasmuch," the judge continued, "as English law insists on giving equal and strict protection to all the religions of the peoples of India, and inasmuch as the offence has been admitted by the defendant Passepartout, who stands convicted of having desecrated with a sacrilegious foot the floor of the pagoda of Malabar Hill in Bombay, on the twentieth of October, I hereby sentence the aforementioned Passepartout to fourteen days' imprisonment and a fine of three hundred pounds."

"Three hundred pounds?" exclaimed Passepartout, to whom only the fine really mattered.

"Silence!" yelped the usher.

"And," added Judge Obadiah, "inasmuch as it is not satisfactorily established that there was no connivance between servant and master, and inasmuch as the latter must in any case be held responsible for the acts of a paid employee, I hereby sentence the aforementioned Phileas Fogg to seven days' imprisonment and a fine of one hundred and fifty pounds. Clerk, call the next case!"

In his corner Fix was filled with indescribable satisfaction. For Phileas Fogg to be detained for a week in Calcutta was more than was needed to give the warrant time to reach him.

Passepartout was dumbfounded. This sentence spelt ruin for his master. A wager of twenty thousand pounds had been lost, and all because, like an utter fool, he had gone into that cursed pagoda!

Phileas Fogg, as composed as if this sentence were nothing to do with him, had not so much as frowned. But just as the clerk was calling the next case, he stood up and said:

"I wish to offer bail."

"You are entitled to do so," replied the judge.

Fix felt a shiver run down his spine, but he regained his composure when he heard the judge, "in view of the status of Phileas Fogg and his servant as travellers", fix bail at the enormous sum of a thousand pounds each.

If Mr Fogg failed to serve his sentence, it would cost him two thousand pounds.

"Here is the money," said that gentleman.

And from the bag Passepartout was carrying he took a wad of banknotes which he placed on the clerk's desk.

"This sum will be returned to you when you leave prison," said the judge. "In the meantime you are released on bail."

"Come along," Phileas Fogg said to his servant.

"They might at least return my shoes," cried Passepartout angrily.

His shoes were given back to him.

"They've cost a tidy sum!" he muttered. "Over a thousand pounds each! And they aren't even comfortable!"

Utterly crestfallen, Passepartout followed Mr Fogg, who had given the young woman his arm. Fix still hoped that his robber would decide against parting with that sum of two thousand pounds and that he would serve his seven days' imprisonment. He accordingly hurried after Fogg.

Mr Fogg took a carriage, and Aouda, Passepartout and he himself promptly climbed into it. Fix ran after the carriage, which soon drew up on one of the quays.

Half a mile out in the roadstead the *Rangoon* lay at anchor, the Blue Peter flying at her masthead. Eleven o'clock was striking. Mr Fogg was an hour ahead of time.

Fix saw him get out of the carriage and into a small boat with Aouda and his servant. The detective stamped his foot.

"The scoundrel is leaving," he exclaimed. "Two thousand pounds thrown away! He's as spendthrift as a thief! Oh, I'll follow him to the ends of the earth if need be, but if he goes on at this rate, there'll be nothing left of the stolen money!"

The police inspector had good grounds for making this remark. For in fact, since leaving London, what with fares, bribes, the purchase of an elephant, fines and bail, Phileas Fogg had already thrown away more than five thousand pounds; and the percentage on the sum recovered which was given to the detectives concerned was steadily decreasing.

CHAPTER SIXTEEN

In which Fix appears to know nothing of what he is told

The *Rangoon*, one of the P & O Line steamers plying in the Chinese and Japanese seas, was an iron screw-propelled boat, of 1,770 tons burden and 400 horsepower. She was as fast as the *Mongolia*, but not as luxurious, so Aouda was not as comfortably accommodated as Phileas Fogg would have liked. But then this passage was only of 3,500 miles, a matter of elevan or twelve days, and the young woman was not a difficult passenger.

During the first few days of the voyage, Aouda became better acquainted with Phileas Fogg, and she took every opportunity of showing him the deepest gratitude. The phlegmatic gentleman listened to her with the most extreme coldness, or so at least it appeared, without betraying the slightest emotion by either voice or gesture. He saw to it that the young woman lacked nothing, and he came regularly at certain hours, if not to chat with her, at least to listen to her. He carried out all the duties which the strictest politeness required, but with as much graciousness and spontaneity as an automaton might have shown whose movements had been planned for that purpose. Aouda did not know what to think, but Passepartout had given her some idea of his master's eccentric character, telling her about the wager which was taking him round the world. This had made Aouda smile, but after all, she owed her life to Phileas Fogg, and her rescuer could only gain by being seen in the light of her gratitude.

Aouda confirmed the account the Hindu guide had given of her touching life story. She did indeed belong to that race which ranks highest among the races of India. Several Parsee merchants had made great fortunes in the Peninsula through the cotton trade. One of them, Sir James Jejeebhoy, had been given a title by the British Government, and Aouda was related to this wealthy personage, who lived in Bombay. In fact it was a cousin of his, the Honourable Jejeeh, whom she hoped to meet in Hong Kong. But would he give her protection and assistance? That she could not say for certain. To this Mr Fogg replied that she had no need to worry, and that everything would be arranged, as he put it, "mathematically".

It is impossible to say whether the young woman understood that horrible adverb. In any case, she gazed at Mr Fogg with her great eyes "as clear as the sacred lakes of Himalaya". But the intractable Fogg, as reserved as ever, did not seem to be the sort of man to throw himself into that lake.

The first part of the voyage was carried out under excellent conditions. The weather was good, and the whole of that part of the huge bay which sailors call "the Bengal Fathoms" favoured the steamer's progress. The *Rangoon* soon came in sight of Great Andaman, the principal island in the group, which navigators can recognize from a very great distance by its picturesque mountain, the Saddle Peak, which rises to a height of 2,400 feet.

The ship kept quite close to the shore, but the Papuan savages of the island, creatures on the lowest rung of the human ladder, but wrongly believed to be cannibals, did not show themselves.

The panorama offered by these islands was superb. The

foreground was filled with vast forests of palms, areca, bamboo, nutmeg, teak, gigantic mimosa and arborescent ferns, while in the background the mountains were gracefully silhouetted against the sky. Along the coast swarmed thousands of those precious swallows whose edible nests are considered a great delicacy in the Celestial Empire. But all this varied scenery of the Andaman Islands was soon out of sight, and the *Rangoon* sped swiftly towards the Malacca Straits, through which she would enter the China seas.

But what was Inspector Fix, haplessly dragged into a journey round the world, doing during this passage? Leaving instructions at Calcutta for the warrant, if it finally arrived, to be sent on to him at Hong Kong, he had managed to embark on the *Rangoon* without being noticed by Passepartout, and he hoped to conceal his presence until the steamer arrived at her destination. It would, after all, be difficult to explain why he was on board without arousing Passepartout's suspicions, as the servant must think he was still in Bombay. But the force of circumstances led him to renew acquaintance with the worthy fellow, as the reader is about to see.

All the inspector's hopes and desires were now concentrated on one spot in the world, namely Hong Kong, for the steamer would not stay at Singapore long enough to enable him to take action there. The arrest must therefore be made at Hong Kong, or the robber would escape him, so to speak, for good.

For Hong Kong, too, was British soil, but the last British soil they would meet with on the journey. Beyond lay China, Japan and America, all offering Fogg a fairly certain refuge. At Hong Kong, if Fix finally found the warrant which was obviously chasing him, he would arrest Fogg and place him in the custody of the local police. There was no difficulty about that. But beyond Hong Kong a mere warrant would no longer be sufficient. He would need an extradition order. That would mean delays, setbacks and all sorts of obstacles, of which the scoundrel would take advantage in order to escape once for all. If the operation failed at Hong Kong, it would be very difficult, if not impossible, to repeat it with any hope of success.

"Consequently," Fix kept telling himself during the long hours he spent in his cabin, "either the warrant will be at Hong Kong, and I arrest my man, or it won't be there, and then I shall have to delay his departure at all costs! I failed in Bombay, and I failed in Calcutta! If I fail at Hong Kong, my reputation is done for! Whatever it costs I must succeed. But if it proves necessary, how am I going to delay that cursed fellow?"

As a last resort, Fix had made up his mind to tell Passepartout everything and let him know what sort of master he was serving, for he was certainly not Fogg's accomplice. Enlightened by this disclosure, Passepartout would doubtless side with Fix, as he would be afraid of being compromised. But this was a risky method, only to be used if everything else had failed. One word from Passepartout to his master would be enough to spoil everything completely.

The inspector was therefore in a state of extreme perplexity when the presence of Aouda on the *Rangoon*, in Phileas Fogg's company, opened up new perspectives.

Who was this woman? What combination of circumstances had made her Fogg's companion? They had obviously met between Bombay and Calcutta, but where? Was it chance that had brought Phileas Fogg and the young woman together, or had he undertaken this journey across India for the express purpose of joining this charming person? For charming she certainly was, as Fix had seen for himself in the courtroom in Calcutta.

It is easy to understand how intrigued the detective was. He wondered whether this business might not involve a criminal abduction. Yes, that must be it! This idea took root in Fix's mind, and he began to realize the advantage he could derive from this new development. Whether the young woman was married or not, it was a case of abduction, and at Hong Kong he might be able to create difficulties for the abductor from which no amount of money could extricate him.

But he must not wait for the *Rangoon* to reach Hong Kong. This fellow Fogg had a deplorable habit of jumping out of one boat into another, and he might be far away before proceedings had been initiated.

It was therefore essential to warn the British authorities and to announce the approach of the *Rangoon* before Fogg landed. Now, nothing was simpler, since the steamer called at Singapore and Singapore was connected by telegraph with the Chinese coast.

However, before taking any action, and in order to make success more certain, Fix decided to question Passepartout. He knew that it was not very difficult to get the fellow to talk, and he made up his mind to emerge from the concealment in which he had remained so far. There was no time to lose, for it was 30th October, and the *Rangoon* was due to put in at Singapore the very next day.

So that day Fix left his cabin and went up on deck with the intention of accosting Passepartout first, with every sign of complete astonishment. Passepartout was strolling about in the bows when the inspector rushed up to him, exclaiming:

"What! You here on the *Rangoon*!"

"Monsieur Fix on board!" replied Passepartout in amazement as he recognized his fellow passenger of the *Mongolia*. "Well, I never! I leave you in Bombay, and I find you on the way to Hong Kong! Are you going round the world too?"

"No, no," answered Fix. "I intend to stop at Hong Kong – for a few days at least."

"I see," said Passepartout, who seemed surprised for a moment. "But how is it I haven't seen you on board since we left Calcutta?"

"Well, I haven't been too well . . . a bit of seasickness . . . I've been lying down in my cabin . . . The Bay of Bengal doesn't suit me as well as the Indian Ocean. But how is your master, Mr Phileas Fogg?"

"In the best of health and as up to date as his itinerary! He isn't a day behind schedule! But there's one thing you don't know, Monsieur Fix, and that is that we have a young lady with us."

"A young lady?" said the detective, looking as if he did not understand what the other meant.

But Passepartout had soon told him all about her. He related the incident of the pagoda in Bombay, the purchase of the elephant for two thousand pounds, the episode of the suttee, the rescue of Aouda, the sentence of the Calcutta court and the release of Phileas Fogg's party on bail. Fix, who was acquainted with the latest of these incidents, pretended to be ignorant of them all, and Passepartout gave himself up to the pleasure of recounting his adventures to a listener who showed so much interest.

"But when all is said and done," asked Fix, "does your master intend to take this young woman to Europe?"

"Oh no, Monsieur Fix, not at all! We are simply going to place her in the care of a relative of hers, a rich merchant of Hong Kong."

"There's nothing to be done about that!" the detective said to himself, hiding his disappointment. "Will you have a glass of gin, Mr Passepartout?"

"With pleasure, Monsieur Fix. The least we can do is to drink to our meeting on board the *Rangoon!*"

CHAPTER SEVENTEEN

*Concerning a variety of matters on the passage between
Singapore and Hong Kong*

Although Passepartout and the detective met frequently
after this, the inspector maintained an attitude of great
reserve towards his companion and made no further
attempt to get him to talk. On only one or two occasions
did he catch a glimpse of Mr Fogg, who remained most of
the time in the saloon, either keeping Aouda company or
playing whist, as was his invariable custom.

As for Passepartout, he had started thinking very
seriously about the strange chance which had once again
placed Fix on the same route as his master. It was certainly
surprising, to say the least. This very pleasant and
undoubtedly most obliging gentleman, whom they had
met first of all at Suez, who had embarked on the
Mongolia, who had disembarked at Bombay, where he
had said he would have to stay, and who had now turned
up again on the *Rangoon*, on his way to Hong Kong, and
who in short was following Mr Fogg's itinerary step by
step, definitely provided food for thought. The coincidence
was striking, to put it mildly. What was this fellow Fix up
to? Passepartout was ready to bet his slippers, which he
had carefully preserved, that Fix would leave Hong Kong
at the same time as they did, and probably on the same
steamer.

If Passepartout had racked his brain for a hundred
years, he would never have guessed the nature of the
detective's mission. He would never have imagined that
Phileas Fogg was being shadowed round the world like a
thief. But as it is only human nature to provide an

explanation for everything, Passepartout, with a sudden flash of intuition, found a highly plausible reason for Fix's perpetual presence. According to him, Fix was not and could not be anything else than an agent put on Mr Fogg's track by his fellow members of the Reform Club, to make sure that this journey round the world was properly carried out along the agreed route.

"It's obvious! It's obvious!" the worthy fellow kept telling himself, full of pride at his perspicacity. "He's a spy those gentlemen have hired to trail us! What a low thing to do! To have an upright, honourable gentleman like Mr Fogg spied on by an agent! Oh, this is going to cost you gentlemen of the Reform Club dear!"

Delighted with his discovery, Passepartout none the less decided to say nothing about it to his master, for he was afraid that the latter would be not unreasonably offended by this distrust on the part of his adversaries. But he made up his mind to chaff Fix whenever he got the chance, with veiled hints which would not compromise him.

In the afternoon of Wednesday, 30th October, the *Rangoon* entered the Malacca Straits, between the peninsula bearing that name and Sumatra. Some extremely picturesque islets with steep mountains hid the big island from view.

At four o'clock the next morning the *Rangoon* put in to Singapore to refuel, having gained half a day on her schedule. Phileas Fogg noted this down in the gains column, and this time he went ashore, to accompany Aouda, who had expressed a desire to go driving for a few hours.

Fix, to whom Fogg's every action seemed suspicious, followed him without letting himself be seen. As for Passepartout, who was secretly amused by the detective's tactics, he went off to do his usual shopping

The island of Singapore is neither large nor impressive. It has no mountains, and hence no profile. However, its

A pretty carriage drawn by two smart horses took Aouda and Mr Fogg through groves of palm trees

flatness has a certain charm, and it resembles a park criss-crossed by fine roads. A pretty carriage drawn by two of those smart horses imported from New Holland took Aouda and Phileas Fogg through groves of palm trees with bright foliage, and of clove trees on which the very buds of the half-open blossoms formed the cloves. Here, pepper bushes took the place of the thorny hedges of the European countryside; sago palms, great ferns with splendid branches, lent variety to the appearance of this tropical region; nutmeg trees with shining leaves filled the air with an all-pervading scent. There was no lack of bands of lively, grimacing monkeys in the woods, and possibly no lack of tigers in the jungle. It might seem surprising that these terrible beasts of prey had not been completely wiped out on such a relatively small island, but in fact more kept coming from Malacca, swimming across the straits.

After a two hours' drive in the country, during which Phileas Fogg looked about him a little but saw nothing, he and Aouda returned to the town, a vast agglomeration of squat, clumsy houses, surrounded by charming gardens in which there grew pineapples, mangosteens and all the finest fruits in the world.

At ten o'clock they re-embarked, unaware that they had been followed all the time by the inspector, who had been obliged to go to the expense of a carriage like theirs.

Passepartout was waiting for them on deck. The good fellow had bought a few dozen mangosteens, a fruit the size of average apples, dark brown outside and bright red inside, with a white flesh which melts between the lips and gives a real gourmet unparalleled pleasure. Passepartout was only too pleased to offer them to Aouda, who thanked him very graciously.

At eleven o'clock the *Rangoon*, her coaling finished, cast off her moorings, and a few hours later her passengers lost sight of the lofty mountains of Malacca, whose forests sheltered the finest tigers in the world.

About thirteen hundred miles separate Singapore from the island of Hong Kong, a small English colony off the Chinese coast. It was important for Phileas Fogg to cover this distance in six days at the most, so as to catch the boat due to leave Hong Kong on 6th November for Yokohama, one of the chief ports of Japan.

The *Rangoon* was heavily loaded, for a large number of passengers had come aboard at Singapore: Hindus, Ceylonese, Chinese, Malays and Portuguese, most of whom were travelling second class.

The weather, which had been fairly fine until then, changed with the last quarter of the moon. The sea became very rough, and the wind at times became a moderate gale, but fortunately it blew from the southeast, and thus favoured the steamer's progress. When it was not blowing too hard, the captain put up canvas. The *Rangoon*, which was rigged like a brig, often sailed under her two topsails and her foresail, and the dual action of steam and wind gave her added speed. In this way, on a choppy and sometimes very trying sea, she skirted the coasts of Annam and Cochin China.

If the journey was tiring, the *Rangoon* was more to blame than the sea, and it was to the steamer that the passengers, most of whom were sick, owed their discomfort. For the ships of the P & O Line plying in the China seas had a serious constructional defect: the ratio between their draught when loaded and their depth had been miscalculated, with the result that they offered little resistance to the sea. Their watertight bulkheads were inadequate, so that they were "drowned", to use sailors' parlance; consequently they only had to ship a little water to be slowed down considerably. These ships were therefore very inferior – in construction, if not in their engines and evaporating apparatus – to the boats of the Messageries Françaises, such as the *Impératrice* and the *Cambodge*. Whereas these vessels, according to the engineers' calculations, could ship a mass of water equal to their own weight before going under, the boats of the P & O Company, the *Golconda*, the *Corea* and the *Rangoon*, could not ship one-sixth of their own weight without sinking.

Consequently in bad weather great precautions had to be taken, and sometimes the Captain had to heave to under easy steam. This meant a loss of time which seemed to leave Phileas Fogg completely unaffected, but which infuriated Passepartout. He blamed the Captain, the Chief Engineer and the Company, and he consigned everyone concerned with conveying travellers to the devil. It is possible, too, that his impatience was due in no small measure to the thought of that gas lamp which was still burning at his expense in the house in Savile Row.

"Are you really in such a hurry to get to Hong Kong?" the detective asked him one day.

"A tremendous hurry!" replied Passepartout.

"You think that Mr Fogg is anxious to catch the boat for Yokohama!"

"Frightfully anxious."

"So now you believe in this peculiar journey round the world?"

"Absolutely. What about you, Monsieur Fix?"

"Me? I don't believe a word of it!"

"You're a sly one!" replied Passepartout with a wink.

This remark made the detective think. The epithet Passepartout had used worried him, though he could not say why. Had the Frenchman seen through him? He did not know what to think. But no one knew he was a detective, so how could Passepartout have found out? And yet the man would not have spoken like that without some ulterior meaning.

On another occasion the good fellow went even further. Try as he might, he could not hold his tongue.

"Tell me, Monsieur Fix," he asked his companion in a teasing tone of voice, "when we get to Hong Kong, are we going to be unlucky enough to leave you there?"

"Well," Fix replied in some embarrassment, "I don't know . . . It's possible that . . ."

"Ah," said Passepartout, "if you came on with us I should be so pleased! Come now, surely an agent of the Peninsular & Oriental Company can't stop half way! You were going no farther than Bombay, and now you'll soon be in China! America isn't far off, and from America to Europe is only a little way!"

Fix was watching his companion intently, and the man's face wore such an amiable expression that he decided to join in the laugh. But Passepartout, who was in high spirits, asked him if his job brought in much money.

"Yes and no," replied Fix, without batting an eyelid.

"There's good business and bad. But you realize of course that I don't travel at my own expense."

"Oh, I'm quite sure of that!" exclaimed Passepartout, laughing more than ever.

When their conversation was over, Fix went back to his cabin and started thinking. He had obviously been found out. Somehow or other the Frenchman had realized that he was a detective. But had he warned his master? What part was he playing in all this? Was he an accomplice or not? Had they seen through the whole thing, in which case the game was up? The detective went through a few difficult hours, sometimes thinking that all was lost, sometimes hoping that Fogg did not realize the situation, and altogether not knowing what to do.

However, he eventually recovered his composure, and decided to be perfectly frank with Passepartout. If he did not find himself in a position to arrest Fogg at Hong Kong, and if Fogg took steps to leave that last piece of British territory, then he, Fix, would tell Passepartout everything. Either the servant was his master's accomplice, in which case the latter knew everything, and the whole project was compromised, or the servant had nothing to do with the robbery, and then it would be in his interest to break with the robber.

Such, then, were the respective positions of these two men, while Phileas Fogg floated above them in majestic indifference. He was orbiting the world in rational fashion, without worrying about the minor planets that gravitated around him.

And yet in his neighbourhood there was − to use the terminology of the astronomers − a disturbing star which should have produced certain tremors in that gentleman's heart. But nothing of the sort happened. To Passepartout's great surprise, Aouda's charm failed to take effect, and the tremors, if they existed at all, would have been more

113

difficult to calculate than those of Uranus which led to the discovery of Neptune.

This was indeed a daily source of astonishment to Passepartout, who could see heartfelt gratitude towards his master in the young woman's eyes. It was obvious that Phileas Fogg had just enough heart to behave heroically, but not enough to fall in love. As for the preoccupations which the hazards of this voyage might have aroused in him, there was no sign of them. Passepartout, on the other hand, lived in a state of perpetual anxiety. One day he was leaning on the engine room railing, watching the powerful engines, which occasionally went mad when the ship pitched heavily and the screw spun round wildly in the air. Then the steam would pour out of the valves, a sight which sent the good fellow into a rage.

"Those valves aren't properly weighted!" he cried. "We aren't moving! That's just like the English! Oh, if this were an American ship, we might blow up, but at least we'd be going faster!"

CHAPTER EIGHTEEN

In which Phileas Fogg, Passepartout and Fix each go about their business

During the last few days of the voyage the weather was rather rough. The wind, blowing steadily from the north-west, grew very strong and hampered the steamer's progress. Owing to her lack of stability, the *Rangoon* rolled heavily, and the passengers had every reason to bear a grudge against the long, nauseating waves which the wind churned up from the open seas.

On 3rd and 4th November there was something like a gale, with squalls lashing the sea in a frenzy. The *Rangoon* was forced to lie for half a day, keeping her course with only ten revolutions of her screw, in such a way as to meet the waves on the slant. All sail had been taken in, and even the rigging whistling in the gusts of wind seemed too much.

Needless to say, the steamer's speed was considerably reduced, and it was estimated that she would reach Hong Kong twenty hours behind time, and even more if the storm did not die down.

Phileas Fogg contemplated this furious sea, which seemed to be fighting against him personally, with his habitual serenity. His brow did not cloud over for a single moment, though a delay of twenty hours would be enough to compromise his journey by making him miss the boat for Yokohama. But the man had no nerves; he felt neither impatience nor boredom. It really seemed as if this storm were part of his programme and had been foreseen. When Aouda discussed this setback with him, she found him as calm as ever.

Fix, for his part, did not see things in the same way. Far from it. This storm delighted him. Indeed, his satisfaction would have known no bounds if the *Rangoon* had been forced to turn and run before the gale. All these delays suited him admirably, for they would oblige Mr Fogg to remain at Hong Kong for a few days. In short, the heavens, with their gusts and squalls, were on his side. Admittedly he was a little seasick, but what did that matter! He ignored his attacks of nausea, and while his body writhed in the agony of seasickness, his spirit exulted with unspeakable satisfaction.

As for Passepartout, it is easy to imagine with what ill-concealed anger he went through this time of trial. So far everything had gone so well! Earth and sea had appeared to be devoted to his master. Steamers and trains alike had obeyed him. Wind and steam had joined forces to speed him on his way. Had the hour of adversity struck at last? Passepartout was as tormented as if the twenty thousand pounds of the wager had to come out of his own pocket. He was exasperated by the storm, infuriated by the squalls, and he would have dearly loved to give the rebellious sea a whipping. Poor fellow! Fix took care to conceal his own satisfaction, and he was wise to do so, for if Passepartout had guessed his secret delight, Fix would have had a hard time of it.

Throughout the storm Passepartout remained on deck, for it would have been impossible for him to stay below. He shinned up the masts, and astonished the crew by showing the agility of a monkey as he helped them with everything. A hundred times he questioned the Captain, officers and sailors, who could not help laughing at seeing somebody in such a state. When he insisted on knowing how long the storm would last, they referred him to the barometer, which showed no signs of rising. He shook it, but neither shaking nor the curses he heaped upon the irresponsible instrument had the slightest effect.

At last the storm abated and during the morning of 4th November the sea grew calmer. The wind shifted two points to the south and became favourable once more.

Passepartout brightened up with the weather. It became possible to hoist the topsails and lower sails, and the *Rangoon* forged ahead once more at great speed.

However, they had to resign themselves to the fact that they could not make good all the time they had lost, and land was not sighted until the 6th, at five in the morning. According to Phileas Fogg's timetable, the steamer was due to arrive on the 5th. He was therefore twenty-four hours late, and was bound to have missed the steamer for Yokohama.

At six o'clock the pilot came on board the *Rangoon* and

took his place on the bridge in order to guide the ship through the channels into Hong Kong harbour.

Passepartout was dying to ask the man if the steamer for Yokohama had left, but he did not dare to do so, preferring to keep a vestige of hope until the last moment. He had confided his anxiety to Fix, who, sly fox that he was, tried to comfort him by telling him that Mr Fogg only had to take the next boat. This of course sent Passepartout into a fury.

But if Passepartout did not venture to question the pilot, Mr Fogg consulted his *Bradshaw* and asked the man in his quiet way if he knew when there would be a boat leaving Hong Kong for Yokohama.

"Tomorrow, on the morning tide," replied the pilot.

"Ah!" said Mr Fogg, without showing the slightest surprise.

Passepartout, who was with them, would have liked to embrace the pilot, while Fix would have gladly wrung his neck.

"What is the ship's name?" asked Mr Fogg.

"The *Carnatic*", the pilot replied.

"Wasn't it yesterday she was due to sail?"

"Yes, sir, but they had to repair one of her boilers, so her sailing was put off till tomorrow."

"Thank you," replied Mr Fogg, who then went down to the saloon again with his automatic step.

As for Passepartout, he gripped the pilot's hand and shook it vigorously, saying:

"Pilot, you're a good sort!"

The pilot probably never found out why his answers had earned him this friendly response. A whistle blew, and he went up again on the bridge to guide the steamer through the flotilla of junks, tankas, fishing boats and ships of all kinds which crowded the approaches to Hong Kong harbour.

By one o'clock the *Rangoon* had been berthed, and the passengers were going ashore.

It must be admitted that on this occasion chance had been singularly kind to Phileas Fogg. If one of her boilers had not needed repairing, the *Carnatic* would have left on 5th November, and the travellers bound for Japan would have had to wait a week for the next steamer. True, Mr Fogg was twenty-four hours late, but this delay was unlikely to have an adverse affect on the rest of the journey, for the steamer which crossed the Pacific from Yokohama to San Francisco connected with the boat from Hong Kong and could not sail before she arrived.

Admittedly there would be a delay of twenty-four hours at Yokohama, but it would be a simple matter to make up for them during the twenty-two days it would take to cross the Pacific. Consequently Phileas Fogg, thirty-five days after leaving London, was only twenty-four hours behind schedule.

As the *Carnatic* was not due to sail until five o'clock the next morning, Mr Fogg had sixteen hours in which to attend to his business, or rather Aouda's. As soon as they came ashore, he offered the young woman his arm and escorted her to a palanquin. He asked the porters to recommend a hotel, and they gave him the name of the Club Hotel. The palanquin set off, followed by Passepartout, and twenty minutes later they reached their destination.

A room was engaged for the young woman, and Phileas Fogg saw to it that she had everything she needed. Then he told Aouda he was going to look for the relative in whose care he was supposed to leave her in Hong Kong. At the same time he told Passepartout to stay at the hotel until he returned, so that the young woman should not be left there alone.

Then he drove to the Stock Exchange, where he felt sure

that a personage such as Jejeeh, one of the richest merchants in the town, would be well known.

Sure enough, the stockbroker whom he approached knew the Parsee merchant, but explained that the latter had not lived in China for the last two years. Having made his fortune, he had gone to live in Europe – in Holland, it was thought, because of the many dealings he had had with that country during his business career.

Phileas Fogg returned to the Club Hotel, and immediately asked if he might see Aouda. Going straight to the point, he told her that the merchant Jejeeh was no longer in Hong Kong, and that he was probably living in Holland.

At first Aouda made no reply. She passed her hand over her forehead, and remained thinking for a few moments. Then she asked in her gentle voice:

"What must I do, Mr Fogg?"

"It is very simple," he replied. "Return with us to Europe."

"But I cannot take advantage . . ."

"You are not taking advantage, and your presence will not inferfere in any way with my programme . . . Passepartout?"

"Monsieur?" replied Passepartout.

"Go to the *Carnatic*, and book three cabins."

Delighted at the prospect of continuing his journey in the company of a young woman who had behaved very graciously towards him, Passepartout promptly left the Club Hotel.

CHAPTER NINETEEN

In which Passepartout takes too keen an interest in his master, and what follows

Hong Kong is a small island which passed into British possession after the war of 1842, under the terms of the Treaty of Nanking. Within a few years the British genius for colonization had founded an important town there and created a port called Victoria. This island is situated at the mouth of the Canton River, only sixty miles from the Portuguese city of Macao on the opposite shore. Hong Kong was bound to defeat Macao in any commercial struggle, and by now the greater part of the Chinese transit trade was carried on through the English town. With its docks, its hospitals, its wharves, its warehouses, its Gothic cathedral, its Government House and its macadamized streets, it looked like a busy town in Kent or Surrey which had gone through the globe and come out at this point in China, almost on the other side of the world.

Passepartout, his hands in his pockets, made his way towards Victoria Port, looking at the palanquins and the wheelbarrows with sails, still in favour in the Celestial Empire, and at the crowds of Chinese, Japanese and Europeans thronging the streets. What the good fellow saw on his way was very much like Bombay, Calcutta or Singapore, all over again. There was as it were a trail of English towns like this all round the world.

Eventually Passepartout reached Victoria Port, where at the mouth of the Canton River, he found a swarm of ships of all nations – English, French, American, Dutch – warships and cargo ships, Japanese or Chinese boats, junks, sampans, tankas and even flower boats looking like floating flowerbeds on the water. As he strolled along, Passepartout noticed a number of natives, all very old, who were dressed in yellow. Going into a barber's shop to get shaved in the Chinese fashion, he learnt from the local Figaro, who spoke English fairly well, that these ancients were all at least eighty years old, and that at that age they were granted the privilege of wearing yellow, the Imperial colour. Passepartout thought this very funny, though he did not quite know why.

After his shave, he went to the quay from which the *Carnatic* was due to sail, and there he was not at all surprised to see Fix walking up and down. But the inspector's face bore an expression of intense disappointment.

"Good!" Passepartout said to himself. "Things are going badly for the gentleman of the Reform Club!" And he greeted Fix with his usual sunny smile, pretending not to notice his companion's look of annoyance.

The detective certainly had good reason to curse the infernal luck which was dogging his footsteps. He still had no warrant! It was clear that the warrant was following him, but that it could not catch up with him unless he stayed a few days in this town. Now Hong Kong was the last British territory on his route, so Mr Fogg was going to escape him for good, unless he could manage to find some way of keeping him there.

"Well, Monsieur Fix, have you decided to come with us as far as America?" asked Passepartout.

"Yes," replied Fix between clenched teeth.

"Get along with you!" cried Passepartout, giving a great burst of laughter. "I knew very well that you couldn't bear to leave us. Come along and book your passage!"

The two of them went into the shipping office and booked four cabins. The clerk informed them that as the *Carnatic*'s repairs had been completed, the steamer would be leaving that very evening at eight o'clock, and not the following morning, as had been announced.

"Splendid!" replied Passepartout. "That will suit my master down to the ground! I'll go and tell him."

At that moment Fix decided on an extreme measure. He resolved to tell Passepartout everything, as this might well be the only way of detaining Phileas Fogg in Hong Kong for a few days.

When they left the office, Fix invited his companion for a drink in a tavern. Passepartout had enough time and accepted the invitation.

There was a pleasant-looking tavern on the quay, and the two of them went in. They found themselves in a large, well decorated room, at the far end of which was a camp bed covered with cushions. On this bed there lay a number of sleeping figures.

In the rest of the room about thirty customers were seated at small tables made of plaited rushes. Some of them were emptying pint mugs of English beer, ale or porter, while others were drinking spirits, gin or brandy. Most of them were also smoking long red clay pipes stuffed with little pellets of opium flavoured with attar of roses. Every now and then one of the smokers, stupefied by the fumes, would slide down under the table, and the waiters, taking him by the head and feet, would carry him over to the camp bed and lay him down beside a fellow sleeper. A score of these inebriates were laid out like this, side by side, in the final stage of intoxication.

Fix and Passepartout realized that they had entered a

smoking den, a haunt of those besotted, emaciated, half-witted wretches from whom debauched England bought every year over ten million pounds' worth of that fatal drug called opium. Deplorable millions those were, derived from one of the deadliest vices known to mankind!

The Chinese Government had tried to check this evil by means of severe laws, but all in vain. From the rich, to whom the use of opium was at first strictly confined, it had spread to the lower classes, and its ravages could no longer be arrested. Opium was smoked all the time and everywhere in the Middle Kingdom. Men and women alike abandoned themselves to this deplorable passion, and once they were accustomed to inhaling this drug, they could not give it up without experiencing horrible stomach cramps. A real addict might smoke as many as eight pipes a day, but he would die within five years.

It was one of these dens, of which there were a vast number, even in Hong Kong, that Fix and Passepartout had entered in search of a drink. Passepartout had no money, but he readily accepted his companion's hospitality, meaning to return it on some future occasion.

They ordered two bottles of port, to which the Frenchman did full justice, while Fix, going more cautiously, watched his companion closely. They chatted about this and that, and above all about Fix's splendid idea of booking a cabin on the *Carnatic*. Talking of that steamer reminded Passepartout that her sailing time had been brought forward a few hours, and as the bottles were empty he got up to go and tell his master.

Fix held him back.

"Just a moment," he said.

"What is it, Monsieur Fix?"

"I want to talk to you about a serious matter."

"A serious matter?" exclaimed Passepartout, gulping down a few drops of wine left at the bottom of his glass.

"Well, we'll talk about that tomorrow. I haven't time today."

"Wait," replied Fix. "It's something to do with your master."

At these words Passepartout looked intently at the other man. The expression on Fix's face struck him as peculiar, and he sat down again.

"What have you got to tell me?" he asked.

Fix laid his hand on his companion's arm, and, lowering his voice, asked:

"You've guessed who I am, haven't you?"

"Of course I have!" said Passepartout with a smile.

"Then I'm going to tell you everything . . ."

"Now that I know everything, my friend! That's a good one! Still fire away. But first let me tell you that those gentlemen of yours are wasting their money!"

"Wasting their money!" said Fix. "It's easy for you to talk. It's clear you don't know how much is involved."

"Oh, yes, I do," replied Passepartout. "Twenty thousand pounds!"

"Fifty-five thousand pounds!" retorted Fix, grasping the Frenchman's hand.

"What!" exclaimed Passepartout. "You mean to say Mr Fogg risked so much! . . . Fifty-five thousand pounds! . . . Well, that's all the more reason for not wasting a moment," he added, getting up once more.

"Fifty-five thousand pounds!" Fix went on, ordering a bottle of brandy and making Passepartout sit down again. "And if I'm successful I get a reward of two thousand pounds. Would you like five hundred of it for helping me?"

"Helping you?" exclaimed Passepartout, his eyes like saucers.

"Yes, helping me to keep Mr Fogg in Hong Kong for a few days."

"What!" cried Passepartout. "What's that you're saying? So, not content with having my master followed and doubting his good faith, those gentlemen now want to put obstacles in his way! Shame on them!"

"Here, what do you mean?" asked Fix.

"What I mean is that this is a dirty trick. They might just as well rob Mr Fogg and take the money out of his pocket!"

"Yes, that's just what we hope to do in the end!"

"But this is an ambush!" exclaimed Passepartout, getting excited under the influence of the brandy which Fix kept pouring out for him, and which he drank without noticing what he was doing. "A real ambush! And they call themselves gentlemen! Colleagues!"

Fix was beginning to feel out of his depth.

"Colleagues!" cried Passepartout. "Members of the Reform Club! Let me tell you, Monsieur Fix, that my master is an honest man and when he makes a bet he means to win it fairly."

"But who do you think I am, then?" asked Fix, gazing hard at Passepartout.

"Why, an agent hired by the members of the Reform Club to check my master's route. That's such a humiliating state of affairs that, although I guessed what you were some time ago, I've been very careful not to tell Mr Fogg."

"Then he doesn't know anything?" Fix asked eagerly.

"Not a thing," replied Passepartout, draining his glass once again.

The police inspector passed his hand across his forehead, hesitating before saying anything more. What should he do? Passepartout's mistake seemed to be genuine, but it made his plan all the more difficult. It was obvious that the fellow was speaking in complete good faith, and that he was not his master's accomplice, as Fix might have feared.

"Well," he said to himself, "since he isn't his accomplice, he'll help me."

Once again the detective had made up his mind. In any

case, he no longer had any time to lose. At all costs he had to arrest Fogg in Hong Kong.

"Listen," Fix said curtly. "Listen to me carefully. I'm not what you think, in other words an agent of the members of the Reform Club."

"Get along with you!" said Passepartout, grinning at him unbelievingly.

"I am a police inspector, sent out from London on a special mission . . ."

"You . . . a police inspector!"

"Yes, and I can prove it," replied Fix. "Here is my warrant card."

And taking a paper out of his wallet, the detective showed his companion a card signed by the Chief of the Metropolitan Police. Completely dumbfounded, Passepartout gazed at Fix, unable to utter a single word.

"Mr Fogg's wager," Fix went on, "is just a trick, which has taken you all in, you and his fellow members of the Reform Club, for it was in his interest to make sure of your innocent complicity."

"But what for?" cried Passepartout.

"Listen. On the twenty-ninth of September, the sum of fifty-five thousand pounds was stolen from the Bank of England by an individual whose description we have been able to obtain. Well, here is that description, which fits that of Mr Fogg feature for feature."

"Nonsense," exclaimed Passepartout, striking the table with his powerful fist. "My master is the most honest man in the world!"

"How do you know?" retorted Fix. "You don't even know him! You entered his service the very day of his departure, and he left in a great hurry on a ridiculous pretext, without any luggage, and taking with him a huge sum in banknotes! And you dare to maintain that he's an honest man!"

"Yes! Yes!" the poor fellow repeated mechanically.

"Then you want to be arrested as his accomplice, do you?"

Passepartout had buried his face in his hands. His features had changed completely, and he did not dare to look at the police inspector. Phileas Fogg a robber – the brave and generous man who had rescued Aouda! And yet there were so many presumptions against him! Passepartout tried to reject the suspicions which were stealing into his mind. He did not want to believe in his master's guilt.

"Well, what do you want me to do?" he asked the detective, controlling his feelings by a supreme effort.

"Listen," replied Fix. "I've shadowed Mr Fogg here, but I haven't yet received the warrant for his arrest which I've asked London to send me. So you must help me to keep him here in Hong Kong . . ."

"Me! You want me to . . ."

"And I'll give you a share of the two thousand pounds reward promised by the Bank of England!"

"Never!" replied Passepartout, who tried to get up but fell back on his chair, feeling his wits and his strength abandoning him at the same time.

"Monsieur Fix," he stammered, "even if everything you've told me is true . . . even if my master is the robber you're looking for . . . and I deny that he is . . . I've been, or rather I am in his service . . . I've seen how good and generous he is . . . Betray him? . . . Never . . . no, not for all the gold in the world. . . . Where I come from they'd rather starve than do a thing like that!"

"You refuse?"

"I refuse."

"Then let's pretend I haven't said anything," suggested Fix, "and let's have another drink."

"Yes, let's have another drink!"

Passepartout felt more and more intoxicated. Realizing that he had to separate him at all costs from his master, Fix decided to finish the job. On the table were a few pipes filled with opium, and Fix slipped one of them into Passepartout's hand. He took it, raised it to his lips, lit it, took a few puffs, and fell back, stupefied by the narcotic.

"At last!" said Fix, seeing Passepartout dead to the world. "Mr Fogg won't be told in time that the *Carnatic* is sailing. And if he does get away, at least he'll go without this cursed Frenchman!"

Then he paid the bill and left the tavern.

CHAPTER TWENTY

In which Fix comes in contact with Phileas Fogg

During this discussion, which threatened to compromise Mr Fogg's future, he and Aouda were walking about the streets of the English quarter. Since Aouda had accepted his offer to take her to Europe, he had had to give his mind to all the little matters involved in such a long voyage. An Englishman like himself might just possibly go round the world with a travelling bag, but no lady could undertake such a journey in those conditions. Consequently clothing and other articles needed for the journey had to be bought. Mr Fogg carried out his task with characteristic calmness, and whenever the young widow, embarrassed by so much kindness, offered apologies or objections, he invariably replied:

"It is in the interests of my journey; it is part of my programme."

After making their purchases, they returned to the hotel and dined sumptuously at the *table d'hôte*. Then Aouda, who was a little tired, went up to her room after shaking hands in the English fashion with her imperturbable rescuer.

The honourable gentleman, for his part, spent the whole evening reading *The Times* and the *Illustrated London News*.

If he had been the sort of man to be surprised at anything, it would have been at not seeing his servant appear at bedtime. But as he knew that the steamer for Yokohama was not due to sail until the following morning, he did not give it a thought. The next morning, however, Passepartout did not appear when Mr Fogg rang for him.

What the honourable gentleman thought when he learnt that his servant had not returned to the hotel, no one could have said. He merely picked up his travelling bag, sent word to Aouda and ordered a palanquin.

It was then eight o'clock, and high tide, which the *Carnatic* had to use to get through the channels, was due at half past nine.

When the palanquin arrived at the entrance to the hotel, Mr Fogg and Aouda got into that comfortable vehicle, and their luggage followed them on a barrow.

Half an hour later the travellers got out on the quay, where Mr Fogg was told that the *Carnatic* had sailed the day before.

He had counted on finding both the steamer and his servant, and now he had to do without either. But no sign of disappointment appeared on his face, and when Aouda looked at him anxiously, he merely said:

"A trifling incident, Madam, nothing more."

At that moment a man who had been watching him closely came up to him. It was Inspector Fix, who raised his hat and said:

"Sir, were you not, like myself, a passenger on the *Rangoon*, which arrived yesterday?"

"Yes, sir," Mr Fogg replied coldly, "but I have not the honour . . ."

"Excuse me, but I expected to find your servant here."

"Do you know where he is, sir?" the young woman asked eagerly.

"What!" exclaimed Fix, pretending to be surprised. "Isn't he with you?"

"No," replied Aouda. "We haven't seen him since yesterday. Do you think he can have sailed on the *Carnatic* without us?"

"Without you, Madam?" said the detective. "But, if you will pardon the question, did you intend to sail on that steamer?"

"Yes, sir."

"So did I, Madam, and I am extremely disappointed. The *Carnatic* completed her repairs and left Hong Kong twelve hours earlier than expected, without telling anyone. Now we shall have to wait a week for the next boat."

As he uttered the words "a week" Fix felt his heart leaping for joy. A week! Fogg kept in Hong Kong for a week! This would give him time to receive the warrant. At last luck was siding with the representative of the law.

It may be imagined therefore how thunderstruck he was when he heard Phileas Fogg say in his usual calm voice:

"But it seems to me there are other ships besides the *Carnatic* in Hong Kong harbour."

And Mr Fogg, offering his arm to Aouda, set off towards the docks in search of a ship about to sail.

Still dazed, Fix followed him as if the two men were tied together by a thread.

All the same, luck really seemed to have deserted the man it had hitherto served so well. For three hours Phileas Fogg searched the harbour from end to end, determined, if necessary, to charter a boat to take him to Yokohama; but all the vessels he saw were either loading or unloading, and consequently were unable to get under sail. Fix began to hope again.

However, Mr Fogg was not discouraged, and he was about to continue his search, even if he had to go as far as Macao, when he was accosted by a sailor in the outer harbour.

"Is your honour looking for a boat?" the sailor asked, taking off his cap.

"Have you a boat ready to sail?" asked Mr Fogg.

"Yes, your honour, a pilot boat. No. 43, the best boat in the harbour."

"She sails fast?"

"Between eight and nine knots, more or less. Would you like to see her?"

"Yes."

"Your honour will be pleased with her. Do you want to go for a trip?"

"No, for a voyage."

"A voyage?"

"Will you agree to take me to Yokohama?"

At these words the sailor stood stock still, with his arms at his sides, and his eyes wide open.

"Your honour must be joking?" he said.

"No. I missed the *Carnatic*, and I must be in Yokohama by the fourteenth at the latest, to catch the steamer for New York."

"I'm sorry," replied the pilot, "but it's impossible."

"I'll pay you a hundred pounds a day, and a bonus of two hundred pounds if I get there in time."

"Are you serious," the pilot asked.

"Quite serious," replied Mr Fogg.

The pilot walked away and looked out to sea, plainly torn between the desire to earn a huge sum of money and the fear of venturing so far. Fix was on tenterhooks.

Meanwhile Fogg had turned towards Aouda.

"You won't be afraid, Madam?" he asked her.

131

"With you, Mr Fogg, no," the young woman replied.

The pilot had once again approached, and was twisting his cap between his hands.

"Well, pilot?" said Mr Fogg.

"Well, your honour," the pilot replied, "I couldn't risk either my men or myself, or you either, on such a long voyage on a boat of barely twenty tons, and at this time of the year too. Anyhow, we shouldn't get there in time, for it's sixteen hundred and fifty miles from Hong Kong to Yokohama."

"Only sixteen hundred," said Mr Fogg.

"It comes to the same thing."

Fix breathed again.

"But," added the pilot, "there might be some other way of managing it."

Fix held his breath.

"How?" asked Phileas Fogg.

"By going to Nagasaki, at the southern end of Japan, eleven hundred miles from here, or just to Shanghai, eight hundred miles away. The Shanghai route wouldn't take us far from the Chinese coast, and that would be a great advantage, especially as the currents run northwards."

"Pilot," replied Phileas Fogg, "it's at Yokohama that I have to catch the American mail, and not at Shanghai or Nagasaki."

"Why not?" asked the pilot. "The San Francisco steamer doesn't start from Yokohama. She calls at Yokohama and Nagasaki, but she starts from Shanghai."

"You are sure of that?"

"Certain."

"And when does the boat leave Shanghai?"

"On the eleventh, at seven in the evening, so we've got four days in front of us. Four days, ninety-six hours, and with an average speed of eight knots, if we're lucky, if the wind stays in the southeast and there's a calm sea, we can cover the eight hundred miles between here and Shanghai."

"And you can start . . .?"

"An hour from now. As soon as I've bought provisions and got sail."

"Then that's settled . . . Are you the master of the boat?"

"Yes — John Bunsby, master of the *Tankadere*."

"Would you like an advance?"

"If that isn't inconvenient for your honour."

"Here are two hundred pounds on account . . . sir," Phileas Fogg added turning to Fix, "if you wish to avail yourself of . . ."

"Sir," Fix replied boldly, "I was going to ask that favour of you."

"Good. In half an hour we shall be on board."

"But that poor fellow . . ." said Aouda, who was concerned about Passepartout's disappearance.

"I shall do everything I can for him," Phileas Fogg replied.

So while Fix, nervous, feverish and fuming with rage, went to find the pilot boat, the two others made their way to the Hong Kong police station, where Phileas Fogg gave a description of Passepartout and left enough money to repatriate him. The same formalities were carried out at the French Consulate, and then the palanquin, after calling at the hotel to collect the luggage, took the travellers back to the outer harbour.

The clock struck three. Pilot boat No. 43, with her crew on board and her provisions loaded, was ready to set sail.

The *Tankadere* was a charming little twenty ton schooner; with her fine bow and trim lines she looked like a racing yacht. Her gleaming brass, her galvanized iron-work, and her deck as white as ivory, showed the care her master, John Bunsby, took to keep her in good condition. Her two masts had a slight sternwards rake; she carried spanker, foresail, fore staysail and jibs, and could put up a crossjack to run before the wind. She looked wonderfully fast, and she had, in fact, already won several prizes in the pilot boat races.

The crew of the *Tankadere* consisted of her master and four of those fearless seamen who went out in all weathers to meet ships and knew the China seas perfectly. John Bunsby was a man of about forty-five, sturdy and sun-tanned, with keen eyes and strong features. Level-headed and thoroughly capable, he would have inspired confidence in the most timid.

Phileas Fogg and Aouda went on board; Fix was already there. Through the stern companionway they went down to a square cabin, whose walls had been fitted with bunks above a circular divan. In the middle was a table lit by a hanging lamp. It was small, but perfectly clean.

"I am sorry I have nothing better to offer you," Mr Fogg told Fix, who bowed without replying. The police inspector felt a sort of humiliation at being placed under an obligation by Mr Fogg.

"I must say," he thought, "he's a very polite scoundrel, but he's a scoundrel all the same!"

At ten past three the sails were hoisted, and the British flag fluttered at the schooner's peak. The passengers were seated on deck, and Fogg and Aouda gave one last glance at the quay to see if there were any sign of Passepartout.

Fix was by no means free of anxiety, for chance might have brought to that very spot the unfortunate fellow he had treated so badly. In that event there would have been an angry explanation which would not have been at all to the detective's advantage. But the Frenchman did not show up; no doubt the stupefying narcotic still held him in its grip.

At last John Bunsby steered for the open sea, and the *Tankadere*, with the wind filling her spanker, foresail and jibs, leapt forward over the waves.

CHAPTER TWENTY-ONE

*In which the Master of the "Tankadere" is in great
danger of losing a bonus of two hundred pounds*

This voyage of eight hundred miles in a twenty ton
schooner was a dangerous venture, especially at that time
of the year. The China seas are usually rough, and are
swept by terrible squalls, particularly during the equi-
noxes; and this was early November.

Since he was being paid by the day, it would obviously
have been to the pilot's advantage to take his passengers
on to Yokohama. But he would have been extremely
foolhardy to attempt such a journey in these conditions;
indeed it was bold enough, not to say rash, to go as far as
Shanghai. But John Bunsby had faith in his *Tankadere*,
which rose to the waves like a seagull, and perhaps he was
justified.

Later in the day the *Tankadere* passed through the
capricious channels leading out of Hong Kong, and
whether she was taking into the wind or running before it,
she behaved admirably.

"There's no need, pilot," said Phileas Fogg as the
schooner emerged into the open sea, "for me to urge you
to make all possible speed."

"Your honour can leave that to me," replied John
Bunsby. "We're carrying all the sail we can in this wind.
If we added to our jibs, it wouldn't help us, but only slow
us up."

"That's your job, pilot, and not mine, and I leave it to
you."

Body erect and feet apart, as steady as a sailor, Phileas
Fogg gazed unperturbed at the rough sea. The young

woman, seated in the stern, was deeply moved at the sight of this ocean, already darkened in the twilight, whose perils she was braving in so frail a boat. Above her head spread the white sails, sweeping her on through space like great wings. Lifted up by the wind, the schooner seemed to be flying through the air.

Night came; and the moon, now entering its first quarter, gave only a dim light which would soon be lost in the mists on the horizon. The clouds were rising from the east and had already invaded part of the sky.

The pilot had lit the vessel's lights – an indispensable precaution in those seas crowded with landward-bound shipping. Collisions there were not uncommon, and at the speed she was going, the schooner would have been smashed at the slightest shock.

Fix, in the bows, was deep in thought. Realizing that Fogg was not given to talking, he was keeping aloof. What was more, he felt a certain repugnance at the idea of speaking to this man, whose help he was accepting. Moreover, he was wondering about the future. He felt quite certain that Mr Fogg would not stop at Yokohama, but that he would immediately take the steamer for San Francisco so as to reach America, in whose vast expanse he would find both impunity and safety. Phileas Fogg's plan struck him as simplicity itself.

Instead of sailing straight from England to the United States, like any common criminal, this man Fogg had done the grand tour and had covered three-quarters of the earth to reach the American continent more surely. There, having thrown the police off the trail, he could live in peace on the bank's money. But once they were on American soil, what was Fix to do? Should he let this man go? No, a hundred times no! Until he managed to obtain an extradition order, he would never let him out of his sight. This was his duty, and he would carry it out to the end. Anyhow, something had already been accomplished;

Passepartout was no longer with his master, and after what Fix had confided to him it was essential that master and servant should never meet again.

Phileas Fogg, too, was thinking about his servant, who had disappeared so strangely. Taking everything into consideration he decided that it was not unlikely that, as the result of some misunderstanding, the poor lad had embarked on the *Carnatic* at the last moment. This, too, was Aouda's opinion: she deeply regretted the absence of that honest servant to whom she owed so much. Perhaps, then, they would find him at Yokohama; if the *Carnatic* had taken him there this would be easy to find out.

About ten o'clock the wind began to rise. It might perhaps have been prudent to take in a reef, but after carefully studying the sky the pilot made no alterations to the sails. Anyhow, the *Tankadere*, which drew a great deal of water, carried her canvas splendidly, and everything was ready to shorten sail quickly in the event of a squall.

At midnight Phileas Fogg and Aouda went down to the cabin. Fix was already there, stretched out in one of the bunks. As for the pilot and his men, they remained all night on deck.

By sunrise the next morning, 8th November, the schooner had sailed more than a hundred miles, and the log, consulted at frequent intervals, showed an average speed of between eight and nine knots. With every sail taking the wind, the *Tankadere* was making her best possible speed. If the wind held, the chances were all in her favour.

Throughout that day she kept close to the coast where the currents favoured her; it was five miles at most off her quarter, its irregular outline sometimes coming into sight through gaps in the mist. As there was an offshore wind, the sea was not so rough, and this was fortunate for the schooner, for small vessels have their speed reduced by the swell, which "kills them", as sailors say.

Towards noon the wind died down somewhat and veered to the southeast. The pilot put up the jibs, but two hours later he had to take them down again for the wind had once again freshened.

Mr Fogg and the young woman, neither of whom, fortunately, was subject to seasickness, enjoyed the ship's preserved food and biscuit with a hearty appetite. Fix, whom they invited to share their meal, had to accept for he knew that ballast is as necessary to stomachs as to ships, but this annoyed him. To travel at this man's expense, and to live on his food, struck him as rather unfair. He did, however, eat – only a morsel, it is true, but eat he did.

Still, after the meal he thought it incumbent on him to take Mr Fogg aside.

"Sir," he said to him.

This "sir" seemed to blister his lips, and it was all he could do to refrain from laying hold of this "gentleman's" collar.

"Sir, it was very kind of you to offer me a place on your ship. But although my resources do not allow me to act as generously as yourself, I insist on paying my share . . ."

"Do not let us discuss that, sir," Mr Fogg replied.

"But I insist . . ."

"No, sir," repeated Fogg in a tone which did not admit of a reply. "This will go down in my general expenses!"

Fix bowed: he felt he was choking and, going forward to lie down in the bows, he said nothing more all day.

As they were making excellent progress, John Bunsby felt very hopeful, and more than once he assured Mr Fogg that they should reach Shanghai in good time. Mr Fogg's only reply was that he was counting on doing so. Besides, the whole crew of the tiny schooner showed the utmost zeal; the good fellows were spurred on by the thought of the promised reward. There was not a sheet which was not kept taut, not a sail which was not stoutly set, not a lurch for which the helmsman could be reproached! The boat could not have been handled more skilfully if she had been competing in a regatta of the Royal Yacht Club.

In the evening the log revealed that two hundred and twenty miles had been covered since they had left Hong Kong, and Phileas Fogg was entitled to hope that when they reached Yokohama he would have no delay to note down in his record. In that case the first real setback which he had suffered since leaving London would probably not interfere with his plans.

During the night, some time before dawn, the *Tankadere* entered the Fo-Kien Straits, which separate Formosa from the Chinese coast, and here she crossed the Tropic of Cancer. In these straits the sea was very rough, full of eddies produced by the countercurrents. The schooner laboured heavily, impeded by the choppy waves, and it became very difficult to stand on deck.

At daybreak the wind increased further, and the look of the sky suggested an approaching gale. The barometer, too, announced an impending change in the weather by its fluctuations, the mercury oscillating capriciously. The sea in the southeast was rising on long waves which suggested a storm was in the offing, and on the previous evening the sun had set in a red mist amid the phosphorescent gleams of the ocean.

The pilot studied the threatening appearance of the sky for a long time and muttered a few unintelligible phrases between his teeth. Then, finding himself near his passenger, he asked in a low voice:

"May I speak freely to your honour?"

"Yes," replied Phileas Fogg.

"Well, we're in for a squall."

"Will it come from the north or the south?" was all that Mr Fogg asked.

"From the south. Look, there's a typhoon coming up!"

139

"I don't mind a typhoon from the south: it will help us on our way," said Mr Fogg.

"If that's the way you look at it," retorted the pilot, "I've nothing to say."

John Bunsby's forebodings proved well-founded. At a less advanced season of the year, the typhoon, as a famous meteorologist put it, would have spent itself like a luminous cascade of electric flames, but near the winter equinox it was to be feared that it would burst upon them with great violence.

The pilot began to take his precautions. He took in all sail and lowered the yards to the deck. The poles were struck and the hatches carefully secured so that not a drop of water could get into the hull. A single triangular sail, a storm jib of strong canvas, was hoisted as a fore stay-sail, to keep the schooner before the wind. Then they waited.

John Bunsby had urged his passengers to go below; but to be imprisoned in a confined space, almost without air, and thrown about by the waves, would not have been at all pleasant. Neither Mr Fogg nor Aouda, nor even Fix, would agree to leave the deck.

At about eight o'clock a squall of wind and rain fell upon them. Although she had only one scrap of sail the *Tankadere* was swept along like a feather by this wind, which defies description when it blows its hardest. To compare its velocity with four times the speed of a locomotive under full steam would be to fall short of the truth.

Throughout the day the vessel scudded northwards, swept along by the enormous waves and fortunately travelling at a speed equal to theirs. A score of times she was almost overwhelmed by one of those mountains of water rising behind her, but catastrophe was averted by a skilful shift of the helm by the pilot. At times the passengers were drenched by the spray, but they took this philosophically. Fix cursed, no doubt; but courageous

Aouda, her eyes fixed on her companion, whose composure she could not help but admire, showed herself worthy of him and braved the tempest by his side. As for Phileas Fogg himself, he gave the impression that the typhoon was part of his programme.

So far the *Tankadere* had been sailing steadily northwards; but towards the evening, as was to be feared, the wind veered round three-quarters to the northwest. The schooner, now broadside on to the waves, was frightfully shaken. The sea struck her with a violence calculated to terrify anyone who did not know how firmly all the parts of a ship are bound together.

With nightfall the storm grew even more violent. Seeing the gale increase in fury as the darkness grew deeper, John Bunsby felt seriously alarmed. He began to wonder if it were not time to put into port, and after consulting his crew he went up to Mr Fogg and said:

"I think, your honour, that we'd do well to make for one of the ports on the coast."

"I think so too," replied Phileas Fogg.

"Oh!" said the pilot. "But which?"

"I know only one," Mr Fogg replied quietly.

"And which is that?"

"Shanghai."

It took the pilot a few moments to realize what this reply meant, and what determination and tenacity it showed. Then he exclaimed:

"Why, yes, your honour is quite right. On to Shanghai!"

And the *Tankadere* sailed imperturbably northwards.

That night was perfectly terrible. It was a miracle that the little schooner did not capsize. Twice she was swept by the seas and everything would have been washed overboard if the gripes had failed. Aouda was utterly exhausted, but she never complained, and more than once Mr Fogg had to rush over to her to protect her against the violence of the waves.

When daylight reappeared the storm was still blowing with extreme fury. Now, however, the wind returned to the southeast; this was a favourable change, and the *Tankadere* swept forward again on this raging sea, whose waves were now contending with those produced by the new direction of the wind. The resulting clash of waves would have crushed any vessel less solidly built.

From time to time the coast came into sight through the mist, but there was not a vessel to be seen. The *Tankadere* was the only one to remain at sea.

At noon there were a few signs that the wind was abating, and as the sun declined towards the horizon, these became more pronounced.

The storm had in fact been too violent to last long. Now at last the passengers, who were completely exhausted, were able to take a little food and to get some rest.

The night was comparatively peaceful, and the pilot rehoisted some of his sails with a few reefs let out. The vessel made considerable progress, and at daybreak the next day, the 11th, after examining the coastline, John Bunsby was able to announce that they were not a hundred miles from Shanghai.

A hundred miles and only one day in which to cover them! Mr Fogg had to reach Shanghai that very evening if he did not want to miss the steamer for Yokohama. But for that storm, during which he had lost several hours, he would now have been less than thirty miles from that port.

The wind was dropping perceptibly, but fortunately so was the sea. All sails were set – jibs, staysails and flying jib – and the sea foamed under the schooner's prow.

By noon the *Tankadere* was not more than forty-five miles from Shanghai, and she still had six hours in which to reach harbour before the steamer for Yokohama set out.

Anxiety gripped the crew, for everyone wanted to get there at all costs, and everyone – Phileas Fogg no doubt excepted – felt his heart beating with impatience. It was essential for the little schooner to keep up an average of nine knots, and the wind was still dropping! It was a fitful breeze, blowing from the coast in capricious gusts, and the sea became smooth as soon as they had passed.

But the vessel was so light, and her lofty sails, woven of fine material, caught the fickle breezes so well, that, helped by the current, John Bunsby reckoned at six o'clock that they were only ten miles from the mouth of the Shanghai River, the town itself being situated at least twelve miles upstream.

At seven o'clock they were still three miles from Shanghai. The pilot gave vent to a terrible oath as he saw the bonus of two hundred pounds escaping him. He looked at Mr Fogg. Mr Fogg was as impassive as ever, although his whole fortune was at stake at that very moment . . .

At that moment, too, a tall black spindle shaped object, crowned by a plume of smoke, appeared on the horizon. It was the American steamer, leaving port at the appointed hour.

"Curse it!" shouted John Bunsby, pushing away the helm with a despairing gesture.

"Signal her!" was all that Phileas Fogg said.

A small bronze cannon stood on the foredeck of the *Tankadere*, which was used to make signals in foggy weather.

The cannon was loaded up to the muzzle; but just as the pilot was about to apply a red-hot coal to the touch-hole Mr Fogg said:

"Put the flag at half-mast."

The flag was lowered to half-mast. This was a signal of distress, and it could well be hoped that on seeing it the American steamer would change her course for a moment to come to the aid of the pilot boat.

"Fire!" said Mr Fogg.

And the explosion of the little bronze cannon rent the air.

CHAPTER TWENTY-TWO

In which Passepartout realizes that, even at the Antipodes, it is wise to have a little money in one's pocket

After leaving Hong Kong on 7th November at half past six in the evening, the *Carnatic* cruised at full steam towards Japan. Though she was fully loaded with cargo and passengers, two cabins in her stern were unoccupied. They were cabins which had been booked in the name of Phileas Fogg.

On the following morning the men in the bows were somewhat surprised to see a passenger with a dazed look in his eyes, a shaky step and tousled hair, emerge from the second class companionway and stagger to a spar on which he sat down.

A few moments after Fix had left the opium den, two of the attendants had picked up Passepartout, who was fast asleep, and had laid him on the bed reserved for the opium smokers. Three hours later, pursued even in his nightmares by one sole idea, Passepartout woke up, struggling against the stupefying influence of the drug. The thought of an unfulfilled duty dispelled his torpor. He left the drunkards' bed and, staggering and leaning against the walls, falling and getting up again, but always irresistibly urged on by a sort of instinct, he came out of the opium den shouting, as if in a dream:

"The *Carnatic*! The *Carnatic*!"

The boat was there, with steam up, and Passepartout

had to take only a few steps. He rushed up the gangway, staggered on to the deck, and fell unconscious in the bows just as the *Carnatic* was casting off.

A few sailors, accustomed to this sort of thing, carried the poor fellow down into a second class cabin, where he did not awake until the following morning, a hundred and fifty miles from China.

And that was why, that morning, Passepartout found himself on the deck of the *Carnatic* gulping down great breaths of sea air. This sobered him, and he began to collect his thoughts. He found this anything but easy work, but at last he recalled the events of the previous evening, Fix's revelations, the opium den, and so on.

"It's obvious", he said to himself, "that I've been terribly drunk. Whatever will Monsieur Fogg say? Anyhow, I haven't missed the boat, and that's the main thing."

Then his thoughts returned to Fix.

"As for that fellow, I very much hope that we're rid of him, and that after his proposal to me he hasn't dared to follow us on to the *Carnatic*. A police inspector, a detective, dogging my master's heels and accusing him of robbing the Bank of England! Rubbish! Monsieur Fogg is no more a thief than I'm a murderer!"

Should he explain all this to his master? Ought he to tell him about the part Fix was playing in this affair? Wouldn't it be better to wait till they got back to London to tell him that an agent of the Metropolitan Police had followed him round the world, and enjoy the joke with him? Probably. In any case, he would have to think it over. The first thing to do was to go to Monsieur Fogg and offer his apologies for his outrageous behaviour.

So Passepartout got up. The sea was rough and the vessel was rolling heavily. Although the good fellow was still rather unsteady on his legs he managed to make his way to the stern.

He failed to see anyone on deck who looked like his master or Aouda.

"That's all right," he said to himself. "At this hour of the day Aouda will still be in bed. As for Monsieur Fogg, he'll have found somebody to play whist with, and as usual . . ."

With these words Passepartout went down to the saloon. Monsieur Fogg was not there. The only thing for him to do was to ask the purser which cabin Monsieur Fogg was in, but the purser replied that he did not know any passenger of that name.

"I beg your pardon," Passepartout insisted. "He's a tall gentleman, rather cold and reserved. He has a young lady with him . . ."

"We have no young lady on board," replied the purser. "What's more, here's the passenger list. You can see for yourself."

Passepartout read through the list . . . His master's name was not there. He felt stunned, but then an idea crossed his mind.

"I am on the *Carnatic*, I suppose?" he asked.

"Yes," answered the purser.

"Bound for Yokohama?"

"That's right."

For a moment Passepartout had been afraid he was on the wrong boat. But though he was on the *Carnatic* it was quite certain that his master wasn't. Thunderstruck, Passepartout slumped into an armchair. Then, all of a sudden, the truth dawned upon him. He remembered that the time of sailing of the Carnatic had been brought forward, that he had been supposed to tell his master of the fact, and that he hadn't done so! So it was his fault that Monsieur Fogg and Aouda had missed the boat!

Yes, it was his fault, but it was even more the fault of the traitor who, to separate him from his master and keep the latter in Hong Kong, had made him drunk. For at last

146

On the 13th the "Carnatic" entered Yokohama harbour

he understood the police inspector's trick. And now Monsieur Fogg was ruined; he had lost his wager; perhaps he had even been arrested and thrown into jail! The thought made Passepartout tear his hair. Oh, if he ever got his hands on Fix, what a settling of scores there would be!

But after the first moment of stupefaction he regained his calm and began to study the situation. It was anything but enviable. Here he was on his way to Japan: he was certain to get there, but how would he get back? His pockets were empty. Not a shilling, not a penny! Admittedly his passage and his meals had been paid for in advance, so he had five or six days before him in which to decide what to do. The way he ate and drank during the voyage beggars description. He ate as if Japan, where he was due to land before long, were a desert, bare of anything to eat.

On the 13th, with the morning tide, the *Carnatic* entered Yokohama harbour. Yokohama is an important port of call in the Pacific. Every boat carrying mail or passengers between North America, China, Japan and the islands of Malaysia, put in there. It is situated in the Bay of Yeddo, not far from that huge city, the second capital of the Japanese Empire, once the residence of the Tycoon, in the period when that civil emperor existed, and a rival of

147

Meako, the great city which is the home of the Mikado, the ecclesiastical emperor descended from the gods.

The *Carnatic* took up her moorings alongside the quay in Yokohama harbour near the jetties and the customs warehouses, amidst a multitude of ships of all nations.

Passepartout set foot without the slightest enthusiasm on this remarkable land of the Rising Sun. He had nothing better to do than to take chance for his guide and wander haphazardly through the streets.

He found himself at first in an absolutely European city, with low-fronted houses with verandas over graceful peristyles, covering the whole area between the Treaty promontory and the river with its streets, squares, docks and warehouses. Here, as in Hong Kong, the streets swarmed with people of all races, Americans, English, Chinese, Dutch, with merchants ready to buy or sell anything, in whose midst the Frenchman felt as much a stranger as if he had been dropped into the land of the Hottentots.

He had admittedly one recourse, which was to apply to the French or English Consul. But he shrank from the idea of relating his story, which was so intimately connected with his master's, and before trying that he wanted to exhaust every other possibility.

So after traversing the European quarter, where chance had not favoured him, he entered the Japanese quarter, determined if necessary to go on to Yeddo.

This native quarter of Yokohama was called Benten, from the name of the sea goddess worshipped on the neighbouring islands. It contained beautiful avenues of firs and cedars, holy gates of strange architecture, bridges hidden in the midst of bamboos and reeds, temples sheltered beneath the vast gloom of age-old cedars, monasteries within whose walls the priests of Buddhism and the sectaries of Confucius vegetated, and endless streets in which one might have garnered a harvest of pink-faced, rosy-cheeked children, little creatures who looked as if they had been cut out of some native screen, and who were playing in the midst of short-legged poodles and yellowish tailless cats with lazy, wheedling ways.

The streets were swarming with people bustling to and fro, processions of bonzes beating their monotonous tom-toms, yakoonins, custom house and police officers in pointed hats encrusted with lacquer, and wearing two swords in their belts, soldiers dressed in blue cotton clothes with white stripes and armed with percussion guns, men-at-arms of the Mikado, trussed up in their silk doublets, with hauberks and coats of mail, and countless other military men of all ranks, for in Japan the soldier's profession is highly esteemed as it is despised in China. Then came mendicant friars, long-robed pilgrims and ordinary civilians with sleek ebony-black hair, big heads, long torsos and thin legs – people of short stature whose complexion ranged from dark copper tints to dull white, but was never yellow like that of the Chinese, from whom the Japanese differ completely. Finally, among the carriages, the palanquins, the horses, the porters, the barrows fitted with sails, the *norimons* with lacquered sides, the luxurious *cangos*, regular litters made of bamboo, a few women could be seen walking along, taking short steps with their small feet, shod in canvas shoes, straw sandals or carved clogs. These women were not pretty, with their flat chests, their slanting eyes, and their teeth blackened in accordance with the prevailing fashion, but they wore gracefully their national garment, the kimono, a sort of dressing gown fastened with a broad silk sash tied behind the back in a huge knot, which the Parisian ladies of today seem to have borrowed from the women of Japan.

For a few hours Passepartout strolled about in the midst of this motley crowd, looking too at the strange, luxurious shops, the bazaars crowded with all the gaudy splendour of Japanese jewellery, the restaurants adorned with streamers and banners which he was in no position to enter, those teahouses in which fragrant hot water was drunk by the cupful together with "sake", a liquor obtained from fermented rice, and those comfortable smoking houses where a very fine tobacco was smoked, and not opium, the use of which was almost unknown in Japan.

Then Passepartout found himself in the country, in the midst of vast paddy fields. There, not on shrubs but on trees, the brilliant blossoms of full-blown camellias were putting forth their last colours and their last perfumes, and within bamboo enclosures, cherry trees, plum trees and apple trees, which the natives grew more for their blossom than for their fruit, and which grimacing scare-crows and screeching whirligigs protected against the beaks of sparrows, pigeons, crows and other voracious birds. There was not a majestic cedar but sheltered some great eagle, not a weeping willow but spread its foliage over some heron sadly perched on one leg; and on all sides there were crows, ducks, hawks, wild geese, and great numbers of those cranes which the Japanese addressed as noble lords and which in their eyes symbolized long life and happiness.

Strolling along like this, Passepartout noticed a few violets in the grass.

"Good!" he said. "Here's my supper."

But when he smelt them he found that they had no scent.

"No luck!" he reflected.

The good fellow had admittedly had the foresight to eat as much as he could before leaving the *Carnatic*, but after wandering about all day he felt as if his stomach were hollow. He had noticed that there was neither mutton, goat-flesh nor pork on the stalls of the native butchers, and as he knew that it was sacrilege to kill cattle, which were strictly reserved for agricultural needs, he had concluded that meat was scarce in Japan. He was quite right; but in default of butcher's meat, his stomach would have done quite well with the joints of wild boar or deer, the partridge or quail, the poultry or fish which, with rice, formed almost the only food of the Japanese. But he had to put a good face on things, and he decided to wait until the next day before looking for food.

At nightfall Passepartout returned to the native quarter, and wandered through the streets lit by multicoloured lanterns. He watched the acrobats performing their amazing feats and the astrologers who, in the open air, were collecting crowds around their telescopes. Then he saw the harbour again, gleaming with the lights of the fishermen, who were attracting the fish with the glow of flaming resin.

At last the streets emptied, and the crowds were replaced by the police making their rounds. These officers, clad in magnificent costumes and in the midst of their attendants, looked like ambassadors, and every time Passepartout came across one of these dazzling patrols he muttered with a grin:

"Hallo, here's another Japanese embassy on its way to Europe!"

CHAPTER TWENTY-THREE

In which Passepartout's nose grows inordinately long

The next day, Passepartout, worn out and famished, decided that at all costs he must get something to eat, and the sooner the better. Admittedly, he could always sell his watch, but he would rather have died of hunger. Now, if ever, was the time to use the strong, if not melodious, voice with which nature had endowed him.

He knew a few French and English tunes, and he decided to try them. The Japanese were bound to be music-lovers, since they did everything to the accompaniment of cymbals, tom-toms and drums, and they could not fail to appreciate the talents of a European virtuoso. Still, it might be a little early for a concert, and the dilettanti, prematurely awakened, might pay the singer in coin which did not bear the Mikado's head.

So Passepartout decided to wait a few hours; but as he wandered along it occurred to him that he might seem too well dressed for a strolling artist, and he hit upon the idea of changing his garments for some old clothes more in harmony with his position. Moreover, this exchange was bound to leave a balance which he could use immediately to satisfy his appetite.

Once taken, this decision had to be carried out, and it was only after a long search that Passepartout discovered a native old clothes dealer, to whom he explained his needs. The European outfit appealed to the dealer, and soon Passepartout left his shop rigged out in an old Japanese robe and a sort of ribbed turban faded with age. On the other hand, a few pieces of silver jingled in his pocket.

"Good!" he reflected. "I'll imagine that I'm in a carnival!"

Thus "Japanesed", Passepartout made it his first task to enter a modest-looking teahouse; and there he breakfasted on the remains of a fowl and a few handfuls of rice, like a man for whom dinner was a problem still to be solved.

"Now," he said to himself, when he had eaten his fill, "I mustn't lose my head. I can't help myself by selling this outfit for one still more Japanese. So I've got to think of some way of leaving this land of the Rising Sun as quickly as I can: in any case, the memories I shall take away with me will be anything but pleasant."

He then had the idea of visiting the steamers leaving for America, offering his services as a cook or a steward, asking in return for only his passage and his food. Once in San Francisco, he would soon find some way of getting out of his difficulties. The great thing was to cross those four thousand seven hundred miles of ocean which lay between Japan and the New World.

Not being the sort of man to let an idea go begging, Passepartout made for the harbour. But the nearer he got to the docks, the more impracticable seemed his plan, which had appeared so simple when he had first thought of it. Why should they need a steward or a cook on an American ship, and what sort of confidence would he inspire in anybody, dressed up as he was? What testimonials could he provide? What references could he give?

As these thoughts were going through his mind, his gaze fell on a huge placard which some sort of clown was carrying through the streets of Yokohama. It was worded in English and read as follows:

HONOURABLE
WILLIAM BATULCAR'S TROUPE
OF JAPANESE ACROBATS
LAST PERFORMANCES
Before Their Departure for the United States
OF THE
LONG LONG NOSES,
UNDER THE SPECIAL PATRONAGE OF THE GOD TINGOU
GREAT ATTRACTION

"The United States of America!" exclaimed Passepartout. "Just what I'm looking for!"

Following the man carrying the notice, he soon found

A huge placard carried by some sort of clown

154

himself back in the Japanese quarter. Soon he stopped in front of a huge building crowned with several clusters of streamers; on its outside walls, in crude colours but without any attempt at perspective, were depicted a whole troupe of jugglers.

This was the establishment of the Honourable William Batulcar, a sort of American Barnum, and the manager of a troupe of contortionists, jugglers, clowns, acrobats, equilibrists and gymnasts who, according to the notice, were giving their last performances before leaving the Land of the Rising Sun for the United States.

Passepartout went in under a peristyle in front of the hall, and asked for Monsieur Batulcar, who appeared in person.

"What do you want?" he asked Passepartout, whom he at first took for a native.

"Do you want a servant?" asked Passepartout

"A servant!" exclaimed the Barnum, stroking the thick grey goatee which sprouted under his chin. "I've got two. They're obedient and faithful, they've never left me, and they serve me for nothing, provided I feed them . . . And here they are," he added, indicating his two strong arms, lined with veins as thick as the strings of a double bass.

"So I can't be of any use to you?"

"None at all."

"Damn! It would have suited me to go away with you."

"Here!" exclaimed the Honourable Batulcar. "You're no more a Japanese than I'm a monkey! So why are you dressed like that?"

"One dresses as well as one can!"

"True enough. You're a Frenchman, aren't you?"

"Yes, a Parisian of Paris."

"Then you must know how to make faces?"

"Dammit," replied Passepartout, annoyed to find his nationality provoking such a question. "Yes, we French

155

can make faces, it's quite true, but no better than the Americans!"

"Quite right. Well, if I don't engage you as a servant, I can give you a job as a clown. You understand, my dear fellow. In France they exhibit foreign clowns, and in foreign countries we exhibit French clowns."

"I see."

"You're a strong fellow, I hope?"

"Especially when I've had a meal."

"And you can sing?"

"Yes," replied Passepartout, who in the past had taken part in a few street concerts.

"But can you sing standing on your head, with a spinning top on the sole of your left foot and a sabre balanced on the sole of your right foot?"

"I certainly can," answered Passepartout, remembering the gymnastic exercises of his youth.

"You see, everything depends on that," said Batulcar, and the engagement was concluded on the spot.

So at last Passepartout had found work; he was employed as an odd-job man in the famous Japanese troupe. This was not a very flattering post, but within a week he would be on his way to San Francisco.

The performance, announced with a great flourish by the Honourable Batulcar, was due to begin at three o'clock, and soon the formidable instruments of a Japanese orchestra, drums and tom-toms, were thundering away at the door, Needless to say, Passepartout had not had time to learn a part, but he was to lend the assistance of his massive shoulders in a grand display of the "Human Pyramid" performed by the Long Noses of the God Tingou. This "great attraction" was to bring the performance to an end.

Before three o'clock the audience crowded into the immense hall. Europeans and natives, Chinese and Japanese, men, women and children rushed to take their places on the narrow benches and in the boxes facing the stage. The musicians had gone inside, and the full orchestra of gongs, tom-toms, bones, flutes, tambourines and big drums was playing frantically.

Though this performance resembled any other acrobatic display, it must be confessed that the Japanese are the best equilibrists in the world. One man, armed with his fan and a few pieces of paper, performed the graceful trick of the butterflies and the flowers. Another used the fragrant smoke of his pipe to trace in the air a series of words paying a compliment to the audience. A third juggled with some lighted candles, which he blew out in succession as they passed in front of his lips and relighted from one another without for a single moment interrupting his marvellous juggling. Another produced the most improbable combinations of humming tops; in his hands these melodious toys seemed, in their endless gyration, to take on a life of their own: they ran along pipe-stems, along the edges of sword blades, along wires no thicker than a hair stretched from one side of the stage to the other; they circled round the rims of crystal vases, they scaled bamboo ladders, they scattered into every corner, producing strange harmonic effects by combining their different notes. The jugglers juggled with them, and they spun in the air; they threw them like shuttlecocks with wooden battledores, and they went on spinning; they thrust them into their pockets and when they took them out they were still spinning – right up to the moment when a spring was released which made them burst open like fireworks.

There is no need to describe the marvellous feats of the troupe's acrobats and gymnasts, on ladders, on poles, on balls, on barrels and so forth, all carried out with remarkable precision. But the principal attraction of the whole performance was the display by the Long Noses, astonishing equilibrists as yet unknown to Europe.

These Long Noses formed a society under the direct

protection of the God Tingou. Clad like medieval heralds, they bore on their shoulders a splendid pair of wings, but their special distinction was the long nose with which each face was embellished, and above all the use they made of it. These noses consisted of bamboo canes five or six or ten feet long, some straight, others curved, some smooth and others covered with warts. It was on these appendages, which were securely fastened, that they performed all their balancing feats. A dozen of these sectaries of the God Tingou lay flat on their backs, and their comrades climbed on to their noses, held as upright as lightning conductors, jumping and vaulting from one to another, and performing the most improbable tricks.

The attention of the public had been specially called to the final attraction, a human pyramid, in which fifty of the Long Noses were to represent the Car of Juggernaut. But instead of forming this pyramid by climbing on one another's shoulders, the Honourable Batulcar's artistes were to use nothing but their noses. Now one of the performers at the base of the Car had left the troupe, and as all that was needed was strength and skill, Passepartout had been selected to take his place.

True, the worthy fellow felt really sorry for himself when – a sad reminder of his youth – he had put on his medieval attire, decorated with multicoloured wings, and a nose six feet long had been clapped on to his face! Still, that nose was his bread and butter, and he resigned himself to putting up with it.

He went on stage and took his place among those of his colleagues who were to form the base of the Car of Juggernaut. They all lay down flat, their noses pointing towards the sky. A second batch of acrobats took up their position on these long appendages, a third placed themselves above these, and then a fourth; and upon these noses, which met only at the tips, a human monument soon rose right to the very top of the theatre.

Then, just as the applause was increasing and the instruments in the orchestra were roaring like thunder, the whole pyramid tottered, its equilibrium was lost, one of the noses at its base was withdrawn, and the monument collapsed like a house of cards.

The fault lay with Passepartout, who, leaving his post, had leapt across the footlights without the help of his wings, clambered up to the right-hand gallery, and fallen at the feet of a member of the audience shouting:

"Oh, my master! My master!"

"Is it you?"

"Yes, it's me!"

"Very well! In that case my lad, come along to the steamer!"

Mr Fogg, Aouda, who was with him, and Passepartout rushed down the corridors, but outside the hall they found the Honourable Batulcar, furious with rage and demanding damages.

Phileas Fogg appeased his fury by throwing him a handful of banknotes, and at half past six, just as she was about to sail, Fogg and Aouda set foot on the American steamer. They were followed by Passepartout, with his wings still fastened to his back, and his face adorned with the six-foot nose he had not yet managed to remove!

CHAPTER TWENTY-FOUR

In which the Pacific Ocean is crossed

What had happened off Shanghai is easy to understand. The *Tankadere*'s signals had been sighted from the Yokohama steamer. The captain, seeing a flag at half-mast, had steered towards the little schooner. A few moments later, Phileas Fogg, paying the agreed sum for his passage, handed Skipper John Bunsby five hundred and fifty pounds. Then the worthy gentleman, accompanied by Aouda and Fix, boarded the steamer, which promptly resumed her course for Nagasaki and Yokohama.

Arriving that morning, 14th November, at the scheduled time, Phileas Fogg left Fix to go about his business, and went aboard the *Carnatic*. There he learned, to the delight of Aouda – and perhaps, though he showed no sign of it, to his own – that the Frenchman Passepartout had indeed arrived in Yokohama the previous day.

Phileas Fogg, who had to leave that very evening for San Francisco, set out at once in search of his servant. He applied without success to the French and English consuls, and after vainly roaming the streets of Yokohama, he was beginning to despair of ever finding Passepartout when chance, or perhaps a sort of presentiment, took him into the Honourable Batulcar's hall. He would certainly never have recognized his servant in his eccentric heraldic garb; but the latter, lying flat on his back, caught sight of his master in the gallery, and could not resist twitching his nose. Hence the loss of equilibrium, and all that ensued.

Passepartout learned of this from Aouda, who then explained how they had succeeded in getting from Hong Kong to Shanghai on the schooner *Tankadere*, in the company of a certain Mr Fix.

At the mention of Fix, Passepartout did not bat an eyelid. He did not think the time had yet come for him to tell his master what had passed between the detective and himself. So in the account he gave of his adventures, he blamed only himself and offered his apologies for having allowed himself to be intoxicated with opium in a Hong Kong smoking den.

Mr Fogg listened to this narrative coldly and without comment; then he advanced his servant a sum of money

160

large enough for him to buy more suitable clothes on board. So within an hour the worthy fellow, having removed his nose and shed his wings, no longer had anything about him to recall the follower of the God Tingou.

The vessel on which they were crossing from Yokohama to San Francisco belonged to the Pacific Mail Steamship Company, and was called the *General Grant*. She was a huge paddle steamer of two thousand five hundred tons, well equipped and very fast. An enormous beam rose and fell regularly above the deck; a piston rod was linked to one end and a connecting rod to the other, which, converting the rectilinear into circular motion, operated the paddle shaft. The *General Grant* was rigged as a three-masted schooner, and she had a large spread of canvas which greatly assisted her steam power. Travelling at twelve knots, she would not take more than three weeks to cross the Pacific, so that Phileas Fogg was entitled to assume that, arriving at San Francisco on 2nd December, he would be in New York on the 11th and in London on the 20th – thus anticipating by a few hours that fateful date of 21st December.

There was a fairly large number of passengers on board, some English people, a great many Americans, a whole crowd of coolies emigrating to America and a certain number of officers of the Indian Army who were using their leave to travel round the world.

From a nautical point of view the voyage was uneventful. The boat, supported by her great paddle wheels and steadied by her huge spread of canvas, rolled but little, and the Pacific justified its name reasonably well. Mr Fogg was as calm and as uncommunicative as ever, and his young companion felt more and more attached to him by bonds other than those of gratitude. His nature, so silent yet so generous, was having a greater effect on her than she realized, and almost unknown to herself she was yielding to emotions to whose influence the enigmatic Fogg seemed completely impervious.

Aouda, moreover, was keenly interested in his plans and worried about the setbacks which might compromise the success of the journey. She often chatted with Passe-partout, who could read between the lines of her heart. The good fellow now had unbounded faith in his master; he was never weary of praising his honesty, his generosity, his devotion; then he would reassure Aouda regarding the outcome of the journey, impressing upon her that the most difficult part was over, that they had left behind those fantastic countries China and Japan, and were on their way back to civilized lands, and that a train from San Francisco to New York and a liner from New York to London would probably be all they needed to complete that impossible journey round the world within the agreed period.

Nine days after leaving Yokohama, Phileas Fogg had journeyed round exactly one half of the globe, for on 23rd November the *General Grant* crossed the 180th meridian, which, in the southern hemisphere, stands at the antipodes of London. Of the eighty days allotted to him, Mr Fogg had, it is true, used up fifty-two, so that he now had only twenty-eight at his disposal. It must be pointed out, however, that if that gentleman was now only half way round according to the meridians, he had really covered more than two-thirds of the whole distance. For consider what a roundabout way he had been obliged to go – from London to Aden, from Aden to Bombay, from Calcutta to Singapore and from Singapore to Yokohama! If he could have followed the fiftieth parallel, which is that of London, the distance would only have been about twelve thousand miles, while Phileas Fogg was compelled, by the vagaries of the various modes of travel, to cover twenty-six thousand. Of these he had now, on 23rd November, covered about seventeen thousand five hundred miles. But from now on his course was straight, and Fix was no longer there to pile up obstacles in his way.

It happened too that on this day of 23rd November, Passepartout had a pleasant surprise. It will be recalled that the stubborn fellow had insisted on keeping his famous family watch set to London time, regarding all the local times of the countries he travelled through as completely wrong. Well, on this day, though he had never put it on or back, his watch now agreed with the ship's chronometer!

It is easy to imagine how exultant he was. He would have liked to know what Fix would have said if he had been there.

"That scoundrel told me a lot of nonsense about the meridians, the sun and the moon!" he reflected. "Oh, those people! If we listened to them, a fine sort of time we should keep! I knew that one of these days the sun would make up its mind to go by my watch!"

What Passepartout did not know was that if the dial of his watch had been divided into twenty-four hours like Italian clocks, he would have had no reason to exult, for when it was nine in the morning on board ship its hands would have shown nine in the evening, or twenty-one hours past midnight – the exact difference between London time and that of the 180th meridian.

But even if Fix had been able to explain this purely physical effect no doubt Passepartout would have been incapable of understanding it, or at least of admitting it. And in any case, if by some impossible chance Fix had unexpectedly appeared on board at that moment, it was likely that Passepartout, who had good reason for resentment, would have discussed quite a different matter with him in quite a different way.

But where was Fix at the moment?

Fix was on board the *General Grant*.

When they had reached Yokohama, the detective had

left Mr Fogg, whom he hoped to rejoin later that day, and had gone at once to the British Consulate. There he had at last found the warrant which had been following him from Bombay and which was now forty days old – the warrant which had been sent to him from Hong Kong on the *Carnatic*, the very ship on which he was supposed to be. The detective's disappointment may well be imagined. The warrant was now useless! Mr Fogg had left British soil, and an extradition order would now be needed to arrest him!

"Very well!" reflected Fix, after his first explosion of anger. "My warrant isn't any good here, but it will be in England. That scoundrel looks like going back to his own country, fancying he has thrown the police off the trail. Very well. I'll follow him there. As for the money, I hope to heaven some of it is left! But what with travelling and bribes and trials and fines and elephants and all sorts of expenses, my man has already got through more than five thousand pounds! Still, the Bank has plenty of money!"

Having made up his mind, he promptly embarked on the *General Grant*, and he was already on board when Mr Fogg and Aouda arrived. To his extreme surprise he recognized Passepartout in his heraldic costume. To avoid an explanation which might ruin everything, he at once took cover in his cabin. Thanks to the large number of passengers, he felt sure he could keep out of his enemy's sight, but that very day he suddenly found himself face to face with him on the foredeck.

Passepartout flew at Fix's throat without further explanation, and to the delight of some Americans, who at once started laying bets on him, he gave the wretched inspector a splendid thrashing which showed the great superiority of the French style of boxing over the English.

When Passepartout had finished, he felt calmer and as it were relieved. Fix got to his feet in a rather battered condition, and looking at his adversary said coldly:

"Have you finished?"

"Yes, for the time being."

"Then come and have a word with me."

"A word with you?"

"In your master's interest."

As though subdued by this cool request, Passepartout followed the police inspector and the two of them sat down in the bows.

"You've given me a thrashing," said Fix. "That's all right. I expected it. But now listen to me. So far I've been against Mr Fogg, but now I'm on his side!"

"At last!" cried Passepartout. "So now you think he's an honest man?"

"No," Fix replied coldly. "I think he's a scoundrel. . . Hush, keep still, and let me speak. So long as Mr Fogg was on British soil, it was in my interest to hold him back while I waited for a warrant for his arrest. I did everything I could to that end. I set the Bombay priests on to him, I made you drunk at Hong Kong, I separated you from your master, I made him miss the Yokohama steamer . . ."

His fists clenched, Passepartout listened.

"Now," Fix continued, "Mr Fogg seems to be going back to England. All right, I'll follow him. But in future I'm going to remove any obstacles from his path as carefully and zealously as I've piled them up till now. I've changed my tactics, you see, and I've changed them because it's in my interest. I may add, that your interest is the same as mine, for it's only in England that you'll be able to find out whether you're in the service of a criminal or an honest man!"

Passepartout had listened to Fix very attentively, and he felt convinced that the man was speaking in good faith.

"Well, are we friends?" asked Fix.

"Friends, no," Passepartout replied. "Allies, yes, but remember this: at the slightest sign of treachery I'll wring your neck."

"Agreed," said the police inspector quietly.

Eleven days later, on 3rd December, the *General Grant* entered Golden Gate Bay and arrived in San Francisco.

So far Mr Fogg had neither gained nor lost a single day.

CHAPTER TWENTY-FIVE

Which affords a brief glimpse of San Francisco on the occasion of a political meeting

It was seven in the morning when Phileas Fogg, Aouda and Passepartout set foot on the American continent – if this name can be given to the floating quay on which they disembarked. These quays, rising and falling with the tide, facilitated the loading and unloading of ships. Alongside them were moored clippers of all sizes, steamers of every nationality, and those steamboats with several decks which plied on the Sacramento and its tributaries. There too were piled up the commodities of a trade which extended as far as Mexico, Peru, Chile, Brazil, Europe, Asia and all the islands in the Pacific.

In his joy at reaching American soil at last, Passepartout thought it incumbent on him to disembark with a somersault in his very best style. But when he landed on the worm-eaten planks of the quay he almost fell through them. Taken aback by the way in which he had "set foot" in the New World, the good fellow let out a tremendous yell, which put to flight a flock of countless cormorants and pelicans, the usual denizens of these floating quays.

As soon as he had landed, Mr Fogg asked at what time the first train would leave for New York, and was told at six o'clock in the evening. So Mr Fogg had a whole day to spend in the Californian city. He ordered a carriage for Aouda and himself, Passepartout climbed up beside the driver, and for three dollars they were driven to the International Hotel.

From his lofty perch Passepartout stared with some curiosity at the great American city, with its wide streets, its neat rows of low houses, its churches and chapels in Anglo-Saxon Gothic, its huge docks and its palatial warehouses, some made of wood and others built of brick. In the streets he saw a great many carriages, omnibuses and tramcars, and on the crowded pavements not only Americans and Europeans, but also Chinese and Indians – enough people, in fact, to make up a population of over two hundred thousand inhabitants.

He was amazed, for he had expected to see the legendary city of the "forty-niners", a city of robbers, incendiaries and murderers who had rushed there in search of nuggets, a huge home for all sorts of down-and-outs, where they gambled for gold dust, a revolver in one hand and a knife in the other. But those "good old days" had gone, and San Francisco now looked like what it was, a great commercial city. The lofty tower of the city hall, where policemen were on the lookout, dominated the whole network of streets and avenues, which intersected each other at right angles, and in the midst of which lay green squares, while beyond was a Chinese quarter which seemed to have been imported from the Celestial Empire in a box of toys. There were no more sombreros, no more red shirts like those of the gold-diggers, no more beplumed Indians, but silk hats and frock coats, worn by large numbers of gentlemen endowed with feverish energy. Some of the streets, such as Montgomery Street – the equivalent of Regent Street in London, the Boulevard des Italiens in Paris and Broadway in New York – were lined with splendid shops, whose windows displayed goods from all over the world.

When Passepartout reached the International Hotel he

felt as if he had never left England. The ground floor of the hotel was taken up by an immense "bar", a kind of refreshment room open gratis to all passers-by. Dried meat, oyster soup, biscuits and cheese were provided without the customer's having to open his purse; all he paid for was his drink, whether ale, port or sherry. Passepartout thought this "very American".

The hotel restaurant was comfortable. Mr Fogg and Aouda sat down at a table and were copiously served on Lilliputian plates by negroes of the darkest hue.

After breakfast Mr Fogg, accompanied by Aouda, left the hotel to go to the British Consulate to have his passport visa'd. Outside he found his servant, who asked him if, before they went on the Pacific Railway, it would not be wise to buy a few dozen Enfield carbines or Colt revolvers, as he had heard of Sioux and Pawnees who held up trains like Spanish brigands. Mr Fogg replied that this was an unnecessary precaution, but that he could please himself. Then he went on towards the Consulate.

He had hardly gone two hundred yards when, "by a complete coincidence", he met Fix. The detective expressed the greatest surprise. What! Mr Fogg and he had crossed the Pacific together and yet they had never met on board. Anyhow, he could not but be honoured to meet once more the gentleman to whom he owed so much, and as his business was taking him back to Europe, he would be delighted if he might continue his journey in such pleasant company.

Mr Fogg replied that the honour would be his, and Fix, who was determined not to lose sight of him, asked his permission to join him in having a look round this strange city of San Francisco. This permission was granted.

So there were Phileas Fogg, Aouda and Fix strolling through the streets together. Soon they found themselves in Montgomery Street, where there were huge crowds of ordinary folk. On the pavements, in the middle of the roadway, on the rails of the tramway – in spite of the constant traffic of coaches and omnibuses – on the thresholds of the shops, at the windows of all the houses, and even on the roofs, were multitudes of people. Sandwich men were making their way through the groups. Banners and streamers were fluttering in the wind. Shouts were bursting forth everywhere.

"Hurrah for Kamerfield!"

"Hurrah for Mandiboy!"

It was a political meeting. Such at least was Fix's opinion, which he passed on to Mr Fogg, adding:

"It might be as well, sir, not to get mixed up in this mob. We might get some nasty blows."

"Yes," replied Phileas Fogg, "and even when they are political, blows are blows!"

Fix thought fit to smile at this comment, and to avoid getting mixed up in the crush he and Aouda and Phileas Fogg took up a position at the top of a flight of steps leading to a terrace overlooking Montgomery Street. In front of them, on the opposite side of the street, between a coal merchant's wharf and a petroleum shop, was a large open-air committee room, towards which the various currents of the crowd seemed to be converging.

What was the purpose of this meeting, and why was it being held? Phileas Fogg had no idea. Was it a question of nominating some high civil or military official, the governor of one of the States or a member of Congress? This was not an unreasonable conjecture, judging by the extraordinary excitement gripping the city.

At this moment there was a stir in the crowd, and all hands were raised. Some were firmly clenched and seemed to shoot up and down in the midst of the shouting – an energetic way, no doubt, of casting a vote. The crowd swayed backwards and forwards. The banners wavered, vanished for a moment and then reappeared in tatters. The human waves reached the steps, with heads tossing on the surface as if on a sea suddenly stirred up by a squall. The black hats were visibly getting fewer, and most of them seemed to have lost their normal height.

"It is obviously a political meeting," said Fix, "and the question at issue must be a very exciting one. I shouldn't be surprised if it were still that *Alabama* business, although it's been settled."

"Possibly," Mr Fogg replied quietly.

"Anyhow," Fix continued, "there are two champions facing one another, Mr Kamerfield and Mr Mandiboy."

Aouda, leaning on Phileas Fogg's arm, was gazing at this tumultuous scene with amazement, and Fix was about to ask one of his neighbours what the cause of this excitement was when the disturbance became more pronounced. The cheers and the insults grew louder. The poles of the banners were converted into offensive weapons. Hands disappeared to give place to fists everywhere. From the tops of the carriages and omnibuses, which had been brought to a halt, countless blows were exchanged. Everything was being used as a missile. Boots and shoes described very low trajectories, and it even seemed as if a few revolvers were adding their national bark to the shouts of the crowd.

The mob swept towards the stairway and flowed up its lower steps. One of the parties had evidently been driven back, but mere spectators could not tell whether the advantage lay with Mandiboy or Kamerfield.

"I think it might be prudent for us to go," said Fix, who did not want "his man" to be hurt or get involved in a scrape. "If this has anything to do with England, and we are recognized, we shall get dragged into it!"

"A British subject ..." replied Phileas Fogg, but he could not finish his sentence. Behind him, from the terrace at the head of the stairway, came a frightful howling. With shouts of "Hip, hip, hurrah for Mandiboy!" a swarm of electors was coming to the rescue of its allies, and was making a flank attack on Kamerfield's supporters.

Mr Fogg, Aouda and Fix found themselves between two fires, and they had no time to get away. This torrent of men, armed with loaded sticks and life preservers, was irresistible. While trying to protect their young companion Phileas Fogg and Fix were roughly jostled. Mr Fogg, as phlegmatic as ever, tried to defend himself with those natural weapons which nature has placed at the end of the arms of every Englishman, but in vain. A huge, broad-shouldered fellow with a red goatee and a ruddy complexion, who seemed to be the leader of the mob, raised his massive fist against Mr Fogg and would have injured him badly if Fix had not devotedly taken the blow in his place. An enormous swelling at once appeared under the detective's silk hat, now transformed into a mere skullcap.

"Yankee!" said Mr Fogg, glaring at his opponent with the utmost contempt.

"Limey!" retorted the other. "We'll meet again!"

"Whenever you please!"

"What's your name?"

"Phileas Fogg. And yours?"

"Colonel Stamp Proctor."

After this exchange the human tide swept by. Fix was knocked over, but got up again without serious injury. However, his overcoat had been ripped into two unequal parts, and his trousers resembled those breeches which certain Indians, as a matter of custom, never wear until they have removed the seat.

Still, Aouda had escaped injury and the only one to suffer had been Fix, with his blow from the American's fist.

As soon as they were clear of the crowd, Mr Fogg thanked the inspector.

"Don't mention it," Fix replied, "but come with me."

"Where to?"

"To a shop that sells ready-made clothes."

Certainly such a visit was opportune, for both Phileas Fogg and Fix were in rags, as if they had been fighting for the benefit of Messrs Kamerfield and Mandiboy.

An hour later, when they were suitable attired, they returned to the International Hotel.

There Passepartout, armed with half a dozen six-shooters, was waiting for his master. When he caught sight of Fix with Mr Fogg his brow darkened, but when Aouda had explained in a few words what had happened he calmed down. Clearly Fix was no longer an enemy; he was an ally. He was keeping his word.

Dinner over, a carriage was called to take the travellers and their luggage to the station. As he was getting in, Mr Fogg asked the detective:

"You haven't seen that Colonel Proctor again, have you?"

"No," replied Fix.

"I shall come back to America to find him," Phileas Fogg said coldly. "It would not be proper for a British citizen to let himself be treated like that."

The detective smiled but did not reply. Clearly Mr Fogg was of that breed of Englishmen who, while they do not allow duelling at home, are ready to fight when they are abroad if their honour in involved.

At a quarter to six the travellers reached the station and found their train ready to leave.

Just as Mr Fogg was about to get aboard, he caught sight of a porter and went over to him.

"My good man," he said to him, "hasn't there been a little rioting in San Francisco today?"

"It was a meeting, sir," the porter replied.

"But I thought I noticed some commotion in the streets."

"It was only a meeting about an election."

"The election of a commander in chief, I suppose?" said Mr Fogg.

"No, sir, a justice of the peace."

Having received this reply, Phileas Fogg got into the carriage and the train set off at full steam.

CHAPTER TWENTY-SIX

In which Phileas Fogg and his party travel by the Pacific Express

"From Ocean to Ocean," say the Americans, and those four words ought to have been the usual term for the grand trunk line which crossed the United States at their broadest part. In fact, however, the Pacific Railroad was divided into two distinct lines: the Central Pacific between San Francisco and Ogden, and the Union Pacific between Ogden and Omaha. There five separate lines branched off, which kept Omaha in frequent communication with New York.

Thus New York and San Francisco were linked at that time by an unbroken metal ribbon measuring not less than 3,786 miles. Between Omaha and the Pacific the railway crossed a region still inhabited by wild beasts and Indians, a vast tract which the Mormons began to colonize about 1845, after they had been expelled from Illinois. The whole journey which, even in the most favourable circumstances, formerly took six months now took seven days.

It was in 1862 that, despite the opposition of the Southern members of Congress, who wanted a more southerly line, it was decided that the railroad should run between the forty-first and forty-second parallels.

President Lincoln, whose memory was still held in affectionate regret, himself chose Omaha, in the State of Nebraska, as the terminus of the new network of railway lines. The work was begun immediately, and continued with that American energy which rejects both paperwork and red tape, but the speed with which the line was laid did not detract in any way from the skill with which the task was carried out. In the prairie the work progressed at the rate of a mile and a half a day. An engine, running on the rails laid down the day before, brought the rails to be laid the following day, and advanced along them as fast as they were put down.

The Pacific Railroad put out several branch lines along its route, in the States of Iowa, Kansas, Colorado and Oregon. On leaving Omaha, it ran along the left bank of the Platte River as far as the mouth of the northern branch, then followed the southern branch, crossed the territory of Laramie and the Wahsatch Mountains, passed round the Great Salt Lake until it reached Salt Lake City, the capital of the Mormons, plunged into the Tuilla Valley, skirted the American Desert, Mount Cedar and Mount Humboldt, the Humboldt River and the Sierra Nevada, and descended by way of Sacramento to the Pacific, without the gradient ever exceeding a hundred and twelve feet to the mile, even in the Rocky Mountains.

Such was the long artery which the trains took seven days to cover and which was going to allow Mr Phileas Fogg – so at least he hoped – to catch the Liverpool steamer from New York on 11th December.

The carriage he occupied was a sort of long omnibus carried by two four-wheel bogies, which enabled it to take sharp curves. It had no compartments; two rows of seats lined its sides, and between them was an aisle which led to the lavatories and dressing rooms with which each carriage was provided. Throughout the length of the train the carriages were linked together by gangways so that the

174

passengers could walk from one end of the convoy to the other. There were saloon cars, observation cars, dining cars and refreshment cars at their disposal. The only things missing were theatre cars, and these would come some day.

Vendors of books and newspapers walked constantly up and down the aisles selling their wares; so too did vendors of food and drink and cigars, and these did not lack customers.

The train left Oakland station at six. It was already night, a cold dark night, the clouds which covered the sky threatening to dissolve into snow. The train was not travelling very fast. Allowing for stops, it was not covering more than twenty miles an hour, a speed which neverthe-less should allow it to cross the United States within the scheduled time.

There was little conversation in the carriage, and besides, drowsiness overtook the passengers before long. Passepartout found that he had been placed beside the detective, but he did not speak to him. After what had recently happened, their relations had grown considerably cooler. There was no more sympathy, no more intimacy between them. Fix had not changed in manner, but Passepartout, on the other hand, maintained a strict reserve, ready at the slightest suspicion to strangle his former friend.

One hour after the train left, snow began to fall, a fine snow which fortunately could not delay its progress. Nothing could be seen through the windows but a vast white sheet, against which the spirals of steam from the engine seemed greyish.

At eight o'clock a steward came in and told the passen-gers that it was time for bed, for the carriage was a sleeping car which could be transformed into a dormitory in a few minutes. The backs of the seats were lowered, carefully packed bunks were unrolled by an ingenious method, berths were improvised in a few moments, and each traveller soon had at his service a comfortable bed, protected against inquisitive glances by thick curtains. The sheets were white and the pillows soft. All that anyone had to do was to go to bed and sleep – which each of them did, just as if he were in the comfortable cabin of a liner – while the train hurtled, now at full speed, across the State of California.

The country between San Francisco and Sacramento is not very hilly. This part of the line, known as the Central Pacific, started at first from Sacramento and was extended eastwards to meet the railroad from Omaha. From San Francisco to the Californian capital the line ran directly northeastwards, skirting the American River, which empties itself into San Pablo Bay. The hundred and twenty miles between these two important cities were covered in six hours, and towards midnight, while they were enjoying their first sleep, the travellers passed through Sacramento. They accordingly saw nothing of this large city, the seat of the Californian State government, neither its fine quays, nor its wide streets, nor its splendid hotels, nor its squares, nor its churches.

After leaving Sacramento and passing through the stations of Rochin, Auburn and Colfax, the train entered the Sierra Nevada. It was seven o'clock in the morning when it went through Cisco station. An hour later the dormitory had become an ordinary carriage once more, and through the windows the travellers could see the picturesque mountain scenery. The track obeyed the whims of the Sierra, here hugging the flanks of the mountain, there hanging over precipices, avoiding the sharp angles by means of bold curves and plunging into narrow gorges from which there seemed to be no exit. The engine, sparkling like a reliquary, with its headlight throwing out a lurid glare, its silvery bell, its protruding cowcatcher, mingled its whistling and roaring with the sound of the torrents and cascades, and entwined its smoke among the dark branches of the fir trees. There were few if any tunnels or bridges on this line; the railway followed the sides of the mountains, not seeking to take the shortest route from point to point and never doing violence to nature.

The train entered the State of Nevada through the Carson Valley about nine o'clock, still following a north-easterly direction. At noon it left Reno, where the passengers had twenty minutes for breakfast.

From this point the railway, skirting the Humboldt River, struck north for a few miles, following the course of the river. Then it turned eastwards, keeping close to the river until it reached the Humboldt Range, where the stream has its source, almost at the eastern extremity of Nevada.

After breakfast Mr Fogg, Aouda and their companions resumed their places in the carriage. Comfortably seated there, they observed the varied scenery passing before their eyes; vast prairies, mountains standing out on the horizon, and creeks with their foaming waters. Occasionally a great herd of bison, massing in the distance, appeared like a moving dike. These countless hosts of ruminants often presented an insurmountable barrier to the trains, thousands of them filing across the track in serried ranks for hours at a time, forcing the engine to stop and wait until the line was clear.

Indeed this was what happened on this occasion. About three o'clock in the afternoon a herd of ten or twelve thousand head blocked the railway. The engine slowed down, and tried to drive its cowcatcher into the side of the immense column, but the impenetrable mass brought it to a stop.

These animals – buffaloes, as they are incorrectly called in America – plodded on at their tranquil pace, sometimes uttering terrible roars. They were larger than the bulls of

The animals brought the train to a standstill

Europe, with short legs and tails, prominent withers forming a muscular hump, the bases of their horns set wide apart, and the head and neck and shoulders covered with long hair.

To try and stop their migration was out of the question. When the bison have decided on a direction, nothing can delay or change their progress. It is a torrent of living flesh which no dike could possible stem.

The travellers stood about on the platforms, watching this strange sight. But the one who should have been in the greatest hurry of all, Phileas Fogg, had stayed in his seat and was philosophically waiting until the buffaloes were pleased to make way for him. Passepartout was furious at the delay produced by this agglomeration of animals, and would have liked to open fire on them with his arsenal of revolvers.

"What a country," he exclaimed, "where trains are stopped by mere cattle, which amble along in a procession, refusing to hurry any more than if they weren't holding up the traffic! By heaven, I'd like to know whether Mr Fogg has allowed for this setback in his programme! And that driver who doesn't dare to send his engine right into those obstructive beasts!"

The driver had not tried to sweep away the obstacle, and he had acted wisely. He would no doubt have crushed the first of the buffaloes he attacked with his cowcatcher; but however powerful his engine might be, it would soon have been halted, and the train would have been derailed and wrecked.

The best thing to do therefore was to wait patiently, and then to make up for lost time by speeding up the train. The procession of the bison lasted three mortal hours, and the track was not cleared until night was falling. Then, when the last ranks of the herd were crossing the rails, the leaders were disappearing below the southern horizon.

So it was eight o'clock when the train passed through the defiles of the Humboldt Range, and half past nine when it entered the territory of Utah, the region of the Great Salt Lake, the strange country of the Mormons.

CHAPTER TWENTY-SEVEN

In which, at a speed of twenty miles an hour, Passepartout attends a lecture on Mormon history

During the night of 5th December, the train ran south-eastwards for about fifty miles, then a similar distance to the northeast, in the direction of the Great Salt Lake.

About nine o'clock in the morning, Passepartout went out on to one of the platforms to get a breath of fresh air. The weather was cold and the sky grey, but it was no longer snowing. Enlarged by the mist, the solar disc looked like a huge cold coin, and Passepartout was trying to calculate its value in pounds sterling when he was diverted from this useful task by the appearance of a somewhat strange-looking personage.

This man, who had boarded the train at Elko station, was tall and very dark; he had a black moustache, black stockings, a black silk hat, a black waistcoat, black trousers and white tie and dogskin gloves, and might have been taken for a clergyman. He was going from one end of the train to the other, and to the door of each carriage he was sticking, by means of sealing wafers, a hand-written notice.

Passepartout went up to one of these notices and read that Elder William Hitch, a Mormon missionary, would take advantage of his presence on Train No. 48 to deliver a lecture on Mormonism in Car No. 117, from eleven to twelve o'clock, and that any gentlemen who were desirous of learning about the mysteries of the religion of the Latter Day Saints were invited to attend.

"I shall certainly go," Passepartout said to himself, for he knew hardly anything about Mormonism except the basis of Mormon society, the custom of polygamy.

The news spread quickly throughout the train, which was carrying about a hundred passengers. Of these, thirty at the most, attracted by the lure of a lecture, were occupying the seats in Car No. 117 at eleven o'clock. In the front row of the faithful sat Passepartout. Neither his master nor Fix had thought fit to bestir themselves.

At the appointed hour Elder William Hitch rose, and in a somewhat angry voice, as though he had already been contradicted, he cried:

"I tell you that Joe Smith is a martyr, that his brother Hiram is a martyr, and that the persecutions of the prophets by the United States Government are going to make a martyr out of Brigham Young! Who dares to maintain the contrary?"

Nobody ventured to contradict the missionary, whose excited manner formed a marked contrast to the natural calmness of his face. But no doubt his anger could be explained by the harsh trials to which Mormonism was then being subjected. For the United States Government had just succeeded, not without some difficulty, in overcoming these independent fanatics. It had made itself master of Utah, and after imprisoning Brigham Young, accused of rebellion and polygamy, had forced that territory to submit to the laws of the Union. Since then the prophet's disciples had redoubled their efforts, and were resisting, by words in default of acts, the demands of Congress.

And here was Elder William Hitch, trying to make converts on the very railways.

Then, emphasizing his words by his raised voice and by the violence of his gestures, he related the history of

Mormonism, from biblical times onwards: how, in Israel, a Mormon prophet of the tribe of Joseph published the annals of the new religion and bequeathed them to his son Morom; how, many centuries later, a translation of this precious book, written in Egyptian hieroglyphics, was produced by Joseph Smith Junior, a farmer in the State of Vermont, who revealed himself as a mystical prophet in 1825; and how, finally, a heavenly messenger appeared to him in a shining forest and gave him the annals of the Lord.

At that moment a few members of the audience, not particularly interested in the missionary's retrospective account, left the carriage. But William Hitch went on to tell how Smith Junior, gathering together his father, his two brothers and a few disciples, founded the religion of the Latter Day Saints – a religion which had been adopted not only in America but also in England, Scandinavia and Germany, and numbered among its followers both artisans and many members of the liberal professions – how a colony was founded in Ohio; how a church was erected at a cost of two hundred thousand dollars and a town built at Kirkland; and how Smith became a daring banker and received from a humble mummy showman a papyrus containing a narrative in the hand of Abraham and other famous Egyptians.

As this story was getting rather long-winded, the ranks of his listeners thinned some more, and the audience was reduced to about twenty persons.

But the Elder, taking no notice of these desertions, related in detail how Joe Smith went bankrupt in 1837; how his ruined shareholders covered him with tar and rolled him in feathers; how he was found again, more honourable and honoured than ever, a few years later, at Independence, in Missouri, where he had become the leader of a flourishing community of at least three thousand disciples; and how then, pursued by the hatred of the gentiles, he had had to flee to the Far West.

There were still ten people in the audience, including the worthy Passepartout, who was listening in utter fascination. It was thus that he learnt how, after long persecutions, Smith reappeared in Illinois, and in 1839, on the banks of the Mississippi, founded the settlement of Nauvoo-la-Belle, whose population rose to twenty-five thousand souls; how Smith became its mayor, chief justice and commander in chief; how he stood as a candidate for the Presidency of the United States in 1843; and how he was finally lured into an ambush at Carthage, thrown into prison and murdered by a gang of masked men.

By now Passepartout was absolutely alone in the carriage, with the Elder looking him straight in the eye and hypnotizing him with his words, reminding him that two years after Smith's assassination, his successor, the inspired prophet Brigham Young, left Nauvoo and settled on the shores of the Great Salt Lake, where, in the midst of that beautiful fertile region, on the route of the emigrants crossing Utah on their way to California, the new colony, thanks to the polygamous principles of Mormonism, had flourished exceedingly.

"And that," added William Hitch, "is why the jealousy of Congress has been directed against us; why the soldiers of the Union have trampled on the soil of Utah; why our leader, the prophet Brigham Young, has been imprisoned in defiance of all justice! Shall we yield to force? Never! Driven out of Vermont, driven out of Illinois, driven out of Ohio, driven out of Missouri, driven out of Utah, we shall find yet another independent territory on which to pitch our tent . . . And you, my faithful friend," added the Elder, fixing an angry gaze upon his solitary listener, "will you pitch yours in the shadow of our flag?"

"No!" Passepartout replied boldly; then he in his turn fled, leaving the fanatic to preach in the wilderness.

During this lecture the train had been speeding on, and at about half past twelve it reached the northwest point of the Great Salt Lake. There the passengers had an extensive view of this inland sea, which is also called the Dead Sea, and into which there flows an American Jordan. It is a splendid lake, framed by magnificent broad-based crags, encrusted with white salt; a superb expanse of water, it formerly covered a greater area, but its shores have gradually risen in the course of time, reducing its surface while increasing its depth.

The Great Salt Lake, about seventy miles long and thirty-five miles wide, is three thousand eight hundred feet above sea level. Very different from Asphaltic Lake, which lies twelve hundred feet below the sea, its salt content is very high, and its water holds a quarter of its weight in solid matter in solution; its specific gravity is 1:170 whereas that of distilled water is 1:000. Consequently fish cannot live in it, and those which are carried into the lake by the Jordan, the Weber and other rivers soon die. On the other hand it is not true that the density of the water is such that a man cannot dive into it.

The country around the lake was very well cultivated, for the Mormons were skilled farmers. Six months later, the travellers would have seen on all sides ranches and corrals for domestic animals, fields of corn, maize and sorghum, lush meadows, hedges of wild rose trees and clumps of acacias and euphorbias; but now the ground was covered with a thin dusting of snow.

At two o'clock the travellers got out at Ogden, and as the train was not due to leave again until six, Mr Fogg and Aouda and their two companions had time to visit the City of the Saints by the small branch line connecting it with Ogden. Two hours sufficed for them to explore this thoroughly American town, built as such on the pattern of all the towns in the Union, like vast chessboards with long cold lines and "the gloomy sadness of right angles", as Victor Hugo put it. For the founder of the City of the Saints was unable to escape from the craving for symmetry which is characteristic of the Anglo-Saxons. In this strange country, where the men were certainly not up to the level of their institutions, everything was done "on the square" – towns, houses and follies.

By three o'clock the travellers were strolling through the streets of the city, which was built between one bank of the Jordan and the foothills of the Wahsatch Range. They noticed few, if any, churches: the only monuments were the prophet's residence, the courthouse and the arsenal. Then came houses built of bluish bricks with verandas and balconies, surrounded with gardens and bordered with acacias, palms and carob trees. A clay and pebble wall, built in 1853, encircled the town; and in the main street, where the market was held, there were a few hotels decked with flags, including Salt Lake House.

The city did not strike Mr Fogg and his companions as densely populated. The streets were almost empty, except those near the temple, which they reached only after passing through several districts surrounded by fences. There were a good many women, a fact which could be explained by the unusual composition of Mormon households. It should not be supposed, however, that all Mormons were polygamous. Everyone might do as he pleased, but it should be pointed out that the ladies of Utah were particularly anxious to get married for, according to the local religion, the Mormon Heaven did not admit to its joys any maiden ladies. These unfortunate creatures did not seem either well-off or happy: a few, the wealthiest no doubt, were clad in black silk jackets open at the waist, under a hood or a very modest shawl. The others all wore print dresses.

As a confirmed bachelor, Passepartout could not behold without certain alarm these Mormon women, several of whom were entrusted with the task of ensuring the happiness of one Mormon man. With his sturdy good sense it was the husband for whom he felt the greatest sympathy. It struck him as a terrible thing to have to guide so many ladies at once through the vicissitudes of life, to have to lead them like that in a bunch to the Mormon paradise, with the prospect of joining them there for eternity in the company of the glorious Smith, who was bound to be the crowning ornament of that delectable abode. He felt most decidedly that he had no vocation for such a life and he thought – though here perhaps he was mistaken – that the ladies of Salt Lake City were regarding his person in a somewhat disquieting way.

Fortunately his stay in the City of the Saints was not to be a very long one. At a few minutes before four, the travellers were back at the station and taking their places again in the train.

The whistle blew; but just as the engine's driving wheels gliding along the rails were beginning to impart a certain speed to the train, cries of "Stop! Stop!" were heard.

A moving train cannot be stopped. The gentleman who had uttered these cries was evidently a belated Mormon. He was running so fast that he was out of breath. Fortunately for him, the station had neither gates nor barriers, so he rushed along the track, jumped on the footboard of the last carriage, and dropped exhausted on one of the seats.

Passepartout, who had been anxiously watching these gymnastics, went over to have a look at this laggard. He was greatly interested when he learnt that this citizen of Utah had taken flight simply as a result of a domestic scene.

When the Mormon had recovered his breath, Passepartout ventured to inquire courteously how many wives he had; from the manner in which he had decamped, he thought he must have at least a score.

"One, sir!" the Mormon replied, raising his arms heaven-wards "One, and that was enough!"

CHAPTER TWENTY-EIGHT

In which Passepartout was unable to make anyone hear reason

After leaving the Great Salt Lake and Ogden station, the train travelled northwards for an hour, as far as the Weber River, about nine hundred miles from San Francisco. From that point it struck east again across the rugged Wahsatch Mountains. It was in the territory between these mountains and the Rocky Mountains proper that the American engineers had had to cope with their most serious difficulties.

Consequently, for this part of the railroad, the Union Government grant had risen to forty-eight thousand dollars a mile, whereas it had been only sixteen thousand dollars in the plain. But the engineers, as we have said before, had not violated nature but tricked her, turning rather than attacking any obstacles they encountered, so that to reach the great basin, only one tunnel, fourteen hundred feet long, had been pierced in the whole course of the railroad.

It was at the Great Salt Lake that the track had reached its highest altitude so far; beyond this point it described a very long curve, descending towards Bitter Creek Valley and then rising to the watershed between the Atlantic and the Pacific. In this mountainous region there were a great many streams, and the Muddy, the Green and others had to be crossed by means of culverts.

The nearer they got to their journey's end the more impatient Passepartout became, but Fix too longed to be out of this difficult country. He feared delays, dreaded accidents, and was more anxious than Phileas Fogg himself to set foot on English soil!

At ten o'clock in the evening the train stopped at Fort Bridger station, which it left again almost immediately. Twenty miles farther on, it entered the State of Wyoming, formerly Dakota, travelling the whole length of Bitter Creek Valley, from which the waters forming the hydrographic system of Colorado drain off.

The next day, 7th December, there was a fifteen-minute halt at Green River station. During the night there had been a fairly heavy fall of snow, but, mixed with rain and half-melted, it could not impede the train's progress. Still, this bad weather did not fail to make Passepartout uneasy, for the accumulation of snow might have seriously compromised the journey by clogging the wheels of the carriages.

"What madness it was," he said to himself, "to travel in winter! Couldn't my master have waited for the summer to improve his chances?"

But while the worthy fellow was concerned only about the state of the sky and the fall in temperature, Aouda felt even more anxious for quite a different reason.

A few passengers had got out of their carriage at Green River and were walking up and down the platform while they waited for the train to start. Through the window the young woman recognized one of them as Colonel Stamp Proctor, the American who had been so insolent to Phileas Fogg at the meeting in San Francisco. Not wanting to be seen, Aouda drew back from the window.

This incident caused her considerable alarm. She had become deeply attached to the man who, however cold he might be, gave daily evidence of the most complete devotion. No doubt she did not realize the depth of the feelings which her rescuer aroused in her, and so far she only called them gratitude, but though she did not know it they went much further than that. So her heart seemed to stop when she recognized the coarse brute from whom Mr Fogg intended, sooner or later, to demand satisfaction. Obviously it was chance alone which had led Colonel Proctor to board this train, but there he was, and at all costs Phileas Fogg must be prevented from recognizing his adversary.

When the train had started again, Aouda took advantage of a moment when Mr Fogg was dozing to inform Fix and Passepartout of the position.

"That fellow Proctor on the train!" exclaimed Fix. "Well, you needn't worry, Madam: before he meets Mr Fogg, he'll have to deal with me! I feel that I was the one he insulted most!"

"And besides," added Passepartout, "I'll look after him, even if he is a colonel!"

"Mr Fix," Aouda went on, "Mr Fogg will not entrust anyone with the task of avenging his honour. He is the sort of person, as he said himself, who will return to America to find the man who insulted him. So if he should catch sight of Colonel Proctor we cannot prevent an encounter which might have deplorable consequences. We must therefore take care that he doesn't see him."

"You're right, Madam," replied Fix. "If they met it might ruin everything. Win or lose, Mr Fogg would be delayed and . . ."

"And," put in Passepartout, "that would play into the hands of the gentlemen of the Reform Club. In four days we'll be in New York, so if for four days my master doesn't leave his carriage, we can hope that chance won't bring him face to face with that accursed American, the devil take him! Surely we can manage to prevent him . . ."

Here the conversation had to be dropped. Mr Fogg had awoken and was looking at the countryside through the snow-spattered window. But later, without being overheard either by his master or by Aouda, Passepartout asked the police inspector:

"Would you really fight for him?"

"I'd do anything," replied Fix quietly in a tone of implacable determination, "to bring him back to Europe alive!"

Passepartout felt a shiver run through his body, but his faith in his master remained unshaken.

Now, was there any method whereby Mr Fogg could be kept in this compartment to prevent any chance of his meeting the Colonel? That shouldn't be a difficult task, as he was neither fidgety nor inquisitive. In any case the police inspector thought he had hit on the desired method, for a few moments later he said to Mr Fogg:

"The hours one spends on a train seem endless, don't they, sir?"

"Yes," replied Mr Fogg, "but they pass all the same."

"On the steamers," the inspector continued, "you used to spend your time playing whist?"

"Yes," answered Phileas Fogg, "but that would be difficult here. I have neither cards nor partners."

"Oh, as for cards we can easily buy some. They sell everything on American trains. As for partners, if this lady plays by any chance . . ."

"Of course, sir," the young woman replied eagerly. "I can play whist. That is part of an English education."

"And I too," said Fix, "think I can claim to play fairly well. So with the three of us and a dummy . . ."

"Just as you please, sir," replied Phileas Fogg, delighted to get back to his favourite game, even on a train.

Passepartout was sent to find the steward, and soon returned with two packs of cards, scoring cards, counters and a folding table with a cloth top. There was nothing lacking, and the game began. Aouda had a reasonable knowledge of whist, and was even complimented by so severe a player as Phileas Fogg. As for the inspector, he was a first-rate and a worthy match for Mr Fogg.

"Now," Passepartout said to himself, "we've got him. He won't move again!"

At eleven o'clock in the morning, the train reached the watershed between the two oceans at Bridger Pass, 7,524 feet above sea level, one of the highest points it would attain while crossing the Rocky Mountains. After about another two hundred miles the travellers would at last reach the vast plains which extended as far as the Atlantic, and which nature has made so suitable for the laying of a railroad.

On the slope of the Atlantic basin the first streams, direct or indirect tributaries of the North Platte River, could already be seen. The whole horizon to the north and east was covered with the vast semicircular curtain which forms the northern portion of the Rocky Mountains, dominated by Laramie Peak. Between the mountain curve and the railway stretched immense, well-irrigated plains. On the right of the railroad rose the first slopes of the mountain range which sweeps round to the south as far as the sources of the Arkansas River, one of the great tributaries of the Missouri.

At half past twelve the passengers caught a glimpse of Fort Hallek, which dominated this region. A few more hours, and they would be across the Rocky Mountains. It was therefore reasonable to hope that no accident would befall the train as it crossed this difficult terrain. The snow had stopped falling, and the weather was turning crisp and cold. Huge birds flew far away, scared by the engine, and no wild animal, wolf or bear, could be seen on the plain. It was the desert in all its vast nakedness.

After a fairly comfortable lunch, served in their carriage, Mr Fogg and his partners had just resumed their interminable game when some loud whistle blasts were heard. Then the train stopped.

Passepartout put his head out of the window, but he could see nothing to account for this stoppage, and there was no station in sight.

Aouda and Fix feared for a moment that Mr Fogg might take it into his head to get down on to the line, but he contented himself with telling his servant:

"Go and see what is happening."

Passepartout jumped out of the carriage. About forty passengers had already left their seats, among them Colonel Stamp Proctor.

The train had pulled up before a signal at red, which blocked the way. The driver and the guard had got down and were talking excitedly with a track-watchman whom the stationmaster at Medicine Bow, the next stop, had sent to meet the train. Some passengers had gone up to them to join in the discussion, and among these was the self-same Colonel Proctor, with his loud voice and dictatorial gestures.

Joining the group, Passepartout heard the watchman say:

"No, there's no way of going on. The bridge at Medicine Bow is shaky and it couldn't take the weight of the train."

The bridge in question was a suspension bridge over some rapids about a mile from the place where the train had stopped. According to the watchman, it was threatening to collapse, for several of its cables had broken, and it was impossible to risk crossing it. The watchman was therefore not exaggerating in the least when he maintained the train could not go on. And carefree as the Americans usually are, when they decide to play safe, it would be sheer madness not to play safe too.

Passepartout, not daring to go and inform his master of what was happening, listened with clenched teeth, as motionless as a statue.

"Here!" protested Colonel Proctor. "We're not going to stay here and take root in the snow, are we?"

"Colonel," the guard replied, "they've telegraphed to Omaha station for a train, but it isn't likely to reach Medicine Bow for another six hours."

"Six hours!" exclaimed Passepartout.

"Probably," said the guard. "Anyhow, it will take us that time to reach the station on foot."

"On foot!" cried all the passengers.

"But how far away is this station?" one of them asked the guard.

"Twelve miles away, on the other side of the river."

"Twelve miles in the snow!" exclaimed Colonel Stamp Proctor.

The colonel let fly a volley of oaths, denouncing both the railway company and the guard, and in his fury Passepartout came close to joining in with him. Here was a material obstacle which was proof, for once, against all his master's banknotes.

What was more, there was widespread disappointment among the passengers, who, quite apart from the delay, saw themselves forced to trudge fifteen or so miles across the snow-covered plain. So there was a hubbub of exclamations and shouts which would certainly have attracted Phileas Fogg's attention if that gentleman had not been absorbed in his game.

But Passepartout was bound to inform him of what was happening, and he was dejectedly making for the carriage when the engine driver, a typical Yankee called Forster, said loudly:

"Gentlemen, there may be a way of getting across."

"Over the bridge?" asked one of the passengers.

"Over the bridge."

"With our train?" asked the colonel.

"With our train."

Passepartout had stopped and was drinking in the driver's words.

"But the bridge is in danger of collapsing!" the guard pointed out.

"That doesn't matter," replied Forster. "I think that if I drive the train at the bridge at full speed, she'll have a chance of getting across."

"The devil!" said Passepartout.

But some of the passengers had been tempted straight away by the idea, notably Colonel Proctor. That hothead considered the suggestion perfectly feasible. He even pointed out that some engineers had thought of crossing "unbridged" rivers with rigid trains driven at full speed. In the end, all those who were interested in the problem took the driver's side.

"We have a fifty per cent chance of getting across," one of them declared.

"Sixty per cent," said another.

"Eighty per cent!"

"Ninety per cent!"

Passepartout was completely taken aback. Although he was ready to try anything to get across Medicine Creek, this method struck him as a little too "American".

"Besides," he reflected, "there's a much simpler way, and none of these people have thought of it . . .!"

"Monsieur," he said to one of the passengers, "the driver's idea seems a bit dangerous to me, but . . ."

"An eighty per cent chance," replied the passenger, turning his back on him.

"I know that," Passepartout replied, turning to another passenger, "but a few minutes' thought . . ."

"No time for thought! It's a waste of time!" retorted the American he had spoken to, shrugging his shoulders. "The driver is certain we can get across."

"I don't doubt we'll get across," Passepartout went on, "but it might be more prudent . . ."

"What do you mean, prudent!" cried Colonel Proctor,

stung by this word he had happened to overhear. "At full speed, I tell you! At full speed!"

"I know . . . I understand . . ." repeated Passepartout, whom nobody would allow to finish his sentence, "but if you don't like the word prudent, at least it would be more natural . . ."

"Who? What? What's that? What does the fellow mean by natural?" cried people on all sides.

The poor man did not know to whom to speak.

"Are you scared?" Colonel Proctor asked him.

"Me, scared!" exclaimed Passepartout. "All right! I'll show these people that a Frenchman can be as American as they are!"

"All aboard! All aboard!" shouted the guard.

"Yes, all aboard!" repeated Passepartout. "All aboard! And quick about it! But you can't stop me from thinking that it would have been more natural to let us cross the bridge on foot first and the train next!"

But nobody heard these wise words. And in any case nobody would have acknowledged their wisdom.

The passengers climbed back in their carriages, and Passepartout returned to his seat without saying anything about what had happened. The card-players were absorbed in their whist.

The engine gave a shrill whistle. The driver, putting the engine into reverse, backed his train for about a mile, like a long jumper getting ready to take a run before leaping.

Then, at a second blast on the whistle, the forward movement began growing faster and faster until it reached a terrifying speed. Soon nothing could be heard but the continuous shriek of the steam; the pistons were doing twenty strokes to the second, and the axles were smoking in the axle-boxes. Hurtling along at a hundred miles an hour, the whole train, so to speak, no longer seemed to be bearing down on the rails, for its speed had almost cancelled out its weight.

And they got across! It was like a flash of lightning. Nobody saw anything of the bridge. It is fair to say that the train leapt from one bank to the other, and the driver did not succeed in stopping his engine until it had gone five miles beyond the station.

But scarcely had the train crossed the river when the bridge, completely destroyed, fell with a roar into the rapids of Medicine Bow.

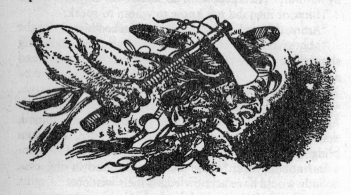

CHAPTER TWENTY-NINE

In which is given an account of various incidents which happen only on American railroads

That evening the train went on without meeting any obstacles, passed Fort Saunders, crossed Cheyenne Pass and came to Evans Pass. Here the railroad reached the highest point of its course, 8,091 feet above sea level; henceforth it had only to descend to the Atlantic, across the boundless plains which nature had levelled.

At this point on the Grand Trunk a line branched off to Denver, the chief town of Colorado, a territory rich in gold and silver mines, where over fifty thousand people had already settled.

In three days and three nights the travellers had covered 1,382 miles from San Francisco, and in all probability another four days and four nights should bring them to New York. So Phileas Fogg was still keeping to his schedule.

During the night the train passed Walbach Camp on the left. Lodge Pole Creek flowed parellel to the line, following the rectilinear frontier between the states of Wyoming and Colorado. At eleven o'clock the travellers entered Nebraska, passing near Sedgwick and close to Julesburgh, situated on the southern branch of the Platte River. It was here that the inauguration of the Union Pacific Railroad, whose chief engineer was General J. M. Dodge, had taken place on 23rd October 1869; here two powerful locomotives had drawn up, bringing nine carriage-loads of guests, including Vice President Thomas C. Durant; here ringing cheers had been raised, Sioux and Pawnees had staged a mock Indian battle, and fireworks had been set off; here, finally, the first issue of the *Railway Pioneer* had been run off a portable printing press. Thus had been celebrated the inauguration of this immense railroad, an instrument of progress and civilization, thrown across the desert and destined to link together cities and town which did not as yet exist. The whistle of the locomotive, more powerful than the lyre of Amphion, was soon going to bid them arise from the American soil.

At eight o'clock in the morning Fort MacPherson was left behind. A distance of three hundred and fifty-seven miles separates this place from Omaha. The line ran along the left bank of the southern branch of the Platte River, following its capricious meanderings. At nine o'clock, the travellers arrived at the important town of North Platte, built between the two arms of the great river, which close again around it to form a single artery, a large tributary whose waters mingle with those of the Missouri a little way above Omaha.

The one hundred and first meridian was crossed.

Mr Fogg and his partners had resumed their game. Not one of them grumbled about the length of the journey — not even the dummy. Fix had begun by winning a few guineas, which he was now losing; but he was showing no less enthusiasm than Mr Fogg. Fortune was particularly kind to the latter that morning: trumps and honours were raining into his hands. At one moment, having prepared a bold stroke, he was about to play a spade when behind his chair a voice was heard to say:

"If I were you, I'd play a diamond . . ."

Mr Fogg, Aouda and Fix looked up. Beside them was Colonel Proctor. Stamp Proctor and Phileas Fogg recognized each other at once.

"So it's you, Mister Limey!" the colonel exclaimed. "It's you who wants to play a spade!"

"And who does play it," Phileas Fogg replied coldly, laying down the ten of that suit.

"Well, I want to make it diamonds," Colonel Proctor retorted in an angry tone of voice.

He made as if to snatch up the card that had been played, and added:

"You don't know anything about this game."

"Perhaps I might be better at another," said Phileas Fogg, standing up.

"You have only to try your hand at it, son of John Bull!" the boorish individual replied.

Aouda had turned pale, the blood rushing to her heart. She had grasped Phileas Fogg's arm, but he gently repulsed her. Passepartout was ready to hurl himself at the American, who was staring at his adversary in the most insulting way.

198

But Fix, too, was on his feet, and going over to Colonel Proctor he said:

"You forget that I am the man you have to deal with, sir. It was I whom you not only insulted but struck!"

"Mr Fix," said Mr Fogg, "I beg your pardon, but this matter concerns me alone. In asserting that I was wrong to play a spade, the colonel has insulted me again, and he shall give me satisfaction for it."

"When you like and where you like!" the American replied. "And with whatever weapon you please!"

Aouda tried in vain to hold Mr Fogg back, and the detective made further futile attempts to take the quarrel upon himself. Passepartout made as if to throw the colonel out of the window, but a sign from his master checked him. Phileas Fogg left the carriage and the American followed him on to the platform.

"Sir," Mr Fogg said to his adversary. "I am in a great hurry to return to Europe and any delay would greatly prejudice my interests."

"Well, what's that got to do with me?" Colonel Proctor retorted.

"Sir," Mr Fogg continued, very courteously, "after our encounter in San Francisco, I made up my mind to come back to America to find you as soon as I had completed the business which calls me back to the Old World."

"Is that so?"

"Will you agree to meet me in six months' time?"

"Why not six years?"

"I said six months," replied Mr Fogg, "and I shall be there without fail."

"That's just a lot of excuses!" cried Stamp Proctor. "It's now or never."

"Very well," replied Mr Fogg. "Are you going to New York?"

"No."

"To Chicago?"

"No."

"To Omaha?"

"That's none of your business! Do you know Plum Creek?"

"No," replied Mr Fogg.

"It's the next station. The train will get there in an hour and it will stop there for ten minutes. Ten minutes is time enough to exchange a few revolver shots."

"Very well," replied Mr Fogg. "I will stop at Plum Creek."

"And I guess you'll stay there too!" added the American with unparalleled insolence.

"Who knows, sir?" answered Mr Fogg; and as cool as ever, he went back into his carriage.

There he began by reassuring Aouda, telling her that boasters were never to be feared. Then he asked Fix to act as his second in the impending duel. Fix could scarcely refuse; and then Phileas Fogg calmly resumed his interrupted game, playing a spade with complete composure.

At eleven o'clock the engine's whistle announced that they were approaching Plum Creek. Mr Fogg got up and, followed by Fix, went out on to the platform. Passepartout accompanied him, carrying a pair of revolvers. Aouda stayed in the carriage, as pale as death.

At that moment the door of the next carriage opened, and Colonel Proctor also appeared on the gangway; he was followed by his second, a Yankee of the same kidney. But just as the two adversaries were going to get down on the line, the guard rushed up and shouted:

"You can't get down, gentlemen."

"Why not?" asked the colonel.

"We're twenty minutes late, and the train isn't stopping here."

"But I have to fight a duel with this gentleman."

"I'm sorry," replied the guard, "but we must be off at once. There's the bell ringing now!"

The bell was indeed ringing, and the train moved on.

"I'm really very sorry, gentlemen," the guard repeated. "In any other circumstances I'd have been able to oblige you. But after all, as you haven't had the time to fight here, what's to keep you from fighting as we go along?"

"That might not suit this gentleman!" sneered Colonel Proctor.

"It suits me perfectly!" replied Phileas Fogg.

"Well, we're in America, and no mistake!" thought Passepartout. "And the guard is a gentleman of the first order!"

And muttering these words, he followed his master.

Preceded by the guard, the two adversaries and their seconds passed along the carriages to the rear of the train. There were only about a dozen passengers in the last carriage, and the guard asked them if they would be kind enough to leave for a few minutes, for the benefit of two gentlemen who had an affair of honour to settle.

By all means! The passengers were only too happy to oblige the two gentlemen, and they withdrew on to the platforms.

The carriage, about fifty feet long, was very suitable for the purpose. The two opponents could advance upon each other between the seats and open fire at their ease. Never had a duel been easier to arrange. Mr Fogg and Colonel Proctor, each equipped with two six-shooters, entered the carriage. Their seconds, who remained outside, shut them in. At the first whistle of the engine they were to open fire ... then, after an interval of two minutes, all that remained of the two gentlemen would be removed from the carriage.

Nothing indeed could be simpler. It was so simple in fact that Fix and Passepartout felt their hearts beating as if they were about to burst.

They were accordingly waiting for the agreed signal, the blast on the whistle, when there came a sudden outburst

201

of savage yells. Explosions rang out, too, but they did not come from the carriage reserved for the duellists. On the contrary, these explosions could be heard along the whole length of the train, right up to the front, while cries of terror came from inside the carriages.

Colonel Proctor and Mr Fogg, revolver in hand, promptly left their carriage, and rushed towards the head of the train, where explosions and shots were loudest. They had realized that the train was being attacked by a band of Sioux.

This was not the first attack by these daring Indians, who had already held up trains more than once. As was their custom, a hundred or so had jumped on to the footboards, without waiting for the train to stop, and had clambered on to the carriages with the ease of a clown leaping on to a galloping horse.

These Sioux were armed with guns: hence the explosions, to which the passengers, most of whom were armed, were replying with revolver shots. First, however, the Indians had jumped on to the engine and had half-killed the driver and the fireman with blows from their tomahawks. A Sioux chief, wanting to stop the train but not knowing how to work the handle of the regulator, had opened the throttle completely instead of shutting it, and the engine was rushing forward at terrific speed.

Meanwhile the Sioux had forced their way into the carriages; they were running about like enraged apes over the roofs, bursting open the doors and fighting hand to hand with the passengers. From the luggage van, which had been forced open and plundered, packages were being hurled on to the line. Cries and shots never ceased.

Yet the travellers were defending themselves bravely. Some of the carriages had been barricaded and were sustaining a siege like travelling forts swept along at a hundred miles an hour.

From the very beginning of the attack, Aouda had

shown great courage. Revolver in hand, she was defending herself heroically, firing through the broken windows whenever one of the savages appeared. A score of Sioux, mortally wounded, had fallen on to the track, and those who slipped on to the rails from the platforms were crushed like worms under the wheels of the carriages.

Several passengers, seriously wounded by bullets or tomahawks, were lying on the seats.

The struggle had to be brought to an end. It had already lasted ten minutes, and unless the train were stopped it could only result in victory for the Sioux. Fort Kearney station was only two miles ahead, and there was an American garrison there. But if the train went beyond Fort Kearney, it would fall into the hands of the Sioux before it reached the next station.

The guard was fighting at Mr Fogg's side when a bullet laid him low. As he fell, he cried:

"If the train doesn't stop within five minutes, we're done for!"

"I shall stop it!" said Phileas Fogg, getting ready to rush out of the carriage.

"Stay here, Monsieur," shouted Passepartout. "That's my business!"

Phileas Fogg had no time to stop the brave fellow who, opening a door without the Indians seeing him, managed to slip under the carriage. Then, while the fight was still going on and the bullets were whizzing over his head, he worked his way forward under the carriages with all the agility and nimbleness of his old acrobatic days. Hanging on to the couplings, helping himself along by means of the brake rods and struts, crawling forward from one carriage to the next with wonderful skill, he finally reached the head of the train. He had not been seen, for nobody could possibly have seen him.

There hanging on by one hand between the luggage van and the tender, he used the other to unhook the safety chains. But because of the pull on the coupling bar, he would not have been able to unscrew it if a sudden jolt of the engine had not jerked it free. Parted from the tender, the train gradually fell behind while the engine raced ahead with increased speed.

Carried forward by its momentum, the train travelled on for a few more minutes, but the brakes were applied inside the carriages, and it finally came to a halt, less than a hundred yards from Kearney station.

There the soldiers from the fort, attracted by the firing, came rushing up. The Sioux had not waited for them, and even before the train had completely stopped the whole band had decamped.

But when the passengers were counted on the station platform, it was discovered that several of their number were missing. Among these was the courageous Frenchman whose devotion had just saved them.

CHAPTER THIRTY

In which Phileas Fogg simply does his duty

Three passengers, including Passepartout, had vanished. Had they been killed in the fight? Were they prisoners in the hands of the Sioux? Nobody could tell as yet.

There were a fair number of wounded, but it was found that none of them was mortally injured. One of the most seriously hurt was Colonel Proctor, who had fought bravely and been brought down by a bullet in the groin. He was carried into the station with other passengers whose condition demanded immediate attention.

Aouda was safe, and Phileas Fogg, who had not spared

himself, had not even a scratch. Fix had been hit in the arm, but the wound was not serious. But Passepartout was missing, and tears were streaming down Aouda's cheeks.

Meanwhile all the passengers had left the train. The wheels of the carriages were stained with blood, and tatters of flesh hung from the naves and spokes. As far as the eye could reach long streaks of blood stained the white plain. The last of the Indians were disappearing from sight to the south, in the direction of the Republican River.

Mr Fogg, his arms folded, stood motionless; he had a serious decision to make. Aouda, standing beside him, looked at him but did not say a word . . . He knew what that look meant. If his servant had been taken prisoner, should he not risk everything to recue him from the Indians?

"I shall find him, dead or alive," he said quietly to Aouda.

"Oh, Mr . . . Mr Fogg," cried the young woman, grasping his hands and moistening them with her tears.

"Alive," Mr Fogg added, "provided we do not waste a single moment!"

By making this decision, Phileas Fogg was sacrificing himself completely. He had just pronounced his own ruin, for even one day's delay would make him miss the steamer at New York. His bet was irrevocably lost. But in the face of the thought: "It is my duty!" he had not hesitated.

The captain in command at Fort Kearney was there. His men — about a hundred in all — had taken up defensive positions in case the Sioux launched a direct attack on the station.

"Sir," Mr Fogg said to the captain, "three passengers have vanished."

"Dead?" asked the captain.

"Dead or prisoners," replied Phileas Fogg. "That is a mystery which has to be cleared up. Do you intend to pursue the Sioux?"

"That's a serious matter, sir," the captain told him. "Those Indians may go on running beyond Arkansas. This fort has been entrusted to me, and I cannot leave it."

"Sir," Phileas Fogg continued, "three men's lives are at stake."

"No doubt . . . but can I risk the lives of fifty to save three?"

"I do not know whether you can, sir, but that is your duty."

"Sir," the captain retorted, "there is nobody here who can teach me my duty."

"Very well," said Phileas Fogg coldly. "I shall go by myself!"

"You, sir!" exclaimed Fix, who had joined them. "You go after the Indians by yourself!"

"Then do you want me to leave that poor wretch to his fate — the man to whom everyone here owes his life? I shall go."

"Well then, you shan't go alone!" exclaimed the captain, moved in spite of himself. "No! You're a brave man! . . . Thirty volunteers!" he added, turning towards his men.

The whole company stepped forward as one, so that the captain had only to choose among these gallant fellows. Thirty men were selected, and an experienced sergeant put himself at their head.

"Thank you, Captain!" said Mr Fogg.

"Will you let me come with you?" asked Fix.

"You can do as you please, sir," replied Phileas Fogg. "But if you really want to do me a service you will stay with this lady. In case anything should happen to me . . ."

A sudden pallor spread over the police inspector's face. Was he to part from this man whom he had followed so persistently step by step? Was he to let him go off like this into that wilderness? Fix looked hard at the gentleman and, in spite of his suspicions and the struggle going on within him, before that calm, frank gaze he lowered his eyes.

"I'll stay," he said.

A few moments later Mr Fogg had pressed the young woman's hand; then, after entrusting her with his precious travelling bag, he went off with the sergeant and his little band. But first he told the soldiers:

"My friends, there will be a thousand pounds for you if we save those prisoners."

It was then a few minutes after midday.

Aouda had gone into a room in the station and there she waited by herself, thinking of Phileas Fogg, of his generosity, of his calm courage. Mr Fogg had sacrificed his fortune and now he was risking his life, and that without hesitation, as a duty, without any fuss. Phileas Fogg was a hero in her eyes.

Inspector Fix, for his part, did not share these thoughts, and could not control his agitation. He strode feverishly up and down the platform. Overborne for a moment, he was not himself again. Now that Fogg had gone, he realized how stupid he had been to let him go. What, had he really allowed that man he had been following around the world to get away? As his real nature took control once more, he blamed and accused himself, treating himself as if he had been the chief of the Metropolitan Police reprimanding a detective caught committing some terrible blunder.

"What a fool I've been!" he reflected. "That other fellow must have told him who I am! He's gone, and he won't come back! Where am I going to lay hands on him again now? But how could I let myself be hypnotized like that – I, Fix, who have a warrant for his arrest in my pocket! I really am an idiot!"

So thought the police inspector while the hours passed all too slowly for his liking. He did not know what to do. At times he was tempted to tell Aouda everything, but he knew how she would treat him. What was he to do? He was tempted to set off across the great white plains in pursuit of Fogg! He didn't think it impossible to find him, for the footprints of the detachment were still impressed on the snow. But soon every trace would disappear under a fresh layer.

Fix was overwhelmed by discouragement. He felt an almost insurmountable longing to give up the whole game, and now he was actually offered a chance to leave Kearney station and to continue his journey, which had hitherto been so disappointing.

For about two o'clock in the afternoon, while the snow was falling heavily, long whistle blasts were heard coming from the east. A huge shadow, preceded by a lurid light, slowly drew nearer, considerably magnified by the mist, which lent it a fantastic appearance.

Yet no train was expected yet from the east. The help which had been summoned by telegraph could not have arrived so soon, and the train from Omaha to San Francisco was not due until the following day.

The mystery was soon explained.

This engine, which was travelling very slowly and whistling loudly, was the one which, after being detached from the train, had continued on its course at such terrifying speed, taking with it the driver and fireman, both of them unconscious. It had travelled several miles; then, as its fire had burned low for lack of fuel, its steam pressure had fallen; and an hour later, after gradually slowing down, it had at last come to a stop about twenty miles beyond Kearney station.

Neither the driver nor the fireman was dead, and after remaining insensible for quite a long time, they had recovered consciousness.

The engine was then at a standstill. When the driver found himelf in the desert, with an engine that no longer had any carriages behind it, he realized what had happened.

He could not imagine how the engine had been detached from the train, but he had no doubt that the train, which had been left behind, was in distress.

The driver did not hesitate as to what he should do. The wisest course of action was to push on in the direction of Omaha, while to return towards the train, which was perhaps still being pillaged by the Indians, was dangerous. All the same, coal and wood were shovelled into the firebox, the fire revived under her boiler, the pressure rose again, and about two o'clock in the afternoon the train started back towards Kearney station. It was her whistle that could be heard in the mist.

The travellers were delighted to see the engine take its place at the head of the train, for now they would be able to continue this journey which had been so unhappily interrupted.

When the locomotive arrived, Aouda had gone out and asked the guard:

"Are you going to leave?"

"At once, Madam."

"But what about those prisoners ... our poor companions?"

"I cannot hold up the service," the guard replied. "We're three hours late already."

"And when will the next train be coming from San Francisco?"

"Tomorrow evening, Madam."

"Tomorrow evening! But that will be too late! You must wait ..."

"That's quite impossible," replied the guard. "If you want to go, take your seat."

"I shall not go," answered the young woman.

Fix had heard this conversation. A few minutes earlier, when he had had no means of getting away, he had been determined to leave Kearney; and now that the train was there ready to start, now that all he had to do was to resume his seat in the carriage, an irresistible force held him rooted to the spot. The platform seemed to be burning his feet, yet he could not tear himself away. The struggle within him was beginning again. He was choked with fury at the idea of failure. He wanted to fight on to the end.

In the meantime the passengers and a few of the wounded – including Colonel Proctor, whose condition was serious – had taken their places in the carriages. The overheated boiler could be heard humming, and steam was escaping through the safety valves. The driver blew the whistle, the train moved off, and soon it disappeared, mingling its white smoke with the whirling snowflakes.

Inspector Fix had stayed behind.

A few hours went by. The weather was very bad, and the cold intense. Seated on a bench in the station, Fix never stirred. One might have thought he was asleep. In spite of the squall, Aouda kept coming out of the room which had been placed at her disposal, walking to the end of the platform, peering through the tempest of snow, trying to pierce the mist which narrowed the horizon round her, and listening for any sound that might be audible. But there was nothing. Then she went back indoors, chilled to the bone, but only to return a few minutes later, and always in vain.

Evening came, and the little detachment had not returned. Where were they? Had they been able to catch up with the Indians? Had there been a fight, or were the men lost in the mist and wandering about at random? The commander of Fort Kearney was very anxious, although he tried to show no sign of his uneasiness.

With night the snow fell less thickly but the cold grew more intense, and not even the bravest men could have looked out into that dark emptiness without a feeling of horror. The plain was wrapped in absolute silence, and neither the flight of any bird nor the movement of any beast disturbed the infinite stillness.

Throughout the night Aouda, her mind obsessed with sinister forebodings, her heart full of anguish, wandered about on the edge of the prairie. Her imagination carried her far away and showed her countless dangers, and what she suffered during those long hours could never be described.

Fix did not move, but he too was unable to sleep. Once a man went up to him and even spoke to him, but the detective shook his head and sent him away.

The night went by like this. At dawn, the dim disc of the sun rose above the misty horizon, and now it was possible to see for a couple of miles. It was towards the south that Phileas Fogg had gone with the detachment, and in the south nothing could be seen. It was then seven in the morning.

The captain, who was extremely anxious, did not know what course to adopt. Should he send another detachment to the help of the first? Should he sacrifice more of his men when there was so little chance of rescuing those whom he had sacrificed already? But his hesitation did not last; having beckoned one of his officers, he was just ordering him to make a reconnaissance towards the south when some shots rang out. Was it a signal? The soldiers dashed out of the fort and half a mile away they caught sight of a small band of men returning in good order.

Mr Fogg was marching at their head, and with him were Passepartout and the two other travellers who had been snatched from the hands of the Sioux.

Ten miles south of Fort Kearney there had been a fight. A few moments before the detachment arrived, Passepartout and his fellow prisoners had already been at grips with their captors and the Frenchman had felled three of them with his fists when his master and the soldiers came rushing to their help.

Rescuers and rescued alike were welcomed with shouts

of joy, and Phileas Fogg distributed the promised reward among the soldiers, while Passepartout murmured, not unreasonably:

"It must be admitted that I'm costing my master a pretty penny!"

Fix looked at Mr Fogg without saying a word, and it would have been no easy matter to analyse the emotions which were struggling in his mind. As for Aouda, she had grasped the gentleman's hand and was pressing it between her own two hands, unable to utter a single word.

Ever since he arrived Passepartout had been looking around the station for the train. He expected to find it there, ready to set off at full speed for Omaha, and he had hoped they would still be able to make up the time they had lost.

"The train! The train!" he cried.

"Gone!" Fix replied.

"And when will the next train come along?" asked Phileas Fogg.

"Not until this evening."

"Ah," was all that the impassive gentleman said.

CHAPTER THIRTY-ONE

In which Inspector Fix takes Phileas Fogg's interests to heart

Phileas Fogg was now twenty hours behind time, and Passepartout, the involuntary cause of this delay, was in despair. He had ruined his master without a doubt!

But then the inspector went up to Mr Fogg and looked him straight in the face.

"Seriously, sir," he asked, "are you in a great hurry?"

"Seriously," replied Phileas Fogg, "I am."

"I really want to know," Fix continued. "Is it really a matter of great importance to you to reach New York on the eleventh, before nine in the evening, the time when the steamer leaves for Liverpool?"

"A matter of supreme importance."

"And if your journey hadn't been interrupted when we were attacked by those Indians, you would have got to New York as early as the morning of the eleventh?"

"Yes, twelve hours before the departure of the steamer."

"Good. Well, you're twenty hours late. The difference between twenty and twelve is eight. That's eight hours you've got to make up. Would you like to try?"

"On foot?" asked Mr Fogg.

"No," Fix replied. "On a sledge. On a sledge with sails. A man has suggested the means of transport to me."

This was the man who had spoken to the police inspector during the night, and whose offer Fix had refused.

Phileas Fogg did not reply; but when Fix had pointed out the man, who was walking up and down in front of the station, he went up to him. A moment later he and this American, whose name was Mudge, went into a hut at the foot of Fort Kearney.

There Mr Fogg examined a strange-looking vehicle. It was a sort of frame built on two long beams, slightly turned up in front like the runners of a sleigh, on which five or six people could find room. From the frame, a third of the way from the prow, rose a very tall mast, to which was attached a huge spanker. This mast, firmly secured by metal cables, supported an iron stay from which could be hoisted a very large jib. At the stern a sort of tiller served to steer the machine.

It was obviously a sledge rigged as a sloop. During the winter, when the trains were held up by the snow, these vehicles could travel very rapidly from station to station across the frozen plains. They carried a prodigious spread of canvas — even more than a racing cutter, with its tendency to capsize — and with a following wind they glided over the surface of the prairies with a speed equal, if not superior, to that of express trains.

Within a few moments a bargain was struck between Mr Fogg and the master of this land-yacht. There was a favourable wind, blowing strongly from the west, the snow was hard, and Mudge was confident that he could get Mr Fogg to Omaha station in a few hours. From Omaha there were a great many lines to Chicago and New York, and frequent trains. It was not impossible that they might make up for the time they had lost, and there could be no hesitation about trying their luck.

Not wanting to expose Aouda to the agony of a journey in the open air, in this cold which their speed would make even more unbearable, Mr Fogg suggested that she should stay with Passepartout at Kearney station. The good fellow would undertake to bring her to Europe by some better route and under more tolerable conditions.

Aouda refused to be separated from Mr Fogg, and Passepartout was delighted with this resolve, for nothing in the world would have induced him to leave his master so long as Fix was with him.

As for what the police inspector thought now, that would have been hard to say. Had his conviction been shaken by Phileas Fogg's return, or did he regard him as an extremely clever scoundrel who felt sure that when his journey round the world had been completed he would be perfectly safe in England? Perhaps his opinion of Phileas Fogg had changed, but he was none the less determined to do his duty, and he showed himself more impatient than all the others to speed up the journey back to England.

By eight o'clock the sledge was ready to start. The travellers — one might almost say the passengers — took their places on it and wrapped their travelling rugs tightly round them. The two huge sails were hoisted, and impelled by the wind the vehicle shot over the snow at a speed of forty miles an hour.

The distance between Fort Kearney and Omaha, in a straight line, is two hundred miles at most. If the wind held, that distance could be covered in five hours, so that if no accident occurred the sledge ought to reach Omaha by one o'clock in the afternoon.

What a journey it was! Huddled together, the travellers could not speak, for the cold, intensified by the speed at which they were going, would have silenced them. The sledge glided over the surface of the plain as lightly as a boat over the surface of the sea . . . but without any swell to slow it down. When the wind blew close to the ground the sledge seemed to be lifted right off the earth by its sails, as by vast wings.

Mudge was at the helm, holding the sledge on course, and with the movement of his tiller he corrected any swerves it tended to make. All the canvas was taut, the jib had been trimmed so as not to be blanketed by the spanker, and a topmast had been fixed so that a flying jib added its driving power to that of the other sails. Though it could not be estimated with mathematical precision the speed of the sledge was certainly not less than forty miles an hour.

"Providing nothing breaks," said Mudge, "we'll get there!"

And certainly it was in his interest to arrive within the agreed time, for Mr Fogg, faithful to his system, had tempted him with a handsome bonus.

The prairie, which the sledge was crossing in a straight line, was as flat as the sea; it might have been an immense frozen pond. The railroad serving this region ran from the southwest to the northwest, passing through Great Island,

Columbus, a large town in Nebraska, Schuyler, Fremont and Omaha. Throughout its course it followed the right bank of the Platte River, but the sledge shortened this route, taking the cord of the bow described by the railway line. Mudge had no fear of being held up by the slight curve of the Platte River before Fremont, as its waters were frozen. The route was thus completely free of any obstacles and Phileas Fogg had only two possibilities to fear: an accident or a change or a fall in the wind.

But the wind did not slacken. On the contrary, it blew strongly enough to bend the mast, which the iron shrouds held firmly in place. These metal ropes sounded like strings of a musical instrument made to vibrate by the touch of a violin bow. The sledge flew on to the accompaniment of a plaintive sound of peculiar intensity.

"Those strings are sounding the fifth and the octave," said Mr Fogg.

These were the only words uttered during the whole journey. Aouda, carefully bundled up in furs and travelling rugs, had been sheltered as much as possible from the attacks of the cold. As for Passepartout, whose face was red as the solar disc when it sets in the mist, he was drinking in the keen air, and with the imperturbable confidence which lay at the bottom of his character he was once again beginning to breathe easily. Instead of reaching New York in the morning, they would get there in the evening, but there was still a chance of doing so before the steamer left for Liverpool.

Passepartout had even felt strongly tempted to shake hands with his ally Fix. He could not forget that it was the inspector himself who had procured the sailing sledge for them, and with it the only method they had of reaching Omaha in time. But, out of some presentiment or other, he kept up his usual reserve.

One thing, in any case, that he would never forget, was the sacrifice that Monsieur Fogg had made, without the slightest hesitation, to snatch him from the hands of the

Sioux. In doing that, Monsieur Fogg had risked his fortune and his life . . . No! That was something his servant would never forget.

While each of the travellers was absorbed in such varied reflections, the sledge was flying over the immense carpet of snow. If it passed by a number of creeks, direct or indirect tributaries of the Little Blue River, no one noticed, for the fields and the watercourses had vanished under a uniform whiteness. The plain was completely deserted, and between the Union Pacific Railroad and the branch line from Kearney to St Joseph it resembled a vast uninhabited island: not a village, not a station, not even a fort was to be seen. Now and then they caught a brief glimpse of some grimacing tree, whose white skeleton was contorted by the gale. Sometimes flocks of wild birds took flight all together. Sometimes, too, large packs of prairie wolves, thin, famished, and urged on by an imperious need, tried to catch up with the sledge, and Passepartout, revolver in hand, held himself in readiness to open fire on those that came closest. If any accident had stopped the sledge, the travellers, attacked by these ferocious beasts, would have been in the greatest danger. But the sledge held to its course; before long it took the lead and soon the whole howling pack had been left behind.

At noon Mudge realized from certain landmarks that he was crossing the frozen course of the Platte River. He said nothing, though he was already certain that twenty miles farther on he would reach Omaha station.

And sure enough, before one o'clock the skilful pilot, leaving the tiller, dashed to the halyards and lowered the sails, while the sledge, carried on by its irresistible momentum, covered another half-mile under bare poles. At last it stopped, and Mudge, pointing to a collection of snow-covered roofs, said:

"Here we are."

There they were, indeed, at that station which numerous

Passepartout was ready to fire on the wolves that came closest

trains kept in daily communication with the eastern part of the United States!

Passepartout and Fix jumped to the ground, stretched their benumbed limbs, and helped Mr Fogg and the young woman to get down. Phileas Fogg paid Mudge generously, Passepartout gave him a friendly handshake, and then they all rushed towards Omaha stations.

This important Nebraska city was the terminus of the Pacific Railroad, properly so called, which linked the Mississippi basin with the great ocean. Omaha was connected with Chicago by the Chicago and Rock Island Railroad, which ran due east and served fifty stations.

There was an express ready to start, and Phileas Fogg and his companions had only just time to clamber into one of the carriages. They had seen nothing of Omaha, but Passepartout told himself that there was nothing to be regretted in that, and that they had more important business than sightseeing.

Travelling at high speed the train entered the State of Iowa, passing through Council Bluffs, Des Moines and Iowa City. During the night it crossed the Mississippi at Davenport, and entered Illinois by Rock Island. The next day, the 10th, at four o'clock in the afternoon, it arrived at Chicago, already risen from its ruins, and standing more proudly than ever on the shores of its beautiful Lake Michigan.

Nine hundred miles separate that town from New York, but there was no shortage of trains at Chicago. Phileas Fogg transferred immediately from one train to another, and the trim locomotive of the Pittsburgh-Fort Wayne-Chicago Railroad set off at full speed, as though it realized that the honourable gentleman had no time to lose. It sped like a flash of lightning across Indiana, Ohio, Pennsylvania and New Jersey, passing through towns with ancient names, a few of which possessed streets and tramcars but not as yet any houses.

At last the Hudson came into sight, and on 11th December at a quarter past eleven in the evening, the train pulled up in the station on the right bank of the river, in front of the very pier of the Cunard Line, otherwise entitled the British and North American Royal Mail Steam Packet Company.

The *China*, bound for Liverpool, had left forty-five minutes earlier!

CHAPTER THIRTY-TWO

In which Phileas Fogg comes to grips with ill-fortune

As she sailed away, the *China* seemed to have taken with her the last hopes of Phileas Fogg, for none of the other ships plying between America and Europe, neither the boats of the French Transatlantic Company, nor the steamers of the White Star Line, the Inman Company, the Hamburg Line and others, could be of any use to him.

The *Pereire*, of the French Transatlantic Company, whose admirable boats were equal in speed and superior in comfort to all those of all the other lines, without exception, was not due to sail until the 14th, that is, two days later. Besides, like the ships of the Hamburg Line, she did not sail directly to Liverpool or London, but to Le Havre, and the delay caused by the extra crossing from Le Havre to Southampton would have nullified Phileas Fogg's latest efforts.

As for the Inman boats, one of which, the *City of Paris*, was due to put to sea the next day, they were out of the question. These ships were especially used for carrying emigrants, their engines were far from powerful, they ran under canvas as much as under steam, and their speed was not great. They took more time crossing from New York to England than Mr Fogg had left in which to win his wager.

This all became perfectly clear to Mr Fogg when he consulted his *Bradshaw*, which gave him, day by day, details of the traffic across the ocean.

Passepartout was overwhelmed. The fact that they had missed the steamer by forty-five minutes appalled him. It was his fault; instead of helping his master, he had never stopped putting obstacles in his path! And when he turned over in his mind all the incidents of the journey, when he added up the sum of money thrown away solely in his interest, when he reflected that this enormous wager, with the addition of the considerable expenses incurred during this journey, which had now proved to be useless, had completely ruined Monsieur Fogg, he heaped reproaches upon himself.

Mr Fogg, however, did not utter the slightest word of blame, and as they left the pier, all he said was:

"We shall decide what to do tomorrow. Come along."

Mr Fogg, Aouda, Fix and Passepartout crossed the Hudson in the Jersey City ferryboat and took a cab to the St Nicholas Hotel on Broadway. Rooms were placed at their disposal, and the night went by, quickly for Phileas Fogg, who slept soundly, but slowly for Aouda and her companions, whose anxiety would not allow them to rest.

The next day was 12th December. From seven in the morning of the 12th to eight forty-five in the evening of the 21st, there remained nine days, thirteen hours and forty-five minutes. So if Phileas Fogg had left the previous day on the *China*, one of the speediest vessels of the Cunard Line, he would have reached first Liverpool and then London within the scheduled period.

Mr Fogg left the hotel alone, after telling his servant to

await his return and to warn Aouda to be ready to leave at any moment.

He went to the banks of the Hudson and searched diligently among the vessels moored to the quay or anchored in the river for any that were about to sail. Several were flying the Blue Peter and were getting ready to put to sea on the morning tide, for in that huge splendid harbour of New York not a day passes without a hundred vessels setting out for every part of the world. But most of them were sailing ships, and they were of no use to Phileas Fogg.

His last attempt seemed to be doomed to failure when he noticed, moored a cable's length at the most off the Battery, a trim, screw-driven merchant ship whose funnel, emitting great puffs of smoke, indicated that she was about to leave.

Phileas Fogg hailed a boat and got into it. A few strokes of the oars took him to the ladder of the *Henrietta*, a steamer with an iron hull, but whose upper works were all made of wood.

Her captain was on board, and when Phileas Fogg climbed on to the deck and asked for him, he came forward at once. He was a man of fifty, a real sea dog, an inveterate grumbler who looked as if he was anything but easy to get on with. With bulging eyes, a complexion the colour of oxidized copper, red hair and a bull neck, he had nothing of the gentleman about him.

"The captain?" asked Mr Fogg.

"That's me."

"I am Phileas Fogg of London."

"And I'm Andrew Speedy of Cardiff."

"You are about to sail?"

"In an hour."

"You are bound for . . . ?"

"Bordeaux."

"And your cargo?"

222

"Stones in the belly. No freight. I'm going on ballast."

"Have you any passengers?"

"No passengers. Never any passengers. Troublesome, arguesome freight."

"Your ship travels fast?"

"Between eleven and twelve knots. The *Henrietta*'s famous for that."

"Will you take me to Liverpool, me and three other passengers?"

"To Liverpool? Why not China?"

"I said to Liverpool."

"No!"

"No?"

"No. I'm bound for Bordeaux, and to Bordeaux I'm going."

"No matter what I offer?"

"No matter what you offer."

The captain had spoken in tones which admitted of no reply.

"But the *Henrietta*'s owners ...!" Phileas Fogg continued.

"The owners — that's me," the captain replied. "The ship belongs to me."

"I will charter her from you."

"No."

"I will buy her from you."

"No."

Phileas Fogg did not bat an eyelid. But the position was serious. New York was not like Hong Kong, nor was the captain of the *Henrietta* like the skipper of the *Tankadere*. So far money had overcome every obstacle. This time money had failed.

Still, some means had to be found of crossing the Atlantic by boat — or by balloon, which would have been very risky, and in any case was impracticable.

It seemed, however, that Phileas Fogg had an idea, for he asked the captain:

"Well, will you take me to Bordeaux?"

"No, even if you paid me two hundred dollars!"

"I am offering you two thousand."

"Per person?"

"Per person."

"And there's four of you?"

"Four."

Captain Speedy began to scratch his head as if he wanted to tear the skin off. Eight thousand dollars to be earned without changing his course made it worth his while to set aside his pronounced antipathy for passengers of any sort. Besides, passengers at two thousand dollars each were no longer passengers, but valuable merchandise.

"I'm going at nine," the captain said simply. "So if you and the others are here . . .?"

"At nine o'clock we shall be on board," replied Mr Fogg just as simply.

It was then half past eight. To leave the *Henrietta*, get into a carriage, go to the St Nicholas Hotel, and fetch Aouda, Passepartout and even the inseparable Fix, to whom he graciously offered a passage, was a task which Mr Fogg accomplished with that calmness which never left him under any circumstances.

By the time the *Henrietta* got under way all four were on board.

When Passepartout learned what this last voyage was going to cost, he uttered one of those prolonged "Oh's" which go all the way down the chromatic scale.

As for Fix, he reflected that the Bank of England was certainly not going to emerge unscathed from this affair. Indeed, assuming that they reached England safely and that Mr Fogg did not throw a few more handfuls into the sea, more than seven thousand pounds would be missing from the bag of banknotes!

CHAPTER THIRTY-THREE

In which Phileas Fogg shows himself equal to the occasion

An hour later the *Henrietta* passed the lightship which marked the mouth of the Hudson, turned the point of Sandy Hook, and put out to sea. During the day she skirted Long Island, cleared the lighthouse on Fire Island, and headed eastwards at full speed.

On the next day, 13th December, at noon, a man went up on the bridge to get his bearings. It is only natural to suppose that this man was Captain Speedy. Nothing of the sort. It was Phileas Fogg, Esq.

As for Captain Speedy, he was quite simply locked in his cabin, and was howling in a way which suggested a perfectly pardonable rage pushed to the point of frenzy.

What had happened was very simple. Phileas Fogg wanted to go to Liverpool; the captain did not want to take him there. Then Phileas Fogg had agreed to take the ship for Bordeaux, but during the thirty hours that he had been on board, he had made such good use of his banknotes that the whole crew, sailors and stokers alike – a scratch crew who were not on the best of terms with the captain – were now devoted to him. And that was why Phileas Fogg was in command in place of Captain Speedy; that was why the captain was locked up in his cabin; and finally that was why the *Henrietta* was making for Liverpool. But it was clear from the way in which Mr Fogg handled the ship that Mr Fogg had once been a sailor.

How all this would end only time would tell. Yet Aouda

felt uneasy, though she said nothing. Fix, for his part, had been completely dumbfounded at first. As for Passepartout, he found the whole thing delightful.

"Between eleven and twelve knots," Captain Speedy had said, and the *Henrietta* was in fact averaging that speed.

So if – for there were still a great many ifs – if the sea did not become too rough, if the wind did not veer to the east, if nothing happened to the boat, if no accident befell the engines, then during the nine days between 12th and 21st December, the *Henrietta* might cover the three thousand miles between New York and Liverpool. It was true that when they arrived, this business of the *Henrietta*, coming on top of that business of the Bank, might lead Mr Fogg further than he wanted to go.

During the first few days the voyage went splendidly. The sea was not too rough, the wind seemed settled in the northeast; the sails were hoisted; and with her trysails set the *Henrietta* forged ahead like a transatlantic liner.

Passepartout was delighted. His master's latest exploit, whose consequences he did not wish to foresee, filled him with enthusiasm. Never had the crew seen anyone more cheerful or more active. He got on the friendliest of terms with the sailors, and astonished them with his acrobatics. He plied them with the most flattering compliments and the most delightful drinks: to his mind they were handling the vessel like gentlemen, and the stokers were stoking like heroes. His good humour was catching and spread to everyone on board. He had forgotten the past with its troubles and dangers, and now thought of nothing but their aim, so nearly achieved. Sometimes he boiled with impatience, as though the *Henrietta*'s boilers were heating him. Often, too, the good fellow hovered round Fix, looking at him with eyes which spoke volumes, but he did not speak to him, for the former intimacy of these onetime friends no longer existed.

As for Fix, it must be said that he could not make head or tail of what was happening. The taking over of the *Henrietta*, the bribing of her crew, this man Fogg handling her like an experienced sailor, all this bewildered him. He no longer knew what to think! But after all, a gentleman who began by stealing fifty-five thousand pounds might well end up stealing a ship. So Fix was naturally led to believe that under Fogg's command the *Henrietta* was not going to Liverpool at all, but to some part of the world where the robber, now turned pirate, would quietly take refuge. This hypothesis, it must be confessed, was extremely plausible, and the detective began quite seriously to regret that he had ever got mixed up in this business.

Captain Speedy, for his part, went on howling in his cabin, and Passepartout, assigned to take him his meals, never performed this duty, strong though he was, without taking the greatest precautions. As for Mr Fogg, he seemed to have completely forgotten that there was a captain on board.

On the 13th they passed the end of the Newfoundland Banks, a dangerous region where, especially during the winter, there are violent squalls. The barometer had fallen suddenly since the previous day, foreshadowing an early change in the weather, and during the night the temperature fell, the cold grew sharper and at the same time the wind veered to the southeast.

This was a misfortune. So as not to have to swerve from his course, Mr Fogg had to shorten sail and make more steam. None the less, because of the state of the sea, whose long waves broke against the ship's prow, her speed was reduced. She pitched violently, and this retarded her progress. The wind gradually became a gale, and already it began to seem likely that the *Henrietta* might no longer be able to make headway against the waves. And if she

227

had to run before the storm, they would be faced with the unknown, with all its grim possibilities.

Passepartout's face grew darker along with the skies, and for two days the good fellow was in a state of fright. But Phileas Fogg was a bold seaman who knew how to fight the seas, and he kept his ship on course without even reducing steam. When the *Henrietta* could not rise to a wave she went right through it, and her deck was swept from end to end. Sometimes, when a mountain of water raised her stern above the waves, her screw was lifted right out of the sea and beat the air with its maddened blades, but the ship still forged ahead.

However, the wind did not blow as fiercely as might have been feared, for this was not one of those hurricanes which sweep along at ninety miles an hour. It was never more than a gale, but unfortunately it stayed obstinately in the southeast, so that no sail could be hoisted. And yet, as will be seen, it would have been a great help if sails had come to the aid of steam!

The 16th of December was the seventy-fifth day since leaving London, and on the whole the *Henrietta* had not yet experienced any disquieting delay. The voyage was almost half over, and the worst regions had been passed. Had it been summer they would have been sure of success, but in winter they were at the mercy of the weather. Passepartout expressed no opinion, but in his heart he was hopeful, and if the wind should fail them he knew they could rely on the steam.

But that very day the engineer came on deck, went up to Mr Fogg, and began a lively conversation with him.

Without quite knowing why – no doubt because of some presentiment – Passepartout began to feel vaguely anxious, and he would have given one of his ears to hear with the other what was being said. Still, he did catch a few words, including these from his master:

"You are sure of what you are saying?"

"Certain, sir," replied the engineer. "You mustn't forget that since we started, we've been keeping all our furnaces going, and while we had enough coal to go from New York to Bordeaux under easy steam, we haven't enough to take us from New York to Liverpool at full."

"I will think it over," replied Mr Fogg.

Passepartout had understood what was wrong, and was seized with mortal anxiety. The coal was giving out!

"Oh, if my master can cope with that," he reflected, "he'll really be a great man!"

Meeting Fix, he could not refrain from telling him how things stood.

"So," replied the detective through clenched teeth, "you really think we're going to Liverpool?"

"Of course!"

"Idiot!" retorted the inspector, and he walked away, shrugging his shoulders.

Passepartout was about to make a sharp retort to this insult, whose real meaning he could not understand. But then he reminded himself that the unfortunate Fix must be greatly disappointed and deeply humiliated in his self-esteem, after so foolishly following a false trail right round the world, and he forbore from condemning him.

And now what was Phileas Fogg going to do? It was hard to imagine what course he could adopt. However, that phlegmatic gentleman seemed to have decided, for that very evening he sent for the engineer and told him:

"Heap up the fires and carry on until the fuel runs out."

A few moments later the *Henrietta*'s funnel was vomiting torrents of smoke.

The vessel accordingly went ahead as before at full speed; but as he had foreseen, two days later, on the 18th, the engineer announced that the coal would run out during the day.

"Don't let the fires get low," replied Mr Fogg. "On the contrary, screw down the valves."

About noon that day, after taking his bearings and calculating the ship's position, Phileas Fogg sent for Passepartout and ordered him to fetch Captain Speedy. This was as good as ordering the good fellow to go and unchain a tiger, and he went down to the poop deck murmuring:

"He'll be like a raving lunatic!"

And indeed, a few minutes later, to the accompaniment of cries and oaths, a bomb arrived on the poop deck. That bomb was Captain Speedy, and it was clear that it was about to explode.

"Where are we?" These were the first words he uttered, choking with rage, and there can be no doubt that if the good man had been at all apoplectic he would never have survived.

"Seven hundred and seventy miles from Liverpool," replied Mr Fogg imperturbably.

"Pirate!" yelled Andrew Speedy.

"I sent for you, sir . . ."

"Buccaneer!"

". . . sir," Phileas Fogg continued, "to ask you to sell me your ship."

"No! By all the devils in hell, no!"

"Because I am going to be obliged to burn her!"

"Burn my ship!"

"Yes – at least her upper works, for we are running out of fuel."

"Burn my ship!" cried Captain Speedy, who could no longer even speak clearly. "A ship worth fifty thousand dollars!"

"Here are sixty thousand," replied Phileas Fogg, offering the captain a roll of banknotes.

The effect on Andrew Speedy was prodigious. No American can remain entirely unmoved at the sight of sixty thousand dollars. In an instant the captain forgot his anger, his imprisonment, all his grievances against his passenger. His ship was twenty years old, and this looked like being the opportunity of a lifetime. The bomb had already been rendered harmless. Mr Fogg had drawn the fuse.

"And the iron hull will be left to me?" he asked in a noticeably milder tone of voice.

"The iron hull and the engine, sir. Done?"

"Done!"

And Andrew Speedy, seizing the roll of banknotes, counted them and slipped them into his pocket.

During this scene Passepartout turned white, and as for Fix, he almost had a stroke. After spending nearly twenty thousand pounds, this fellow Fogg was letting the vendor keep the hull and the engine, in other words almost the whole value of the ship! It was true, though, that the amount stolen from the Bank was fifty-five thousand pounds.

When Speedy had pocketed the money, Mr Fogg said to him:

"All this will not surprise you, sir, when I tell you that unless I am back in London on the 21st of December at eight forty-five in the evening, I shall lose twenty thousand pounds. Now, I had missed the steamer at New York, and as you refused to take me to Liverpool . . ."

"And by the fifty thousand devils in hell, it's a good thing I did," exclaimed Andrew Speedy, "for I've made at least forty thousand dollars as a result."

Then he added more calmly:

"You know something, Captain . . .?"

"Fogg."

"Well, Captain Fogg, there's something of the Yankee about you."

And having paid his passenger what he regarded as a compliment, he was going away when Phileas Fogg asked him:

"And now this vessel belongs to me?"

231

"Certainly, from her keel to the truck of her masts — that is, everything that's made of wood, of course."

"Good. Have all the interior fittings broken up and the pieces used as fuel."

It may be imagined how much of this dry wood had to be burned to keep up the pressure. That day the poop, the deckhouses, the cabins, the berths, and the spar deck were all sacrificed.

On the following day, 19th December, the masts, booms and spars were burned, the masts being brought down and hacked to pieces. The crew showed incredible zeal and Passepartout, hewing, cutting and sawing, did the work of ten men. It was an absolute frenzy of demolition.

On the 20th the rails, the bulwarks, the upper works, and the greater part of the deck were burnt up. The *Henrietta* had been razed till she was no more than a pontoon. But that day the Irish coast and the Fastnet Lighthouse were sighted. By ten in the evening, however, the ship was only just abreast of Queenstown. Phileas Fogg had only twenty-four hours to reach London! And that was the time it would take the *Henrietta* to get to Liverpool — even if she kept on under full steam. And the daring gentleman was at last going to find himself with no steam at all.

"Sir," said Captain Speedy, who had ended up by getting interested in his project, "I'm really sorry for you. You've got everything against you! We're only off Queenstown."

"Oh," said Mr Fogg. "Is that Queenstown, those lights we can see?"

"Yes."

"Can we enter the harbour?"

"Not for three hours. Only at high tide."

"We shall wait," Phileas Fogg replied calmly, without letting his expression show that by a supreme inspiration he was going to try yet again to overcome his ill-luck.

Queenstown is a port on the Irish coast where the transatlantic liners from the United States unloaded their mailbags. This mail was then sent on to Dublin by express trains which were always ready to start. From Dublin it crossed to Liverpool by fast steamers, thus gaining hours on the swiftest boats of the transatlantic lines.

Those twelve hours gained by the American mail, Phileas Fogg hoped to gain in the same way. Instead of reaching Liverpool the next evening on the *Henrietta*, he would be there at noon, and so he would have time to get to London before eight forty-five in the evening.

Towards one in the morning, the *Henrietta* entered Queenstown harbour on the high tide. Then Phileas Fogg, after receiving a vigorous handshake from Captain Speedy, left him on the razed carcass of his ship, which was still worth half the sum he had sold it for.

The passengers disembarked at once, and Fix was sorely tempted to arrest Mr Fogg. Yet he did not do so. Why? What struggle was going on within him? Had he changed his mind about Phileas Fogg? Had he at last realized that he was mistaken?

Whatever the truth of the matter, Fix did not leave him.

With Fix, Aouda and Passepartout, who hardly dared to breathe, Mr Fogg boarded the train from Queenstown at half past one in the morning. He reached Dublin at dawn, and at once embarked on one of those steamers which were regular steel spindles, nothing but engine, and which, disdaining to rise to the waves, invariably passed right through them.

At twenty to twelve on 21st December, Phileas Fogg finally landed on the quay at Liverpool. He was now only six hours from London. But at that moment Fix went up to him, put his hand on his shoulder, and showing him his warrant, said:

"You really are Mr Phileas Fogg?"

"Yes, sir."
"In the Queen's name, I arrest you!"

CHAPTER THIRTY-FOUR

Which gives Passepartout the opportunity to make an atrocious, but possibly novel, pun

Phileas Fogg was in prison. He had been locked up in the Custom House cells, where he was to spend the night before being taken to London

When he saw his master being arrested, Passepartout had tried to hurl himself upon the detective, but some policeman held him back. Aouda, horrified by the brutality of the incident and knowing nothing of the circumstances, was utterly bewildered. Passepartout enlightened her, explaining that Mr Fogg, that honest and courageous gentleman to whom she owed her life, had been arrested as a thief. The young woman protested against this monstrous allegation, her heart was filled with indignation, and tears flowed from her eyes when she realized that she could do nothing, attempt nothing, to rescue her rescuer.

As for Fix, he had arrested the gentleman because it was his duty to arrest him, innocent or guilty. That would be for the court to decide.

Then a thought occurred to Passepartout, the terrible realization that it was he who had been the cause of this misfortune! Why had he hidden the truth from Mr Fogg? When Fix had revealed his status as a police inspector and the task with which he was entrusted, why had he taken it upon himself not to inform his master? Forewarned, the latter would no doubt have given Fix proof of his innocence, he would have shown the man his mistake; in any case he would not have conveyed at his heels, and at his own expense, this troublesome detective whose first thought had been to arrest him as soon as he set foot on the soil of the United Kingdom. When he remembered his blunders and his rash behaviour, the poor fellow was overwhelmed with remorse. He wept piteously, and felt like dashing his head to pieces.

In spite of the cold, he and Aouda had stayed under the portico of the Custom House. Neither of them would leave, for both wanted to see Mr Fogg once again.

As for that gentleman, he was well and truly ruined, and that at the very moment when he was about to reach his goal. This arrest spelt the end of his hopes. Arriving at Liverpool at twenty to twelve on 21st December, he had till a quarter to nine to appear at the Reform Club, in other words just over nine hours – and he needed only six to get to London.

If anyone had entered the Custom House cells at that moment he would have found Mr Fogg sitting motionless on a wooden bench, not showing any sign of anger and quite imperturbable. Whether he was resigned nobody could tell, but this final blow had not, to all appearances at least, caused him any emotion. Was one of those secret rages boiling up in him which are all the more terrible because they are repressed, and which explode at the very last moment with irresistible violence? No one can say. But Phileas Fogg was there calmly waiting for ... what? Was he still cherishing some hope? Did he still believe that success was possible, now that this prison door had closed upon him?

Be that as it may, Mr Fogg had carefully placed his watch on a table and he was following the movement of its hands. Not a word escaped his lips, but his gaze was strangely set.

His position was in any case a terrible one, and for anyone who could not read his conscience it could be summed up as follows:

If he was an honest man, Phileas Fogg was ruined.

If he was a criminal, he had been caught.

Did the thought of flight occur to him? Did he think of trying to find out whether there was any practicable means of exit from the cells? Did he consider the idea of escaping? One might be tempted to think so, for at one stage he walked all round the cell. But the door was safely locked and the window was barred. So he went back to his seat and took the itinerary of his journey out of his wallet. On the line which bore the words, "Saturday 21st December, Liverpool," he added, "80th day, 11.40 a.m." and waited. The Custom House clock struck one, and Mr Fogg observed that his watch was two minutes fast by that clock.

Two o'clock! If that very moment he could board an express, he could still reach London and the Reform Club before eight forty-five in the evening. His forehead wrinkled slightly . . .

At two thirty-three a noise was heard outside, the clatter of doors opening. Two voices could be heard, that of Passepartout and that of Fix.

Phileas Fogg's eyes gleamed for a moment.

The cell door opened and he saw Aouda, Passepartout and Fix rushing towards him . . .

Fix was out of breath, his hair dishevelled. . . . He could not speak.

"Sir," he stammered, "sir . . . forgive me . . . an unfortunate resemblance . . . robber arrested three days ago . . . you . . . free!"

Phileas Fogg was free! He went up to the detective. He looked him full in the face, and, making the only sudden movement he had ever made, or would ever make, in his life, he drew back his arms, and then, with the precision

Mr Fogg hit the inspector with both fists

of an automaton, hit the unfortunate inspector with both fists.

"Well hit!" exclaimed Passepartout. Then indulging in an atrocious pun, well worthy of a Frenchman, he added:

"By heaven! That's what you might call a fine application of *poings d'Angleterre!*"[1]

Fix, prostrate on the floor, did not say a word; he had only got his deserts. But Mr Fogg, Aouda and Passepartout promptly left the Custom House, jumped into a cab, and in a few minutes arrived at Liverpool station.

Phileas Fogg asked if there was an express about to leave for London.

It was twenty to three . . . The express had gone thirty-five minutes before.

Phileas Fogg then ordered a special train.

There were several express engines with steam up, but

[1] "English fists." *Point d'Angleterre*, "English point", is a type of needle-point lace (Trans.).

regular traffic requirements prevented the special train from starting until three o'clock.

At three o'clock, after saying a few words to the engine driver about a certain bonus he might earn, Phileas Fogg set off for London together with the young woman and his faithful servant.

He had to cover the distance between Liverpool and London in five and a half hours – something which is perfectly feasible when the whole of the line is clear. But there were unavoidable delays, and when he reached the terminus all the clocks in London were pointing to ten to nine.

After completing his journey round the world, Phileas Fogg had arrived five minutes late!

He had lost.

CHAPTER THIRTY-FIVE

In which Passepartout does not need to be told twice what his master wishes him to do

The next day the inhabitants of Savile Row would have been very surprised if they had been told that Mr Fogg had returned home. All the doors and windows were shut, and nothing had changed in the outward appearance of the house.

After leaving the station Phileas Fogg had told Passepartout to buy some provisions, and then he had gone home.

He had received with his usual imperturbability the blow which had struck him. Ruined! And all because of that blundering fool of an inspector. After treading that long road with a sure step, after overcoming countless obstacles and braving countless perils, and still finding time to do a little good on the way, to be shipwrecked in harbour by an act of brute force which he could not have foreseen and against which he was unarmed, was really terrible!

Of the large sum he had taken with him there remained only an insignificant residue. His fortune now consisted only of the twenty thousand pounds he owed to his fellow members of the Reform Club. After so many expenses, the wager, if he had won it, would certainly not have enriched him, and in all probability he had not wanted to enrich himself – he was the sort of man who lays a wager for honour's sake – but losing it had completely ruined him. What was more, his mind was made up. He knew what he had to do.

A room in the house in Savile Row had been set apart for Aouda, who was in despair. From certain words which Mr Fogg had let fall she had realized that he was contemplating some dreadful project.

It is indeed well known to what deplorable extremities these English monomaniacs are sometimes driven when obsessed by a fixed idea. So, without appearing to do so, Passepartout kept a close watch upon his master.

First of all, however, the good fellow had gone up to his room and turned off the gas, which had been burning for eighty days. He had found in the letterbox a bill from the gas company, and he thought it was high time to put an end to this expense, for which he was responsible.

The night went by: Mr Fogg had gone to bed, but did he sleep? As for Aouda, she could not get so much as a moment's rest. Passepartout, for his part, watched outside his master's door like a dog.

The following day Mr Fogg sent for him and told him somewhat curtly to see to Aouda's breakfast. He himself would be satisfied with a cup of tea and some toast. He hoped Aouda would be good enough to excuse his absence from lunch and dinner, as all his time would be devoted to putting his affairs in order. He would not come downstairs, but he would be grateful if Aouda would grant him a few minutes' conversation in the evening.

Having thus been given the day's programme, Passepartout had only to conform to it. He looked at his imperturbable master and could not make up his mind to leave the room. His heart was heavy, his conscience tormented with remorse, for he felt more than ever guilty of this irreparable disaster. Yes, if he had warned Monsieur Fogg, if he had disclosed the detective's plans to him, then Monsieur Fogg would not have taken the detective with him to Liverpool, and then . . .

Passepartout could not stand it any longer.

"Master! Monsieur Fogg!" he cried. "Curse me! It's all my fault that . . ."

"I blame nobody," replied Phileas Fogg in his calmest voice. "Go."

Passepartout left the room and went to see the young woman, whom he informed of his master's plans.

"Madame," he added, "I can't do anything myself – anything! I haven't any influence over my master's mind. Perhaps you . . ."

"And what influence would I have?" Aouda replied. "Mr Fogg is never influenced by anyone! Has he ever realized that the gratitude I feel towards him is ready to overflow? Has he ever been able to read my heart? My friend, you mustn't leave him, not even for a moment! You say that he has expressed a wish to speak to me this evening?"

"Yes, Madame. No doubt it's a question of safeguarding your position in England."

"We must wait and see," replied the young woman, remaining very pensive.

So during the whole of that Sunday the house in Savile Row seemed to be uninhabited, and, for the first time since he had lived there, Phileas Fogg did not go to his club when Big Ben struck half past eleven.

And why should he appear at the Reform Club? His fellow members were no longer waiting there for him. As on the previous day, that fateful date of Saturday, 21st December, Phileas Fogg had failed to appear in the morning room of the Reform Club at eight forty-five in the evening, he had lost his wager. There was not even any need for him to visit his banker to withdraw that sum of twenty thousand pounds. His adversaries held a cheque he had signed, and a mere endorsement would enable Baring Brothers to transfer the twenty thousand pounds to their credit.

So Mr Fogg was not obliged to go out, and he did not go out. He stayed in his room and put his affairs in order, while Passepartout never stopped going up and down the stairs of the house in Savile Row. For that poor fellow time seemed to have stopped. He kept listening at his master's door and did not think he was committing the slightest indiscretion. He even looked through the keyhole, and felt that he was perfectly justified in doing so. Every moment he feared some catastrophe.

He sometimes thought of Fix, but now his attitude towards the man had changed completely. He no longer bore a grudge against the police inspector. Like everybody else, Fix had misjudged Phileas Fogg, and in shadowing him, in arresting him, he had done no more than his duty, while he himself . . . The thought overwhelmed him, and he regarded himself as the most contemptible wretch on earth.

When at last he grew too unhappy to bear his own company, he knocked at Aouda's door, entered her room, sat down in a corner without saying a word, and looked at the young woman, who was still wrapped in thought.

About half past seven Mr Fogg sent word to ask if

Aouda could receive him, and a few minutes later the two of them were alone in her room.

Phileas Fogg took the chair and sat down opposite Aouda near the fireplace. His face showed no emotion whatever. The Fogg who had returned was indistinguishable from the Fogg who had gone away. The same calm, the same impassivity.

He sat there for five minutes without speaking. Then he looked up at Aouda and said:

"Madam, will you forgive me for bringing you to England?"

"I, Mr Fogg!" replied Aouda, trying to check the beating of her heart.

"Please allow me to finish," continued Mr Fogg. "When I conceived the idea of taking you far from that country of yours which had become so dangerous for you, I was rich, and I intended to place a part of my fortune at your service. Your life would have been free and happy. Now I am ruined."

"I know that, Mr Fogg," replied the young woman, "and now it is my turn to ask you: Will you forgive me for having accompanied you and – who knows? – perhaps contributed to your ruin by delaying you?"

"You could not have stayed in India, Madam, and the only way of ensuring your safety was to take you so far away that those fanatics could not recapture you."

"So, Mr Fogg," Aouda continued, "not content with saving me from a horrible death, you also felt it your duty to secure my position in a foreign land?"

"Yes, Madam," Fogg agreed, "but events have turned against me. Still, I ask your permission to place the little that is left to me at your disposal."

"But you, Mr Fogg?" asked Aouda. "What is to become of you?"

"Me, Madam?" he replied coldly. "I do not need anything."

"But how, sir, are you going to face the future?"

"As it should be faced," replied Mr Fogg.

"In any case," Aouda went on, "a man like you is beyond the reach of poverty. Your friends . . ."

"I have no friends, Madam."

"Your relatives . . ."

"I have no relatives left."

"Then I am sorry for you, Mr Fogg, for loneliness is a sad thing. What, not a soul to share your troubles! Yet they say that even poverty is bearable when there are two of you."

"So they say, Madam."

"Mr Fogg," said Aouda, standing up and holding out her hand, "would you care to have a relative who is also a friend? Will you have me for your wife?"

On hearing these words Mr Fogg stood up too. There was an unwonted brightness in his eyes, and something like a tremor on his lips.

Aouda gazed at him. The sincerity, uprightness, firmness and sweetness evident in the eyes of this noble woman, who would dare all to save the man to whom she owed everything, first astonished him, then touched him. For a moment he shut his eyes, as if to prevent this gaze from entering deeper still into his heart. When he opened them again, he said simply:

"I love you! Yes, indeed, by everything in the world I hold most sacred, I love you and I am yours!"

"Oh!" exclaimed Aouda, placing her hand on her heart.

Passepartout was summoned and appeared at once. Mr Fogg was still holding Aouda's hand in his.

Passepartout understood, and his round face beamed like the tropical sun at its height.

Mr Fogg asked him if it would not be too late to go and give notice to the Reverend Samuel Wilson, of the parish of Marylebone.

Passepartout smiled his very best smile.

"It's never too late," he said.

It was only five past eight.

"Will it be tomorrow, Monday?" he asked.

"Tomorrow, Monday?" asked Mr Fogg, looking at Aouda.

"Tomorrow, Monday!" replied Aouda.

And Passepartout went off at a run.

CHAPTER THIRTY-SIX

In which Phileas Fogg shares are again at a premium

It is now time to explain what a complete change had taken place in English public opinion when it became known that the bank robber, a certain James Strand, had been arrested in Edinburgh on 17th December.

Three days before, Phileas Fogg had been a criminal whom the police were doing everything in their power to catch. Now he was the most honest of gentlemen, mathematically carrying out his eccentric journey round the world.

What a stir there was, what a fuss in the papers! All who had laid bets for or against him, and had already forgotten the whole business, came forward again as though by magic. All the old transactions became valid once more, all the old engagements were recognized, and, it must be added, new bets were laid with fresh energy. The name of Phileas Fogg was again at a premium on the Exchange.

At the Reform Club his five fellow members spent those three days in a state of some anxiety. That Phileas Fogg whom they had forgotten had been brought to their notice again. Where was he now? On 17th December – the day on which James Strand had been arrested – Phileas Fogg had been gone seventy-six days, and there had been absolutely no news of him. Was he dead? Had he given up the struggle, or was he pursuing his journey along the agreed route? And on Saturday, 21st December, would he reappear, like the god of punctuality, on the threshold of the Reform Club's morning room?

It is impossible to describe the anxiety into which English society was plunged for three days. Telegrams were sent to America and Asia asking for tidings of Phileas Fogg! Every morning and evening someone went to look at the house in Savile Row. Nothing!

Even the police did not know what had become of the detective Fix, who had set off so unfortunately on a false trail. This did not prevent more bets being laid on a vastly increased scale. Like any racehorse, Phileas Fogg was coming round the last bend. The odds against him were no longer quoted at a hundred, but at twenty, at ten, at five to one, and paralytic old Lord Albemarle, for his part, laid bets at even money.

So on the Saturday evening Pall Mall and the adjoining streets were crowded, as if a multitude of brokers were permanently installed around the Reform Club. Traffic was held up as people debated and argued and shouted quotations of "Phileas Foggs" as if they were Government stock. The police had great difficulty in controlling the crowd, and as the hour at which Phileas Fogg was due to arrive drew nearer, the excitement became indescribable.

That evening his five fellow members had been together in the morning room of the Reform Club for nine hours. The two bankers, John Sullivan and Samuel Fallentin; the engineer, Andrew Stuart; Walter Ralph, the director of the Bank of England; and the brewer, Thomas Flanagan, were all waiting anxiously.

When the clock in the morning room marked eight twenty-five, Andrew Stuart stood up and said:

"Gentlemen, in twenty minutes the time we agreed on with Mr Phileas Fogg will expire."

"What time did the last train get in from Liverpool?" asked Thomas Flanagan.

"At seven twenty-three," replied Walter Ralph, "and the next train doesn't get in till ten past twelve."

"Well, gentlemen," Andrew Stuart continued, "if Phileas Fogg had arrived by the seven twenty-three train, he would be here by now. So we can take it that we have won our bet."

"We must wait. We can't say yet," replied Samuel Fallentin. "You must know that our fellow member is an eccentric of the first order. His precision in all things is well known. He never arrives too late or too early. And I wouldn't be at all surprised if he turned up here at the last minute."

"As for me," said Andrew Stuart, who was as nervous as usual, "if I saw him appear, I wouldn't believe my eyes."

"Nor would I," said Thomas Flanagan, "for Phileas Fogg's project was sheer madness. However punctual he might be, he could not prevent inevitable delays occurring, and a delay of only two or three days would be enough to compromise his journey."

"You will observe, too," added John Sullivan, "that we have received no communication from our fellow member, although there is no shortage of telegraph lines along his route."

"He has lost, gentlemen," continued Andrew Stuart, "he has lost a hundred times over! You know, too, that the *China* – the only liner from New York that he could have taken to reach Liverpool in time – arrived yesterday. Well, here is the passenger list, published by the *Shipping Gazette*, and Phileas Fogg's name isn't on it. Even granted the most favourable chances, he can only just have arrived in America. By my reckoning, he will arrive at least twenty days late, and old Lord Albemarle too will be the poorer by five thousand pounds."

"That's obvious," replied Walter Ralph, "and all we shall have to do tomorrow is to present Mr Fogg's cheque at Baring's."

At that moment the hands of the clock pointed to twenty to nine.

"Five minutes more," said Andrew Stuart.

The five men looked at one another. It may be supposed that their hearts were beating a little more rapidly, for even for such bold gamblers the stake was a large one. But they must have wished to conceal their excitement, for, at Samuel Fallentin's suggestion, they took their places at a card table.

"I wouldn't give up my four thousand pounds share in the wager," Andrew Stuart declared as he sat down, "even if someone offered me three thousand nine hundred and ninety-nine pounds!"

At that moment the hands of the clock showed eight forty-two.

The players had taken up their cards, but their eyes kept straying to the clock. It is safe to say that, however confident they might feel, they had never found minutes so long!

"Eight forty-three," said Thomas Flanagan, as he cut the pack which Walter Ralph handed him.

There was a moment's silence. The vast morning room was quiet. But outside they could hear the hubbub of the crowd, dominated now and then by a shrill cry. The pendulum of the clock beat the seconds with mathematical regularity and each of the players could count the strokes as they reached his ear.

"Eight forty-four!" said John Sullivan in a voice which betrayed his involuntary excitement.

Only one minute more and the wager was won. Andrew Stuart and his companions had stopped playing. They had laid down their cards. They were counting the seconds!

At the fortieth second, nothing. At the fiftieth still nothing!

At the fifty-fifth they heard outside a sound like thunder, applause, cheers and even oaths, merging into a continuous roar.

The players rose to their feet.

At the fifty-seventh second the door opened, and the pendulum had not beaten the sixtieth second when Phileas Fogg appeared, followed by a delirious crowd which had forced its way into the club, and in his calm voice said:

"Here I am, gentlemen."

CHAPTER THIRTY-SEVEN

In which it is shown that Phileas Fogg won nothing by travelling around the world, unless it were happiness

Yes – Phileas Fogg in person.

It will be recalled that at five past eight in the evening – about twenty-three hours after the travellers arrived in London – Passepartout had been instructed by his master to make arrangements with the Reverend Samuel Wilson for a certain marriage which was to take place on the very next day.

Passepartout had set out delightedly. He hurried to the Reverend Samuel Wilson's house, but found that the ergyman was out. He naturally waited, though he had to it twenty good minutes at least.

short it was eight thirty-five when he left. But what a

"Here I am, gentlemen"

state he was in! His hair dishevelled, his hat had fallen off and he was running, running, as no one had ever run within living memory, knocking over passers-by and rushing along the pavements like a tornado!

In three minutes he was back at the house in Savile Row, where he staggered exhausted in Mr Fogg's room.

He could not speak.

"What is the matter?" asked Mr Fogg.

"Master . . ." stammered Passepartout, . . . "marriage . . . impossible . . ."

"Impossible?"

"Impossible . . . tomorrow."

"Why?"

"Because tomorrow . . . is Sunday!"

"Monday," said Mr Fogg.

"No . . . today . . . Saturday."

"Saturday? Impossible!"

"It is, it is!" cried Passepartout. "You're one day out! We got back twenty-four hours early . . . but there's only ten minutes left . . . !"

Passepartout had gripped his master by the collar and was rushing him along with irresistible force.

Thus kidnapped, Phileas Fogg, without having time to think, left his room, left his house, jumped into a cab, promised the driver a hundred pounds, and after running over two dogs and colliding with five carriages, reached the Reform Club.

The clock pointed to eight forty-five when he appeared in the morning-room . . .

Phileas Fogg had accomplished the journey round the world in eighty days!

Phileas Fogg had won his bet of twenty thousand ounds!

And now, how was it that a man so exact, so meticu- , could possibly have made this error of one day? How he have thought that he had reached London on the evening of Saturday, 21st December, whereas it was Friday, 20th December, only seventy-nine days after his departure?

The reason for his mistake is quite simple.

Phileas Fogg had, without realizing it, gained one day during his journey – and that simply because he had made his journey round the world by travelling towards the east. He would, on the other hand, have lost a day by going in the opposite direction, towards the west.

In short, by travelling eastwards, Phileas Fogg had gone towards the sun, and as a result the days had become four minutes shorter for him every time he crossed a degree in that direction. Well, there are 360 degrees on the circumference of the earth, and these 360 degrees, multiplied by four minutes, make exactly twenty-four hours – that is, the day he had gained without knowing it.

In other words, while Phileas Fogg, travelling towards the east, saw the sun cross the meridian *eighty* times, his fellow members of the Reform Club who had stayed in London had only seen it cross *seventy-nine* times. That is why on that very day, which was the Saturday and not, as Mr Fogg believed, the Sunday, they were waiting for him in the morning room of the Reform Club.

And Passepartout's famous watch – which had always kept London time – would have revealed this, if as well as showing the minutes and the hours it had also shown the days!

Phileas Fogg had thus won his twenty thousand pounds, but as, during his journey, he had spent about nineteen thousand, his pecuniary gain was mediocre. Still, as has already been explained, the eccentric gentleman's object had been sport, not wealth. And indeed, he shared the remaining thousand pounds between the worthy Passepartout and the hapless Fix, against whom he was incapable of bearing malice. However, simply as a matter of principle, he deducted from Passepartout's share the cost of the nineteen hundred and twenty hours of gas wasted through his negligence.

That very evening Mr Fogg, as imperturbable and phlegmatic as ever, asked Aouda:

"And does this marriage still suit you, Madam?"

"Mr Fogg," she replied, "it is for me to ask you that question. You were ruined and now you are rich . . ."

"Excuse me, Madam, that fortune belongs to you. If the idea of this marriage had not occurred to you, my servant would never have gone to the Reverend Samuel Wilson's house, and I should never have been informed of my mistake, and . . ."

"Dear Mr Fogg . . ." said the young woman.

"Dear Aouda . . ." replied Phileas Fogg.

It goes without saying that the marriage was celebrated forty-eight hours later, and that Passepartout, superb, resplendent, dazzling, gave the bride away. Had he not rescued her, and did he not deserve that honour?

Early next morning, however, he knocked loudly at his master's door.

The door opened and the imperturbable gentleman appeared.

"What is it, Passepartout?"

"What is it, sir? It's that I've just found out . . ."

"What?"

"That we could have made the journey round the world in only seventy-eight days."

"No doubt," agreed Fogg, "by not going through India. But if I had not gone through India, I should not have saved Aouda, she would not have become my wife, and . . ."

And Mr Fogg quietly shut the door.

Thus Phileas Fogg had won his bet. In eighty days he had completed this journey around the world! To this end had made use of every means of transport, steamers, railways, carriages, yachts, merchant ships, sledges, elephants. The eccentric gentleman had displayed in the course of this enterprise his marvellous gifts of coolness and exactitude. But with what result? What had he gained from all this travelling? What had he brought back from this journey?

Nothing, you may say? Nothing, agreed, unless it be a charming woman who – however improbable it might seem – made him the happiest of men.

And indeed, would not anyone travel around the world for less?